pick up on this new series now
ReviewingTheEvidence.com

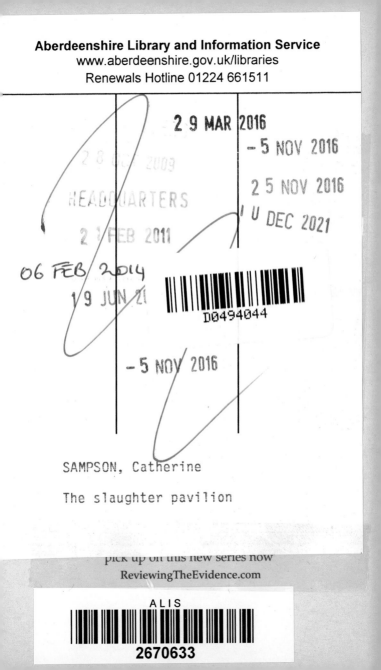

THE SLAUGHTER PAVILION

Catherine Sampson started her career in the BBC
and has worked as Beijing correspondent for *The Times*.
She now lives in Beijing with her husband and
three children. *The Slaughter Pavilion* is
Catherine's fourth novel.

Also by Catherine Sampson

FALLING OFF AIR

OUT OF MIND

THE POOL OF UNEASE

Catherine Sampson

THE SLAUGHTER PAVILION

135798642

A CIP catalogue record for this book is available from the British Library

Typeset by SetSystems Ltd, Saffron Walden, Essex
Printed in the UK by CPI Mackays, Chatham ME5 8TD

PAN BOOKS

First published 2008 by Macmillan

This paperback edition first published 2009 by Pan Books
an imprint of Pan Macmillan Ltd
Pan Macmillan, 20 New Wharf Road, London N1 9RR
Basingstoke and Oxford
Associated companies throughout the world
www.panmacmillan.com

ISBN 978-0-330-44822-2

Visit www.panmacmillan.com to read more about all our books
and to buy them. You will also find features, author interviews and
news of any author events, and you can sign up for e-newsletters
so that you're always first to hear about our new releases.

FOR ALISTAIR, RACHEL AND KIRSTY

ACKNOWLEDGEMENTS

I would like to thank my editors at Pan Macmillan, first Anna Valdinger and now Trisha Jackson, as well as my agent Amanda Pearson, for all their help and support as this series has morphed into something new. My husband, James Miles, has fed me a constant diet of crime-related news items that he knows will interest me. Mark Benecke sent answers and gruesome photographs in response to my queries on forensic pathology. My good friends Martha Huang, Kathy Wilhelm, Jen Schwerin and Lucy Cavender gave me invaluable feedback on early drafts.

This is a work of fiction. The events and people I describe are all imaginary. Beijing exists, of course, but I invented Yidong Village and Wanmei County. I do intend, however, that the stories I make up are believable, by which I mean that they shouldn't seem incredible to someone who knows China. The events described in the first chapter, for instance, are based loosely on an incident which happened in Beijing when a man climbed to the top of an office block carrying the frozen body of a child. I thank those who witnessed that incident for describing it to me.

One

It began with an electronic chirrup and a vibration in his fingertips. He surfaced only briefly, and sank back towards sleep. Then he reached out, fumbling for the mobile where it had slipped out of his hand in the night. He opened one eye to peer at the message on the screen.

the world will witness my despair

Song closed his eyes but it was too late. He recognized the number. He flung the sheet away and tried to get comfortable, turning first onto his side, then onto his stomach. The man had rung a dozen times after Song had thrown him out. The sun was seeping between the curtains, and already the room was oppressively hot. He reached for the bottle of water by the bed, took a mouthful, then splashed some over his face and head – he'd had his scalp shorn almost bald to combat the summer heat.

Another chirrup heralded the arrival of a second message. Again Song tried to ignore it and failed.

the roof international trade tower 0800

He groaned, rolled over, tucking his mobile phone under the pillow. Why couldn't the man leave him alone? A scrap of humanity who couldn't afford a bowl of soup, let alone Song's fees. There was still time for a lie-in. His mind spiralled down towards sleep ... he was about to dive into a cool pool of water. A woman was waiting for him, blue water lapping around her pale breasts. She was looking up at him expectantly, but he couldn't see her face. He dived.

the world will witness my despair ... the roof ...

All at once he was wide awake.

Office workers arrived in waves, disgorged by buses and subway. They headed through revolving glass doors and into the marble-lined lobby to crowd into the lifts that would carry them up into the air-conditioned offices above. His job required that he be able to blend in to almost any environment, but this morning urgency had put paid to that. Dressing quickly, Song had pulled on jeans and a T-shirt, the first clothes that came to hand, and he didn't belong in this brisk, polished world. The security guard was watching him.

Song's eyes skimmed over the women's legs flashing past beneath pastel skirts. He liked the summer. He liked the way women shed their layers of padding and looked the shape they really were. Foreign men and women passed in suits, chattering into their mobile phones. He was looking for a small skinny peasant. A man who, when he opened his mouth, spoke so fast you couldn't stop him. He remembered the man's desperation, how he'd reached the threshold of Song's office and then fallen to his knees, pressing his hands together in entreaty.

'I was told you could help . . . I'll give you everything I have, I'll sign over my house to you, you're my last hope, please help . . .'

A pretty woman stopped in front of him, distracting him. She had a wide mouth, and a curtain of silky hair swung across her face.

'I'm lost,' she said, smiling up at him. 'I'm looking for Starbucks?'

He couldn't help himself. He smiled back at her and started to reply. Then all of a sudden he caught a strange movement out of the corner of his eye and swung around. There was a commotion over by the revolving glass doors. Song couldn't see what was happening because of the numbers of people entering the building, but he could hear a raised voice. 'Move on! You can't go in there!' Song ran towards the disturbance.

He grabbed a woman by her shoulder. She wheeled around.

'Which way did he go?'

She pointed wordlessly towards the entrance. The revolving door slowed him down and then he found himself inside, bathed in cool air. A young security guard was speaking urgently on his walkie-talkie.

'Did he go up?' Song shouted, heading for the lifts,

and the security guard gave a distracted jerk of the head in confirmation.

He had to wait again, and then the lift doors opened in front of him. There was a large foreign woman already in there, white shirt straining over her bust, grey skirt, a laminated security pass hanging on a chain around her plump neck. Song hit the button for the top floor.

The lift moved swiftly upwards. He saw the woman's eyes upon him, reflected in the mirrored walls. He could see his agitation was making her nervous. He glanced up, spotting the CCTV-camera in the corner of the lift. Silently he cursed himself for getting involved and he cursed the peasant for involving him.

'Do you have business in this building?' the woman challenged him in Chinese.

'I'm going to stop a man throwing himself off the roof,' he replied. When her mouth fell open her shock was reflected all around them.

The lift doors opened on the top floor – the thirty-sixth – and Song burst out into the corridor then hesitated, turning on his heel, searching for the fire exit and the staircase which would lead to the roof.

A heavy metal door at the top yielded under his pressure, opening onto a heat-baked roof, the cement blinding under the hazy white sky. Song stepped outside, shading his eyes. The roof of the tower block was as big as a park. The construction noise of the entire city rose up to deafen him with its drilling and pounding. He let his eyes run over satellite dishes and huts that

4

housed electrical facilities. From the edge of the roof rose a gigantic advertising hoarding as high as a two-storey building. From where he stood this hoarding was all scaffolding, a black silhouette against the glare of the sky. A man was clinging precariously to this structure, inching his way up the metal strut which extended from the roof. His clutching, faltering progress was hampered by the fact that he had a child on his back, the smaller body supported in a papoose strapped around the climber's waist and shoulders and tied in a knot in front. The child was not a baby although he carried it like one.

Song's palms were sweating and his heart was pounding. He started to walk towards the scaffolding. If he ran he would alarm the man.

'Hey, Li,' he shouted, finding his voice unreliable, trying again. 'Li, that's not a good idea. Come back down.'

The man peered down at the rooftop, searching for the source of the sound. He saw Song standing there, face raised towards him. For a moment the man didn't move. He continued to cling, like an insect on a stalk. Then his hand reached up and he hauled himself higher.

'Don't take the child up there,' Song yelled. 'I'll help you work things out, come on down.'

Balancing himself in the right angles of the frame where he was more secure, Li began to undo the cloth that held the child to him.

'Don't worry,' he shouted down. Even his voice was thin. 'There's no other way. This way everybody will know.'

Song moved towards the scaffolding and swung himself upwards. Li appeared to be talking to the child. Carefully he tied the papoose to the structure, winding the cloth in and out of the metal struts and securing it with a series of knots until the tiny figure was hanging, suspended, over the side of the building. The child must be asleep, Song thought, or immobilized with terror, because it didn't move.

Below Song the sound of feet exploded onto the roof. There were shouts of surprise, and half a dozen security guards launched themselves towards the hoarding.

'Hold back,' Song yelled down. 'Wait, don't scare him.'

One of the youngest leaped onto the scaffolding and pulled himself up, shouting, 'Come down! You're not allowed up there, come down!'

Li bent his head over the child for a moment and then moved slowly away. He edged along the scaffolding, holding on with both hands, looking down at the guard who was climbing nearer, and now Song could see his fear.

Song pulled himself along the scaffolding towards the child, who was safe only as long as the cloth binding held. The wind was strong. Song felt it buffeting him.

He heard a shout and turned to see the young guard swiping at Li, trying to grab him. Li slipped, losing his footing. For a moment he clung to the steel girder, his legs scissoring wildly in mid-air. Slowly his grip loosened. Screaming, he fell.

*

Far below, traffic came to a juddering halt. Pedestrians stopped in their stride and recoiled. A crowd began to gather.

Song shifted awkwardly on the scaffolding. If he lost his grip he too would die. He anchored himself as well as he could and then, with one hand, he reached for the child's papoose. Seizing the fabric he pulled it towards himself, fighting gravity to haul the child over the parapet. He clasped the bundle to him and at once felt its stillness. He pushed a fold of cloth away from the face. It was a girl, perhaps five or six years old. Her eyes were closed, eyelashes resting on puckered skin. Her mouth was straight and still. For this child the danger was long past. Sapped of life, her complexion was like meat that had been drained of blood. He touched her cheek and sensed deep, deep cold beneath the sun-thawed skin.

Two

He carried her down. There didn't seem any alternative, although his heart was heavy just at the sight of her. Carefully, freeing one hand at a time while the other grasped the scaffolding rods, he slipped the straps of the papoose over his own shoulders while the weight of the child's corpse was still held by the advertising hoarding. Then, shifting his footing, he twisted around to begin climbing down. As he did so something brushed against his face and, swaying wildly, he snatched at it. Catching it and trying to grab the scaffolding all at once, he crushed a flimsy piece of paper in his fist. He slipped the crumpled ball into his pocket so that he had both hands free to steady himself. As he glanced down – a mistake, almost causing him to lose his balance entirely – he saw a flock of the fragile papers, like the wings of tiny translucent birds, fluttering slowly into the abyss. He had seen these papers before, when Li had begged Song to read his petition.

He slid one foot slowly ahead of the other on the rail and shifted his weight, trying to find his new centre of balance as gusts of wind threatened to topple him. He made a shuffling, sliding progress then stopped to take stock, clinging to the scaffolding with one hand, trying not to look down. Angry blasts of horn rose from gridlocked traffic below and voices reached him through loudhailers.

He lowered himself slowly towards the roof. Below him guards were gathering, shouting up at him to come down. The roof had filled with office workers, foreign and Chinese, and several of them had raised their mobile phones to photograph his descent.

He lowered himself onto the roof and instantly he was surrounded by guards. They pulled at him, wresting the child from his back, then recoiling as they touched her, letting her body fall, their voices rising in shock. 'She's dead – frozen solid!'

Song backed away. He thought that with any luck he could take advantage of their consternation to leave unnoticed. But then the guards turned in his direction. He had carried the child down. He was as suspect as the corpse was repellent. Nobody wanted to touch the child, whose body lay on the ground at their feet, but they all wanted to grab him.

An hour later, Song sat in the Dongcheng District police station. They had put him in a whitewashed interrogation room and for the moment at least he was on his own. He had given up smoking six months before but he craved a cigarette now. He leaned his arms on the table in front of him, spreading his fingers on the wooden surface. His hands had not stopped shaking and this seemed as good a way as any of keeping them still. He listened. Sounds came to him from the corridor outside. There were raised voices, hurrying footsteps, ringing phones, the sounds of crisis.

That a peasant had been able to hang the corpse of a frozen child from a skyscraper at the heart of Beijing's business district in front of appalled foreigners was a huge loss of face for the authorities. He remembered the mobile phones raised to photograph the child and thought it would be impossible to keep the morning's events off the Internet. These days the smallest incident made it into China's chat rooms and blogs at least briefly, sometimes with photographs and video footage. The Internet police would try to delete it of course, but not before thousands of people had seen it and copied it and emailed it on.

Song cursed himself for getting involved. His intervention had done no one any good. The child had been dead all along, and the man had fallen to his death. He had done too little and too late.

He could feel the ball of paper in his pocket. It crackled slightly as he moved. He wondered what sweat and crushing had done to it. He was familiar with petitions. Peasants had been writing them from time immemorial, hoping in the face of local injustice that they would find justice with the emperor or, later, the Party centre. Wherever there was a peasant with a grievance, there was a peasant with a petition. Their testimony was transcribed with painful precision. Of course, they could wave these papers until they were blue in the face but the authorities rarely so much as glanced at them, let alone took action. Recently, petitioners had started to band together to try to make more of an impact, but the government's response had been the opposite of the desired effect. Instead of responding to peasants' concerns they had issued regulations strictly limiting gatherings. They had even banned petitioners from committing suicide as an act of protest.

The door swung open and a uniformed officer strode in. He was in his early thirties, tall, with strong, intelligent features. He was on the fast track, Song thought, just as he himself had been almost a decade ago, before the fall. Song got slowly to his feet and held out his hand. The officer ignored it and jerked his head to tell him to sit down. In his own time, Song settled himself back on the chair.

'Name?'

'Song Ren.'

The officer frowned, trying to work out where he'd heard it before. 'Place of work?'

'Anjialou Investigation and Legal Research Agency.'

'What is an investigation and legal research agency?'

'It's an agency,' Song said vaguely, 'that pursues investigation and research of information.'

'What information?' The officer spat the question.

'Financial information,' Song said firmly. He was forbidden by law from involvement in criminal cases, but in fact most of the things that he did were not exactly legal.

'Are you a private detective?'

'I'm an investigator,' Song sidestepped the question. The description 'private detective' was best avoided. Officially China had no need of private detectives. They grew like fungus in the grey sludge that washed up around the edges of the harmonious socialist society.

'Are you hired by women to follow their husbands?' the officer asked point-blank.

'On occasion,' Song confessed, since the game was apparently up.

'So you're a private detective.' The officer threw him a look of contempt.

'I used,' Song said, 'to be a police officer just like you.'

The officer stared at him.

'Why did you go to the International Trade Tower this morning?'

'I arranged to meet a friend in Starbucks,' Song lied smoothly. 'I saw the man and I thought he must have abducted the child so I gave chase.'

He wasn't going to tell the officer about the text message. Then he'd have to tell him the rest.

'You'd been hired to follow him, hadn't you?'

Song almost laughed, the officer was so far off the mark. Instead he said, 'I just wanted to get the kid down. How was I supposed to know she was dead? You should give me a medal. The Party should designate me a model citizen.'

'Don't fuck with me. Don't tell me you didn't know him.'

*

Song's assistant, Wolf, had left the gate open again. The man had shuffled through the courtyard, rapped on the office door. When Song went to open it he observed the man's shabby clothes and his concave belly.

'How can I help you?' Song remembered asking him. It was his standard greeting but in this case he hadn't meant it. While he spoke, Song stood in the doorway, blocking the man's way.

The man had fallen to his knees.

'My name is Li,' he said. 'I was told you could help me . . .'

'Who said I'd help you?'

'He said it didn't matter that I have no money. I'll give you everything I have, I'll sign over my house to you. You're my last hope, please help . . .'

The words had run out of him fast, tumbling over each other. Song caught something about the death of a child, about official involvement. That had made up his mind. The agency was running close enough to the wind. Get involved in murder and police cover-ups, and they'd close him down.

Still on his knees, the man had delved with shaking hands into a battered bag and brought out a sheaf of papers, head bowed, extending them towards Song as if offering a treasure. Song had pushed them away, but the man had continued to kneel there clutching the papers and moving his arms up and down in a gesture of supplication.

'Please, please take my petition. When you've read it you'll understand my despair . . .'

'Get out of here, old man,' Song said softly. 'There's no way I can help you. I'll lose my licence if I start investigating murder.'

*Song turned and headed back inside the office, closing the
door behind him. Then he sat down at his desk and stared at
his computer screen. From the corner of his eye he saw the
man rise slowly to his feet and walk away.*

'Who was he?' The officer was standing, leaning his
knuckles on the table in between them, barking questions at him. 'Why was he at the Trade Tower?'

'He was wearing rags,' Song said. 'I think he was
from out of town. And I think the child was his own
child. You should have seen the way he talked to her.
He loved her.'

The officer shook his head angrily.

'I don't want your speculation.' His voice became
shrill. 'Clearly this had nothing to do with love. He was
a madman. His actions endangered Beijing citizens as
they were going about their daily business, it interfered
with traffic . . .'

'From what you've said,' Song interrupted, speaking
slowly, 'you already have some information about the
man's unstable state of mind. Probably you know more
than I do. I don't know who he was. I don't know where
he came from, or why.'

'If you're concealing anything from me . . .' the officer
started to say.

The door opened and a young man in uniform burst
in. In his hand he held several sheets of crumpled paper
of exactly the kind that Song remembered from the
petition: delicate paper covered in spidery handwritten
characters. The younger man gestured at the officer

frantically to leave the room. The officer leaned over to speak in Song's face. 'This is highly sensitive. If you get involved, you'll end up doing hard labour.'

When the officer had gone, Song sat and waited. He assumed they would want to take a statement. After fifteen minutes no one had come to pursue the interrogation and he concluded that he was free to go. He got to his feet and opened the door into the hallway. He was in no hurry to commit to paper the lies he'd told the officer. If the officer had wanted him to stick around, he should have said so. He wasn't going to do their job for them. Song made his way out into the street and hailed a taxi.

Three

The fierce sun had softened, but the air was still hot and the sky bright. Song got a taxi as far as Anjialou, then got out and walked the last bit of the way through the hutongs. Anjialou was a village that had been swallowed up by the city, and its low buildings were a welcome respite from the grandiose architecture of most of the metropolis. In the past it had been quicker to navigate the narrow alleyways on foot than by car, especially in the early evening when the locals got home from work and thronged around the pancake stalls and the noodle bars.

In a few months the web of alleys would be replaced by a department store, or an office skyscraper, or luxury flats. Several streets had already been razed, and everyone had received their notice to quit in the form of posters pasted on walls.

Many had already piled trucks with their belongings and left. If they kicked up a fuss, the developer would kick back, and harder. There were only a handful of celebrated cases in which developers had accorded big compensation rewards to homeowners who had fought tooth and nail, braving beatings and death threats.

Song stopped and joined a small crowd watching a

team of demolition workers on Alley Number Seven. On the wall behind him red posters covered in black painted characters urged cooperation with the authorities and support for the demolition work. Some of the posters had been torn down or defaced – it was one thing to tolerate your house being destroyed, another to be told by some faceless bureaucrat to like it. Still, the demolition had become summer evening entertainment, a soap opera in which former neighbours' houses were levelled and the neighbours themselves, by their very absence, became fodder for reminiscence and gossip.

Atop a mound of rubble a mechanical scavenger was pulling and pushing at the debris. A row of carts were lined up along the roadside, mules balefully eyeing the hot tarmacadam. Peasant women were picking through the ruins, piling bricks on top of the mule carts.

Song stopped in at the convenience store on the corner of Alley Number Ten to buy a packet of cigarettes. The woman who served him had dyed red hair and a pretty, plump face. She always blushed when he came in. Sometimes they spoke. He knew that she was from rural Henan Province and that she had followed cousins to find work in the capital.

'What are you going to do when they knock this place down?' he asked her, jerking his head in the direction of the demolition team.

'I'm going to go home,' she said. 'I haven't seen my mother for two years.'

'And then?'

'I'll come back, find another job somewhere else.'

He nodded. For most people this wouldn't be a disaster. It was just a matter of starting all over again, as it so often was.

'And you?' she asked, her eyes bright.

He shrugged. 'I don't know, I haven't had any time to think about it.'

'You have to find a new place,' she said. 'Or what will you do when they come to knock the alley down?'

'Don't worry, I'll think of something,' he said, smiling at her despite the events of the day, liking her concern.

Inside the office Song surveyed his staff of two. Wolf, his second cousin, had been with him ever since he'd set up the agency. Wolf was a qualified lawyer but an eccentric one, with silver-dyed hair that flopped on his forehead over the tattoo of the single character, *lang*, that gave him his nickname. A few months earlier, Song had hired Blue, who was tiny, with hair that reached to her waist. He'd taken her on because she spoke good English, but she revealed a pleasing talent for hacking into official websites and a thirst for information to go with it. She could dig gold from the ether. Song had observed that Blue was in love with Wolf, and at first he'd thought Wolf reciprocated. There had been several weeks when Song had dreaded stepping into the office because of the vibrations of thinly veiled lust that seemed to rebound off the walls and zing in the air. But something had gone wrong, he didn't know what. Wolf had been dating other women, and Blue had been suffering. Whatever had happened, it was good news for the agency. Song could step into the office without cringing in embarrassment, and Blue's lack of social life meant she was ideally placed to sit and stare at a screen well past midnight.

Wolf had fallen asleep with his silver head on his arms. Blue, however, was awake and as usual had her eyes glued to her computer monitor.

'It's like a furnace in here,' Song exclaimed.

Wolf gave a startled snore and at the sound of his voice Blue swung around in her office chair.

'Is this you?' she asked Song, pointing at her screen. 'He looks like you.'

'I said it's like a furnace in here,' Song persisted. 'What happened to the air conditioning?'

'It broke down. Wolf said he was going to get it fixed, but then he fell asleep. Don't tell him off, please, he's very tired. Is this you? A man climbed up the . . .'

'I know.'

'So it *was* you. It's all over the Internet. Why were you there? Who was he? Why did he have a . . . ?'

He shook his head savagely, and she knew him well enough to shut up. He went and stood behind her and watched the screen as she scrolled down through photos and video images taken by mobile phones. Song did not recognize himself as the man in the pictures. He thought perhaps it had all happened to someone else and he had dreamt his own involvement.

'It's all been coming online in the last few minutes,' Blue murmured. 'They've got to take it down soon, they can't leave it up.'

'The police say he was a madman,' he said quietly.

'And was he?'

'I don't know.'

Song couldn't face any more. He went and sat at his desk. A mosquito whined past his ear. Every noise, every bright light, they all seemed swollen and exaggerated, assaulting his ears and his eyes. He tried to concentrate on his computer screen but he had to close his eyes against its glare. Then he heard the man's voice, as though he was still here in the doorway to the office.

'I was told you could help.'

'Who told you?'

'You're right,' Blue's voice broke in on his thoughts. She was reading from something on the screen, her finger tracing the words. 'The relevant official said the man was known to have mental problems.' She turned towards him. 'It's always mental problems. Who drove him mad? That's what I want to know.'

Song nodded at her distractedly. Blue was going to England in a few days, her first trip out of the country. She'd got an uncle to wangle her a business visa, although she was actually going for the wedding of a foreign friend, a journalist called Robin Ballantyne who had visited Beijing the year before. Blue had worked as Robin's interpreter, and the crime they investigated had drawn Song in too. That was how Song had come to meet Blue. Until now, Song had been worrying about how he and Wolf would do without her – Wolf's response to the air-conditioning crisis was typically unhelpful – but right now he wished her gone already so that he could sit here in silence with his thoughts.

'People want to know how he could reach Beijing with the corpse of a child,' Blue went on relentlessly. 'They want to know why no one noticed. One man thinks the man killed the child and then killed himself from shame.'

'He fell,' Song said, without thinking. 'He didn't jump.'

Blue turned pleading eyes on him. She didn't have to speak to let him know that she wanted him to tell her everything that had happened. It was cruel to torment her like this. Abruptly, Song pushed back his chair and stood up.

'I'm sorry,' he said.

He opened the door that divided his personal quarters from the office, went inside, and closed the door quietly behind him. There was just a bed, a shelf of books and a wardrobe. Most of his waking hours were spent working. This room was all the private space he needed, but soon this would be gone, demolished under the wrecker's ball. Everything would be gone, the agency that he'd built up from nothing, the home that was this one room.

It was stifling hot. He removed his shoes and lay on the bed with his eyes closed. He saw the transience of things, the homes destroyed, the man losing his grip on the scaffolding, his stomach-churning fall, the flock of papers floating towards the earth. When he saw the face of the frozen child he opened his eyes and stared at the ceiling. He felt sick at the weight of knowing he had turned the man away. He pulled the crumpled page from his pocket, and groaned at the sight of the paper, it was so mangled. He rolled over onto his stomach and placed the paper on the pillow so that he could tease it open gently, stroking at the creases with his fingertips.

The paper was lined, and filled with small, perfectly formed characters, but there were tears which made some sections illegible. He sat on the edge of the bed and switched on his reading light, examining the document. It was as he had thought, one sheet of a petition wrenched from its surrounding pages. It was a liability. If a security guard had seen him grab the paper and slip it into his pocket then the police would come looking for it. At the police station the young officer had carried those scraps of paper as though they were gold dust – officers must have collected them from the streets or from witnesses who'd picked them up as they fluttered down from the rooftop. Whatever the truth was behind such a shameful incident – and Song held a portion of it in his hand – the Party would issue orders that it should be kept secret. Song peered closely at the page, struggling to make sense of the characters.

> . . . but although I waited overnight, sleeping on the ground at their gate, no one would agree to see me. I returned home. I was . . . [illegible] distressed, but I found my wife even more distraught. During my absence

she said she had had a visit from a man called Xu, who
works at the village police station. He demanded . . .
[illegible] our daughter's body. At first she agreed,
because she thought he meant there was to be an investigation into her death. Then . . . [illegible] no investigation, but it was illegal to keep the body at home.
Because of what had happened she did not trust Xu, and
refused to give up our daughter's body. Xu left, threatening her, saying he would return the next day with
other officers to take the body by force, and that she
would be fined for refusing to give up the body. I agreed
with my wife's decision not to surrender her body, which
was our only evidence of murder. But I told her that we
could not leave our child lying . . . [illegible] and that
soon, despite the cold weather, her body would start to
decompose. That night, under cover of darkness, my wife
and I carried our daughter's body to the house of a friend
who had the facilities necessary to preserve her body
until . . . [rest of the page illegible.]

Still Song did not know who the man was, or where
he had come from, or why he had sought him out.
Nor did he know how the frozen child had died. But
he did know that the man was not crazy. Hungry now
for more information, he scoured the rest of the page for
characters he could decipher.

Teacher Ding brought us food and money collected at
the school . . . [illegible] . . . when they see our grief they
fear for their own children and no longer allow . . .
[illegible] . . . address this petition to Chen Dalei at the
Ministry of Public Security . . .

The name Chen Dalei struck Song like a blow from a fist. His father-in-law . . . no, his *former* father-in-law. He hated the man. He let the paper fall onto the floor and stood, pacing the small space up and down. Now he knew why someone had sent the peasant to him with his petition. He knew why that someone – but who? – might have expected him to help the man, if only he'd read the damn thing.

This scrap of paper – which was already a liability – was now a potential jail sentence. Song had sworn to the police that he had nothing to do with Li, but here was his former father-in-law's name in Li's own handwriting. He could be charged with lying to the police as well as withholding evidence. Even without a formal charge the police could make him disappear. Song didn't know how Chen was involved in Li's tragedy, but he didn't have to know. His former father-in-law's name was always an augury of disaster.

He picked up a lighter from his bedside table, and then he bent to pick up the paper from the floor. Holding it by a corner over the metal waste bin, he held up the flame and watched until the document had been consumed. He would not forget what it had said.

Four

YIDONG VILLAGE

Yanhua was startled from sleep. Her shoulder was being shaken back and forth, her muscles offering no resistance. She was never ready to be woken up, but it was five thirty and the sky outside was already light. She could see the sun shining through the piece of cloth that covered the window. Still she couldn't move. The heat from yesterday's sun remained heavy inside her home. Her little sister's sweaty forehead rested against her back. Her father let go of her and patted her sister's arm. Yanhua knew to roll out of the way as Meimei wailed and flailed her arms to protest.

'Come on, get up, I've prepared your breakfast for you,' their father said. He always spoke in a low voice at this time of the morning so as not to wake their mother.

Yanhua was so tired that the smell of the rice porridge made her nauseous. She had slept badly again. For the past few months she'd been having nightmares. She hadn't told anyone about them; everyone was worried enough without her making a fuss about her dreams. Still, she woke every day feeling exhausted, with fragments of nightmare still shifting in her head. She forced herself first to sit upright on the edge of the *kang* where the whole family slept, then to place her feet into the flip-flops that lay waiting on the dirt floor.

Groggily she exchanged ragged pyjamas for a grimy T-shirt which had once been orange, and for fraying shorts from which her mosquito-ravaged legs extended in a mass of scabs and red weals.

She sat at the small scratched piece of furniture which served as dining table and desk, watching her father pick up her little sister and seat her on a chair, where she slumped forward, letting her head fall heavily on her arms. Her father put bowls of porridge in front of each of them, the plump pieces of rice gleaming stickily in the liquid. Their mother was still sleeping on her side, her back rising and falling. Yanhua had heard her parents whispering late into the night. They were talking about Li Hetian.

'He was crazy to try something like that,' she'd heard her father say.

'I'd have done the same,' her mother had replied grimly. Something very bad had happened again, Yanhua could tell from their voices.

'Feed your brain,' her father said softly now. 'It will make our fortune.' Mechanically, Yanhua lifted the bowl. She started to spoon the food into her mouth, but then she thought that she would retch, and she pushed it away from her. She waited while her father persuaded her sister to eat a few mouthfuls, and then she lifted her school bag onto her back.

Her mother pushed herself up in bed, frowning and blinking.

'You're letting them go?' she asked her husband, alarmed.

'They have to go,' he said miserably. 'We've paid the fees, they must go to school while they can.'

'Please,' she wailed. 'Don't send them to school today, keep them at home with us. If we lose them . . .'

'There's no risk if they're sensible,' her father replied. 'They know how to behave.'

'But Li . . .' her mother cried. 'His poor frozen child . . .'

'Don't talk of that in front of the children!'

'I've got to go to school,' Yanhua protested, 'I need to. Don't make me stay at home. What will I do here all day?'

Her mother fell back on her bed with a moan of despair, and her father gazed at his wife for several long moments before taking a breath and heading them towards the door.

'Go, but stick to the path and be careful,' he urged. 'Always stay together.'

Out of the house, turn towards the east, cross a field of stubble, join the dirt path that ran along the ditch, shoes getting scuffed in the dust. Meimei was being a pain in the neck, refusing to hold Yanhua's hand. Now she had woken up she wanted to play silly childish games, prancing along the road and singing. It made Yanhua nervous.

'You heard what Baba said,' she complained to her little sister. 'You should be at my side.'

'There's nothing to be afraid of,' Meimei laughed, 'you can still see me, nothing can happen.'

Yanhua kept walking, head down. Her school bag was heavy on her back, weighed down with books. She was thinking about what her father had said that morning. 'We've paid the fees, they must go to school while they can.'

She had done this walk to school so many times she could do it in her sleep. They passed the mine, where the outbuildings were guarded by dogs. Meimei always stuck close by her side here, although the dogs were chained. Their teachers had warned them about rabies. It wasn't just the dogs that scared them, it was the men. A miserable queue of them were always lined up waiting to go down the shaft, or they were emerging, covered in black coaldust, their eyeballs the only clean thing about them. Yanhua didn't want to think about going down that shaft or spending all day down there in the dark. Some of the men waved at them, but Yanhua never waved back. Her mother had warned her about these men – they were strangers, they had come from places where the peasants had nothing or else they wouldn't risk their lives like this.

One of them was walking towards them along the path. This had happened the past few days when they'd been on their way to school, almost as though he had timed it so that they would meet. He looked very young, no more than a boy, perhaps sixteen years old, with dark skin and shaggy hair that covered his ears. His clothing was ragged. His singlet was torn and his flies half undone, his trousers held up with a belt. As he approached, he smiled broadly and said what he'd said the day before and the day before that.

'Good morning. Do you want to come and play at the mine?'

'No,' Yanhua said firmly, as she had said for the past few days. She didn't stop, she just kept on walking. She thought it was a really bad idea to play at a mine.

They had almost reached the amusement park. Yanhua averted her eyes. It was the part of the walk that scared her the most, although she couldn't say why. An amusement park should be fun, she told herself. But nobody in the village seemed to think of it as fun. Some villagers thought it was the best chance at prosperity they'd had. Of course, Chief Bo had demanded they surrender their farming land to it, but they would set up stalls to sell trinkets outside the amusement park gates when the tourists started to roll in. Other villagers said that only Chief Bo and his cronies would make money out of the amusement park. After all, they'd made nothing out of his other projects. Yanhua had once asked her father what Chief Bo was chief *of*, and he'd grimaced and said he was chief of everything in the village, that meant chief of the government, chief of the Communist Party and chief of most of the enterprises round about. That, he told her, meant people got angry at Chief Bo for turning them off their land, then they got grateful to him for giving them a job, then they got terrified that he'd sack them. Or, her mother added darkly, that he would vanish with the proceeds of his latest money-making project in a suitcase. Their mother worked in Chief Bo's household. She was the one who knew the man best.

Still, although she knew her parents disapproved, and although she knew that people had been thrown off their land for it, she and Meimei couldn't help feeling excited when they saw the roller coaster being erected, and the big wheel and the ticket office with its golden roof. They squealed when they heard that there was to be a pool of crocodiles inside, and then one day an advertisement had appeared on the wall outside, with a picture of a vast, snapping crocodile jaw, and ticket prices printed underneath. That night, their father had lost his temper.

'You think people like us can afford to buy tickets for thirty *yuan* each?' he shouted, enraged by their chatter. There had been tears, recriminations, it had been awful. It was the night she realized with a sickening clarity that her parents might not be able to afford to continue to send both her and Meimei to school. Most of her father's land had been taken away from him and what was left was so dry that nothing much grew there. He'd found himself a job as a mechanic in a workshop on the road to Wanmei County, but it only brought in about 400 *yuan* a month. Their mother worked as a cook at the household of Chief Bo, who was a gourmand. He kept his own pigs for pork, and a menagerie of other, rarer, animals that ended up on his table. Sometimes in the evening, as Yanhua and Meimei sat and ate a bowl of rice and cabbage, their mother would describe the latest thing she'd been required to cook for Chief Bo. There had been snakes and cats, and part of a camel. But what was important was that Yanhua's mother earned 300 *yuan* a month. Yanhua was twelve and Meimei was seven. One of them might have to be taken out of school. They wouldn't starve, but her father had always wanted more for them than that. That was why her father had yelled.

After all that, the amusement park had never even opened. Her father was more furious than ever. He said it was an insult to the families who'd lost their land. According to him – and he was a man who kept his ear to the ground – the project had gone over budget and the investors had lost interest. At one point he heard that the amusement-park management company had already bought the crocodiles, transporting them up from a zoo in the south of the country. Then he heard they were going to slaughter them because there was no food for them. Next he heard that the crocodiles had hidden in the muck at the bottom of their pool and refused to be captured and slaughtered, so they were living wild in there.

Yanhua had never met anyone who had seen one of the crocodiles. Still, at around the same time she realized she might have to leave school, their green, snapping jaws had taken up residence in her dreams. Despite herself, Yanhua glanced towards the ticket office. The girl who'd dropped out of school – Stupid Girl – was there. She was carrying a pail of water and a mop. She was three years older than Yanhua, and she had a job as a janitor at the amusement park. Whatever the weather, she always wore jeans that were tight around her sturdy thighs. Her sleeveless T-shirt showed strong plump arms, and her teenage body was already like a woman's. She'd got the nickname Stupid Girl because she'd done badly at school. When she left, people sneered and whispered things about her family. But after Yanhua's parents had told her that she too might have to leave school, Yanhua had started to look at Stupid Girl with eyes full of appalled sympathy. She felt so sorry for her. The girl was only stupid because she couldn't afford to go to school, and she must be so brave to work all on her own in the amusement park, not knowing whether there were crocodiles still there or not. Yanhua wouldn't have worked in the amusement park even if they'd paid her a fortune, and you could see that no one was paying Stupid Girl a fortune.

Stupid Girl was watching Yanhua. Yanhua raised her hand in acknowledgement.

She turned away to glance back at Meimei, who she'd assumed was running around behind her, but there was no sign of her. Yanhua's heart started to pound. She turned full circle, scouring the landscape with her eyes, and then again, shouting for her sister.

'Meimei,' she yelled, with all the air in her lungs. 'Meimei!'

Meimei wasn't frightened by the amusement park. Meimei was always begging Yanhua to sneak inside with her. Perhaps she'd taken advantage of her sister's distraction to do just that. There was nothing for it. Yanhua started to run towards the amusement park. Stupid Girl was still standing there with her mop in her hand, and Yanhua ran towards her, shouting, 'Have you seen my little sister?'

Stupid Girl didn't answer right away, and Yanhua went right up to her and said to her, face to face, 'Have you seen my little sister?'

She was so slow, Yanhua thought in frustration. Didn't she understand how urgent the situation was? Then Stupid Girl's broad face broke into a smile and she raised her hand to point. Yanhua turned to look and saw Meimei running towards her, laughing.

'I can't believe you couldn't see me,' the younger girl said, panting as she came to a halt in front of her older sister.

'Never, ever, do that again!' Yanhua screamed. She slapped her sister's face, and Meimei's grin dissolved into tears.

Five

He drifted in and out of sleep all night, troubled by dreams and mosquitoes but most of all by his former father-in-law. Waking suddenly from a dream he thought he must have hallucinated the name. He looked frantically for the petition on his bedside table until he remembered that he had burnt it.

In his lucid moments, he tried to think the thing through. The petition could have referred to some other Chen Dalei, of course. There would be other people, hundreds and thousands of people, with the same name. But surely the reference to the Ministry of Public Security and the fact that the man with the frozen child had been sent to Song meant it could not be anyone but his Chen Dalei.

He had hoped never to see his former father-in-law again. The Communist Party's Central Discipline Inspection Commission was investigating Chen for corruption, and with any luck the man would be put behind bars for good. Twice Song had received visits from the Commission's investigators requesting that he give evidence against his former father-in-law. So far Song had persuaded them that he had no useful evidence to bring. His hatred for Detective Chen had obsessed him in the past, but he had seen the destruction that obsessions wrought. He was safer staying away from the man. There were other complications, too. His ex-wife loved her father – well, that no longer had to concern Song. But his son, Doudou, loved his grandfather. How could Song testify against him?

There were people, too many of them, who knew that Song hated Chen. One of them – but *who?* – had sent the man with the frozen corpse to him.

For nearly a decade Song had worked under Detective Chen Dalei, and the man's cruelty and corruption had sickened him. It was a pity, of course, that Song had married Chen's daughter before he'd realized just how bad her father was, and how devoted his daughter was to him. Song had tried to hold it together, but it wasn't just Chen. His former father-in-law had surrounded himself with like-minded officers, and he had corrupted many of the others, so that Song found himself isolated. Chen's deputy, Psycho Wang, was nicknamed for his brutality. In the end, Song had buried his fist in Psycho Wang's belly and he'd walked out on the job. Then he'd walked out on the marriage. Now in the middle of the night he tossed and turned, reliving it all. The contempt and the anger and the frustration came back to him as real as if he was living it still, and now linked in some unfathomable way, and through some anonymous agent, with the frozen corpse of a child.

Somewhere in the early hours of the morning, Song knew two things. First that he would willingly murder Chen for giving him this sleepless night, and for his many crimes. Second, that he had to see him.

As soon as it was light, he called his ex-wife, Lina. It was too early for her, of course. He could hear it in her sleepy voice.

'Where's your father?' he asked. He had intended slipping the question in more discreetly, but he'd never been a diplomat and a night without sleep had only made things worse.

'At the police sanatorium in Huairou District,' she answered, and he thought that sleep had dulled her senses or she would not have given so much information so freely. Usually she treated everything he said with suspicion.

'Why's he in a sanatorium?'

'He needs rest,' she said, her voice already taking on the whine he remembered so well. 'He's being harassed. His health isn't good.'

'He's too sick to stand trial, is he?' Song asked acidly, then wished he'd kept his mouth shut.

'Don't talk about Daddy like that,' Lina complained. 'They can't put him on trial, he's done nothing wrong.'

'Of course you're right,' Song tried to backtrack. 'I'm just concerned about him because of the rumours I hear. I hope his health doesn't suffer.'

'Why are you ringing?' Now Song could hear the suspicion in Lina's voice. She was waking up.

'It's a lovely day,' Song said, forcing enthusiasm, looking out of the window at the brilliant blue sky. It was rare to have a day like this. 'I keep telling Doudou I'll take him out. I've cleared my desk, I thought it would be a good day to take a drive.'

He waited nervously. He was a good liar, but very little ever got past Lina.

'Why did you ask about Daddy?'

'Doudou's already eleven years old, he's growing up fast, he should see more of his grandfather. The boy needs role models.' The words made him want to wash his mouth out.

'So you're saying . . .' She was incredulous. No one knew better how much he hated the man. 'You mean you'll take us to see Daddy?'

The use of the word 'us' drew Song up short, but only for an instant. She'd been to the sanatorium before. She would at least be able to guide him there.

'All right,' Lina said slowly, 'we can have a walk, climb a hill, it will be good for Doudou.'

Song waited in the car park, watching in the rear-view mirror for his ex-wife and son to emerge from the building. When he saw them, he thought they looked like strangers, this skinny, pretty woman, always over-dressed and in clothes that were too young for her. Today she was in a short yellow sun dress, and gold stilettos (he wondered which hill she was going to climb in those) and she carried a patent leather bag. At her side an eleven-year-old boy, taller than ever and fatter too, thighs rubbing together, waddling rather than walking. He got out of the car to greet them.

'Hello, Son.' Song attempted a paternal smile.

'Hello, Father.' Doudou climbed into the back seat along with his mother.

Lina demanded that the air conditioning be turned up to maximum, and Song and Doudou held a stilted conversation about school. Lina interrupted constantly: 'He's getting bullied because he's so fat', 'His teacher says he's sleepy in class and asks whether it's because he's fat', 'He won't do PE any more, he says he doesn't like getting changed in front of the other boys because they see his fat'.

'You're getting bullied?' Song pulled this one fact out of the torrent.

'Mummy told me to hit them,' Doudou said quietly.

'Kick them, not hit them. I want him to take kick-boxing classes,' Lina said. 'Don't you think that's a good idea?'

Song's eyes met Doudou's in the rear-view mirror. Neither Song nor, it seemed, Doudou himself, could see him fighting. Song thought that if Doudou tried to kick anyone, he would fall over.

'You've got to do some regular exercise,' Song said gently. 'And eat less. It's the only way to do it.'

In the back seat, Doudou nodded miserably. Even his face was padded with fat. Song found himself wondering what the boy's face would look like if he slimmed down. As it was, it was difficult to determine whether he looked like either one of them.

'If you want him to lose some weight, you should take him in hand yourself,' Lina hissed at him. 'You're the one who used to be a full-time athlete, you know about bodybuilding.'

'That was a long time ago,' Song protested. But she was right, he could do it if he put the effort in. He could set up a training schedule for the boy, get him swimming – that was Song's sport – even get him eating healthily, although that was more of a challenge after years of Lina's indulgence. The next time he looked in the mirror Song saw that Doudou was eating sweets from a packet in his pocket.

'When you were training, there were drugs to make you faster,' Lina said conspiratorially. 'There must be drugs that could make him thinner. I asked a friend who's a kind of doctor, and he said that roundworms might work. He said some film stars buy a solution of their eggs, and drink it . . .'

'Roundworms?' Song – who suddenly realized what he was hearing – nearly drove off the road. 'Are you mad?'

'I'm only telling you what he said. I said I'd think . . .'

Song's mobile rang, and he took the call because it was Blue.

'The police were just here looking for you,' she said. 'They said witnesses saw you take something from the scene. They're very angry.'

'Don't worry,' Song told her. 'I'll sort it out.'

'There's another thing. On the Internet a man says he picked up a scrap of paper from the ground near where the man fell. He handed it in to the police, but he took a look at it first, and the man who fell is from Yidong. Do you know it? It's in Hebei province, 150 kilometres north-east of Beijing.'

'I've heard of it.' He was about to hang up, when he remembered to add, 'Thank you.' Blue was constantly trying to improve his manners.

'Also,' her tone of voice made his heart sink, 'they've started knocking the street down.'

'How far have they got?'

'They just demolished the corner shop, but they already came and banged on the gate and when I went out to speak to them they said we had to move out at once, or . . .'

'Or what?'

'Their attitude was threatening.'

Song thought that if you were as short as a ten-year-old, as Blue was, then anyone of even average height might look threatening. Still, it was rare that anything scared her.

'I'm sure we've got a bit of time,' he said. 'I'll sort it out when I get back.'

Song hung up. As he drove, his thoughts were on Anjialou and the imminent destruction of his office. He had no idea what he was going to do. He couldn't talk to Lina about it. He couldn't talk to her about anything.

They soon reached the edge of the city. The expressway took them north-east, and the plains gave way to mountains. This was poor countryside, and the peasants were supplementing the income they scraped from the land with tourism cash. A river dawdled through the valley, and the road was lined with restaurants.

'Tell me about your father's situation,' Song said when he saw in the mirror that Doudou had fallen asleep.

'He says the political wind is changing and his accusers will soon be in trouble,' Lina said. Detective Chen was clutching at straws, Song thought.

'I don't know why they're investigating him,' Lina carried on. 'He hasn't done anything that everyone else hasn't done too.'

'Not everyone,' Song said quietly.

'Everyone,' Lina insisted. 'He's being punished for being a good man. He helped people, and they gave him presents as a mark of respect. What's wrong with taking someone out for a meal . . . or giving them a camera . . . or a computer?'

Or a Buick, Song thought to himself, or a flat, or a roomful of women? Lina was right, though, her father wasn't the only one. But he'd made himself vulnerable because he was ostentatious in his corruption. He'd made enemies.

At the gates to the sanatorium there were high walls and a plaque announcing that this was a model government institution. Lina gave her father's name to the guards at the gate, and Song drove in. The building was modern, all mirrored windows and steel. It would have been expensive to build. There were signs to guest rooms, to restaurants, to tennis and squash courts and to a swimming pool. There were extensive landscaped grounds. Lina called her father on her mobile phone while Song parked. He had gone for a walk, they would find him on the hill behind the sanatorium. There was a pavilion there, part of an ancient imperial tomb complex that lay within the grounds.

They walked up the slope, Doudou wheezing like a pig in the scorching heat, and found the pavilion, its red roof and pillars battered by centuries of harsh weather, the swings from extreme winter to extreme summer wreaking devastation on the wood. Chen was sitting on a bench, looking out over the valley, a cigarette in his mouth and stubs littering the ground at his feet. He had been a big man, an imposing man, but he had shrunk so much that he was almost skeletal now. His face was gaunt, his skin an unhealthy purplish-red.

'The Slaughter Pavilion,' Doudou read from a sign. 'This pavilion was used to sacrifice animals in honour of Prince Cui, who is buried here.'

'Meat to the slaughter to honour the imperial household,' Detective Chen said, laughing harshly, 'I'm glad I sat here, it's the right place for me. I shall sit and wait for the knife to fall.' He took the cigarette from his mouth and crushed it alongside the others on the ground.

'What do you think, Doudou?' Detective Chen addressed his grandson. 'Do you feel hungry for some sacrificial lamb? Would you like to wield the cleaver? You want to take the first bite? You can chew on my arm, but there's not much flesh there.'

He thrust his arm towards the boy, who stepped sharply backwards. Lina seized her son's shoulders and pulled him away.

'Don't talk like that in front of the boy,' Song said, trying to keep his tone even.

Detective Chen staggered slightly as he rose from his chair.

'What brings *you* here?' Detective Chen looked at Song, recognizing him for the first time. 'Are you trying to get into her pants again? Too late. Someone else is in there.'

Song shook his head and walked off ahead of them to the car. He'd made a mistake, he thought as he walked, he'd thought he could stand the man's presence long enough to find out what he needed to, but just a few moments and he wanted to hit him.

They drove to the riverside and chose a restaurant which had its own fish pool. The place was heaving with people. Half the city seemed to have decided to take advantage of the good weather to drive out into the country. As they parked and got out of the car, a man approached them leading horses.

'Want a ride?' he shouted at them. 'This one's very strong. The fat one can ride on him if he wants.'

'Go on,' Chen urged his grandson. 'Let's see if he's right. He can't blame us if the thing drops dead.'

Doudou shook his head angrily and walked away from them.

'Leave the boy alone,' Song told Chen.

'Suddenly you're a father?' Lina asked spitefully. 'Doudou can take a joke. I know him better than you do.'

The restaurant had turned itself into a resort. There were young couples splashing in the swimming pool and abseiling down a climbing wall. Song and Doudou borrowed rods and went to try their luck in the fish pond. At first they stood in silence. Song had no more idea how to fish than Doudou did, so they just let their lines sit in the water.

'I don't mind being fat,' Doudou said after a few minutes, 'but when they laugh at me I feel like I might explode.'

Song didn't know what to say, so he said nothing. He knew what his son meant, that he felt he might explode with furious rage. That made him uneasy. Quickness to anger was a weakness that he did not wish to pass on.

When Doudou caught a fish, Song slapped him on the back to congratulate him and Doudou gave him a smile that transformed his face. It was, Song thought, the most physical contact they'd had in years, and the first smile he'd seen from Doudou in almost as long.

They ate Doudou's fish, barbecued with spices, as well as a donkey-meat stew that melted in the mouth, and pheasant diced and sautéed with chestnuts. Song found it hard to eat at the same table as his former father-in-law. Chen asked for a bottle of *maotai*, and drank the entire bottle himself, so that by the end of the meal he was red-faced and belching alcohol and barely able to sit upright in his chair. When Doudou asked to go and play crazy golf, Song suggested that Lina should take him.

'I want to talk to you about something,' Song said, when the two of them were alone.

'I want to talk to you about something,' Chen mimicked unpleasantly.

'What do you know about Yidong?'

'Yidong?' Chen slurred the word.

'Let me refresh your memory. You received a petition about an incident there from a man surnamed Li.'

'Who the fuck cares about incidents in bloody Yidong?'

'The incident was the murder of a little girl,' Song said quietly. 'Do you remember how she died?'

'Let me see. Was she playing in the middle of the road? Did she drink poison they'd put out for the rats? Drown in the fish pond? Let me see, what do piss-poor peasant brats usually die of?'

'Are you telling me you didn't receive the petition?'

Chen shrugged. 'That's very possible.'

'Things are different now,' Song told his former father-in-law. 'Things can't be covered up like they used to be. The girl's father ... well, he's stirred up public attention. Pieces of information about the case are appearing on the Internet. If you know anything, it's bound to come out.'

For a moment Chen appeared to be considering this. Then he smiled.

'An information research agency, is that what you call yourself? You want my information? You and everyone else. And none of you can have it. I'm safe.'

'You're safe? You?' Song heard himself laugh unpleasantly.

'I've built myself a panic room.'

'A what?'

Song took a cigarette from Chen's carton. He lit it. He'd given up smoking again that morning, but now he needed something to calm him down.

'It's American. A room made out of reinforced steel, the whole thing, eight centimetres thick, the floors, the ceiling, the walls. If I lock myself in, they can't get me out. They can shoot at the door for hours and they won't get in.'

'Very good,' Song drew on the cigarette. 'You've built your own sarcophagus.'

'Why would I die? It has its own electricity, its own air conditioning. They can burn the house down around me and it will still be standing.'

'A cell then, a prison cell!' Song raised his voice. He could feel the other diners' eyes on him.

'I have a safe in there,' Chen spoke quietly. 'I've filled it with documents detailing my transactions, original documents, photocopies, microfilms, tapes of conversations. My papers are safe there.'

Song shook his head.

'All my so-called friends who are calling for my head should know what's in those files,' Detective Chen said slowly. 'They've eaten at my table, they've praised me for my loyalty, enjoyed my protection, they've shaken my hand. It's all in there. All the reasons they have to thank me. If anything happens to me it will all come out.'

He reached out and grabbed Song's hand with fingers that were like driftwood, they had so little strength in them.

'I gave you my daughter and you betrayed me ... They told me you're going to testify against me, you ungrateful bastard. Do you know who she's sleeping with now?'

Again Song shook his head. He didn't care. He stubbed out the cigarette. It wasn't helping.

'Wang Rong,' Chen said.

Song's head started to spin. Wang Rong was the name Psycho Wang's doting parents had given him before they'd realized he was a psychopath. Chen must be mistaken. How could Lina even consider ...

Song felt a tap on his shoulder. Startled, he twisted in his chair.

'Daddy, I beat Mummy.' Doudou was grinning from ear to ear.

'It's true,' Lina said, walking up behind him. She was smiling too. 'You beat me fair and square.'

Song stared at his former wife. An image of her with Psycho Wang forced itself into his head.

'I'm just telling your dad about your new Uncle Wang,' Detective Chen said to Doudou.

The boy cast an agonized glance at Song. Then he turned from his family and walked away.

Six

YIDONG VILLAGE

Yanhua delivered her little sister to her ramshackle classroom. On the threshold, the smaller girl seized her big sister's hand and gripped it tight.

'I don't want to go to school,' she complained. 'I want to go home to Mama.'

'Don't be silly.' Yanhua pulled her hand away and gave the girl a push. 'You have to go to school.'

'But I miss Mama!' The little girl was wailing now, tears oozing from her eyes, snot dribbling from her nose. She had planted her feet firmly outside the classroom and lunged to throw her arms around Yanhua's waist.

Yanhua tugged at her little sister's arms, loosening the child's hold on her. She shoved her through the doorway, then crossed the courtyard to her own classroom and took her place in the front row.

Yanhua knew she had been nasty to her sister, but her father's words were still resonating in her head. 'We've paid the fees, they must go to school while they can.' He must have meant that soon one of them would have to drop out. Soon her parents would break it to her. She was the eldest, she had already had some schooling, it would be Meimei's turn, and she would end up like Stupid Girl with a mop and a bucket. She couldn't bear the thought.

'Your brain will make our fortune.' Her father's words echoed in her head. How could he have said that to her if he was planning to take her out of school? She didn't know anything about fortunes, except that they were hard to come by. But her brain amazed and excited her. It absorbed information like rice soaking in a pan, becoming fat and full and shiny. It was the way she could repeat everything she had seen once on a page that had astounded and excited her father and had made him borrow money to pay for her school fees.

Yanhua wasn't interested in her photographic memory except as a tool. The thing that electrified her was the way her brain could make connections, the way she was finding that she was ahead of her teachers, the way that something she learned in one class would jump out at her in another class as her brain seized upon one morsel of information and engaged it with another to make a whole.

She had seen a brain crushed once, its grey matter all mashed with bits of bone when the mine roof had collapsed and three men had died, and she'd watched them dug out. The brain had looked like nothing at all, like rotting bean curd or congealing porridge. Who would have thought that a brain could bring such joy?

*

She tried not to watch as her classmates filed in. It used to be the case that no one missed school unless they were really sick. Now there were two empty chairs. The girls weren't sick, she knew that much, but she had heard that they were being kept at home. It was in the nature of Yanhua's mind to question, but she couldn't bear to think too hard about why their parents would choose to keep them at home. Instead of thinking, she arranged her books on the desk in front of her and readied herself for the start of the class, her hands gripping the edge of her chair. In a few minutes, when the teacher began asking his questions, the synapses would start firing in her head and her arm would shoot into the air.

There was an extra empty chair. The fact struck her just as Teacher Ding walked into the classroom. Fengfeng was missing. Where was she? Fengfeng's parents weren't the sort to keep her home because of rumours, they were too eager for her to succeed. Fengfeng was Yanhua's biggest rival in class, and they didn't like each other much. There was too much at stake.

Teacher Ding greeted the class and the class chorused a greeting in return. He had come to the school the year before. He was bespectacled and bookish, and Yanhua thought he looked nice. She liked it when he smiled at her and praised her, and she liked to see his bare arms resting on the table, so pale and slender and smooth compared to the dark hard muscles of the men in the village. He marked the register. Yanhua noticed that the heat had produced beads of sweat on his forehead and that his shirt was clinging to his back.

'Anyone know where those girls are?' He nodded his head in the direction of the empty chairs.

'Girls are frightened crybabies,' one boy shouted out. It was the kind of contribution that would usually have raised a snigger or two and an angry retort from the teacher. But today the boy's voice landed into silence.

'Well, we'll begin with a passage from your cultural studies textbook,' Teacher Ding told the class in his quiet voice. 'Yanhua, will you read?'

She was his favourite, she knew she was, especially with Fengfeng away. She gave him a little nod and leaped to her feet, eager to please, eager to lift the shadow of worry from his face.

'Paris is the capital of France,' she read fluently. 'It is the home of scenic attractions such as the Eiffel Tower and the River Seine, as well as the site of many famous museums such as the Louvre . . .'

She let her tongue roll over the foreign names, loving them. She would never see the Eiffel Tower or the Louvre. She accepted that. European travel was beyond her wildest dreams. The most she could expect was a good job in the county town, perhaps in the government offices.

'You read very well,' Teacher Ding complimented her. 'Your classmates should emulate you.'

Yanhua sat down, trying to keep a smile off her face. She could feel jealous eyes upon her, but she was used to it. Teacher Ding often praised her, but he didn't intend to be mean to the others, she knew that. It was just that she was his favourite.

At break time she didn't feel like running outside to play. Instead she stayed sitting at her desk and opened her textbook.

'Aren't you going to play?' Teacher Ding asked her as he gathered her books.

'I don't feel like it,' she said, raising her face towards him.

He walked over to her desk and stopped in front of her.

'Yanhua, is there anything wrong?' he asked.

'No,' she said. 'Nothing's wrong.'

He started to walk away and she called after him.

'Teacher Ding, do you think a girl who doesn't go to school can learn everything from books?'

'Everything?' he smiled. 'That's very ambitious.'

She bit her lip and lowered her head. Her words had come out sounding ridiculous, as she had feared.

'Yanhua, you are a very clever girl, but you think too much. Go outside and play.'

Yanhua stared for a moment at her book, then nodded and smiled. He was right. She thought about things too much. She got up and followed Teacher Ding out into the yard.

When she returned to class later and took her seat again she knew she must put everything else from her, her annoying little sister, the jaws that snapped shut around her in her nightmares, the empty seats in the classroom, the possibility that her school life might end. None of this existed, only her brain and the teacher and the blackboard and the answers that sprang to her mouth.

That evening, when she had returned home and was eating her supper with Meimei and with her parents, the news hit them. It began with a banging on the door and an urgent male voice calling her father's name. Her father, grumbling about leaving his food, went to answer the door. Whoever it was must have asked him to step outside, which he did. A few moments later he stuck his head around the door and, looking grim, summoned Yanhua's mother.

'What's happened?' Meimei asked with her mouth full.

'How should I know?' Yanhua retorted. But her heart was pounding. She was one step ahead. Anyone could add two and two together and get four, but her brain could do it in half the time. Now she added together the empty chair, the urgent pounding on the door, her father's expression as he summoned her mother. She could feel great green jaws closing around her . . .

'Fengfeng's missing.'

Her mother had come back into the house and was standing in front of her daughters, eyes wide with fear. Their father came back into the house shaking his head.

'Don't tell them, don't frighten them,' he said.

'They have to know,' his wife said and carried on, speaking quickly as if she wanted to tell them everything before their father could stop her. 'She didn't come back home, and when they rang the school, the teacher said she hadn't been at school all day.'

The great green jaws of terror closed around her with a crunch. She had known. She had known all along, she had seen the empty chair. Her brain had put it all together long ago.

'But she left home this morning as normal.' Her mother carried on talking, too distressed to notice her daughter's expression. 'Why didn't anyone raise the alarm?'

'Doesn't she take the same route as you girls?' her father asked.

They nodded, mute with fear.

'Sometimes we meet her on the way to school,' Yanhua whispered. But even when they met, they didn't walk together. One of them would speed up or one of them would slow down so they didn't have to walk in silence side by side.

'And this morning?' her father asked.

Yanhua shook her head. If they had been friends, Yanhua thought, would she have raised the alarm when Fengfeng didn't come to school?

'We only saw one of the miners,' Yanhua said.

'A miner?' her father repeated.

'He's very young. He's sometimes on that path, I don't know why.' Yanhua said it defensively. She didn't even know why she'd mentioned him, except that she needed to feel as though she had been in some way helpful.

Her mother and father exchanged a glance.

'Did he say anything?' her mother asked.

'He asked us if we wanted to go and play at the mine,' Meimei piped up.

'What did you reply?' their mother asked.

'I just said no, of course.'

Yanhua was proud that she had said the right thing.

'Why would he have been on that path?' her father asked, but none of them could come up with a reason.

Their father told them that Fengfeng's uncle had asked all the men in the village to gather together to share whatever information they had and to form search parties. Shortly afterwards he left the house, telling their mother to lock the door after he had gone.

Seven

Rain cascaded against the window, cocooning her inside the dry office. Blue was alone at her desk, her face illuminated by the glow of her desktop monitor. Neither Song nor Wolf had felt it necessary to furnish the agency with curtains, and with its stark white walls and neon strip lighting it was not a welcoming place. She knew other young women who would have shuddered at the thought of being on their own in an office at night, especially when the demolition of the neighbourhood meant that the streets were deserted. But it was the only place in her universe that was peaceful. Sometimes she remembered that Song had his own quarters next door, but often he was out in the evening. Even when he was in, he kept himself to himself. She liked being alone here.

If Wolf had been at his desk, which was opposite hers, she would not have been reading what she was reading. Wolf's date blog was a list of the women he had dated that week, complete with statistics: age, estimated height, estimated weight, estimated income, educational attainment, an assessment of the success or otherwise of the date. Finally, there was a grade.

Tuesday. Liang XX, PR, foreign enterprise, 27 years old, 1.7m tall, 50 kilos, RMB 8,000+, university graduate. Warm-hearted and energetic in bed. Overall grade: A−

Blue frowned at the screen. Why had he marked Miss Liang down from an A? What flaw had provoked the minus? She sighed. When she had first come to work in the office, Wolf had found every excuse he could to be with her and she had been surprised to realize that he was attracted to her. He was the embodiment of cool, as far as she could see, and she knew herself to be entirely lacking in cool. Her previous boyfriend had left her because she was too short, and she had resigned herself to a life of spinsterhood. At first Wolf's attention had embarrassed her − she suspected that he was making fun of her − but soon she'd found herself swept up in a wave of romance and desire. Because they worked together there had been a sense in which their love was forbidden. They would kiss, only to have Song walk in on them, or touch when they were going through files together.

Then one day she had gone with Wolf to his mother's house. It was a last-minute arrangement and very informal. She hadn't had time to be apprehensive. But when she walked into the flat with Wolf, his mother's face fell. She greeted Blue civilly but without warmth and sat Blue down in the sitting room in front of the television while she took Wolf by the elbow and led him into the kitchen. Blue heard raised voices and turned down the volume on the television so that she could hear.

'So short!' she heard Wolf's mother say. 'Why do you want to go out with a girl like that? You're so tall and good-looking, and you qualified at one of our best universities. You're a good catch. She's got nothing to offer a man like you.'

'Don't talk about her like that . . .' Wolf's voice was pained.

'She's not even very pretty. Just average.'

'Ma, keep your voice down!'

But it got worse. The next thing that Blue had heard was the sound of weeping.

'Before your father died he comforted me by saying that you would look after me,' Wolf's mother wailed. 'He told me that you would bring me a grandson and that your family would be prosperous. She's so tiny. How will she ever have a baby?'

'Ma, she's sweet and she's clever, why can't you just look at her as . . .'

'If she does manage to give birth to a baby it will be a runt.'

'Ma, stop talking about babies. I don't give a damn about babies. She's just a friend. Nothing more. We haven't even talked about getting married, or babies . . . I'll find someone else for all that . . .'

That was when Blue had got up from the sofa and quietly left the flat.

Later, she thought Wolf must have realized that she had heard everything, because when she next saw him in the office his face was contorted with shame. She thought it would be easier for him if she didn't make any mention of it. As hours turned into days and weeks, she realized that it would never be mentioned again. It was as though the whole thing had never happened. Not their romance, not their visit to his mother's flat, or the conversation in the kitchen. None of it.

Blue exited Wolf's blog and began her nightly scavenge for news. She rarely bothered with the online edition of the *People's Daily*, which set her teeth on edge. Instead, she gathered information piecemeal from sites around the country and from individual bloggers. Ever since she was a teenager she had felt frustrated, not only by her short stature but because she wanted to know so much about the world. At last, here in this bare office, her computer plucked invisible strands of information and dropped them in front of her. Because she understood English, she could read newspapers from all over the world. She found she could learn about the domestic politics of America and Australia and Canada. She could even learn a lot about China's politics from these foreign publications, more than from her own country's newspapers. Most Chinese newspapers were also available online, but censorship was so tight that learning anything from them was like conducting an archaeological dig. For the past month she had been reading the online editions of *The Times* and the *Guardian* in preparation for her trip to England.

The door rattled in its frame. She lifted her head.

Shadows moved outside the window and for a moment she thought she heard footsteps splashing through the deluge. She shook her head. It was just the wind and the rain. She turned her eyes back to the monitor.

She typed a few characters into the Baidu search engine. She always had to think carefully before she did that. If she searched for the religious sect 'Falungong', she'd be shown results only from official newspapers. Her aunt had a friend who had been a believer in Falungong. She said her friend was slightly batty, but a danger to no one, except perhaps herself. Still, she'd taken part in a sit-in and been detained by the police, and she hadn't been seen since. One had to apply caution across the board: the words 'Tiananmen Massacre', or even just 'democracy', or 'human rights' all set off alarm bells – as though you could ban the concept at the same time as the word. In the bad old days, some poor artist used to sit in a workshop painstakingly airbrushing Lin Biao out of pictures depicting Chairman Mao. Nowadays banks of computers hummed away filtering Internet traffic from abroad and thousands of eyes skimmed millions of words. All to the same purpose, which was the creation of an alternative reality. These days people weren't so compliant. Netizens found ways to wiggle and slide around the bans, splitting words to fool the filters, or replacing them with pictures. But it was a dangerous game.

All the photographs of the frozen child had already been purged from the Chinese sites. If there was video, it might have found its way out of China and onto

YouTube, but this evening Blue couldn't bring YouTube up on her screen, and she thought perhaps it was censored tonight. You could never tell. Things came and went at the whim of the authorities.

Something banged against the window and she jumped half out of her chair. Then, cautiously, she went to look. Outside, all she could see was black sky and hurling rain. One of the metal gates had blown open, and it was swinging against the wall. Perhaps it was that she had heard, or something falling from the roof washed down by the rain. She thought about going outside to close the gate – Song was scrupulous about security – but she couldn't face getting soaked. If she was honest, she was a little scared too. Maybe she would go home. Then, looking out into the darkness, she thought that maybe she would stay and sleep on the sofa instead. Neither option was good. For the first time ever, she felt trapped in the office.

She returned to her computer.

Chat rooms were still awash with speculation about the case of the frozen child. After scrolling through the comments for a few minutes, Blue closed her eyes, but the glare of the screen was burned onto her retina. She opened them again, and couldn't stop herself reading on although even she had had enough.

A brick came hurtling through the window, spraying glass around it, and landed in front of Blue's desk. She screamed and leaped to her feet. But there was no time to recover. A second brick followed the first, this one on a different trajectory, breaking a second window, landing on the sofa. Wind whistled through the broken glass. Outside Blue could see figures moving, heading towards the door.

Blue ran to the door to Song's quarters. She had never been in there, would never have dreamt of entering except in such circumstances as these. She thought, with her heart sinking, that he had probably locked the door. But when she tried the handle the door opened, and she slipped inside. She didn't dare turn the light on. In the darkness she realized with a leap of relief that she could lock the door from inside by turning a small lever. This she did, and then held herself as still and as quietly as she could.

She could hear them bursting into the office. There was a lot of banging around.

'Come on out, don't hide!' a man's voice shouted. It was rough, uneducated, with a Beijing burr.

'She was in here. Hey! Lady! Where are you? We want to meet you.'

Footsteps approached the door behind which she hid. Someone rattled the door handle. Every muscle in her tensed. Her heart was pounding so hard she thought they must be able to hear it.

'She's locked it.'

Something hit the door. A foot? A chair? The door would not hold. It was as flimsy as everything else in the office, bought for economy, not to last. The banging on the door stopped. For a few moments it seemed they had gone, there was so little noise. Then all hell broke loose. Blue, paralysed with fear, knew that they –

whoever they were – were smashing up the office. She could hear the splitting of wood, the smashing of glass, heavy objects hurled around. Blue closed her eyes tight, but in her mind's eye she saw hands seize her beloved computer and throw it to the floor ... she could not bear it. Blue threw open the door and stepped into the devastation of the office.

'Stop it,' she begged. 'You're hooligans. Stop it.'

They paused in their work of destruction, and they started to laugh at her. Then one of them stepped towards her swinging a wooden club, and that was the last that she knew.

Eight

It was Song who found her. He walked through the office door and stopped dead, gazing around him at the devastation first with incomprehension and then in shock. He saw Blue lying on the floor with blood oozing from a gash in her head and he hurried over to her. He knelt down next to her and touched her cheek. Her eyes opened and her face crumpled in pain.

'What happened?'

'They smashed it . . .' she whispered. She tried to move and succeeded in pushing herself up onto one elbow. She looked around her and moaned before collapsing once more onto the floor. Song was seized by cold fury. Desks and chairs were scattered in pieces, their legs broken off. The computers were a mountain of shattered plastic panelling and pulverized innards. Daubed on the wall in black paint was a circle and inside it the character *chai*: 'demolish'. Attacks on property weren't unusual, it was a quick way of getting people out of their homes in a hurry. But this was unusually violent.

Blue touched her forehead, then stared at the blood on her fingers.

'Did you know them?' Song asked urgently.

Blinking, she shook her head.

'How many were there?'

She closed her eyes.

'. . . not sure . . . three or four . . .'

'Did they say anything?'

But this time she couldn't even summon the energy to shake her head.

'OK, let's talk later. We should get you to the hospital, you're going to need stitches.'

She moaned a protest, but she was in no condition to fight. He pressed a clean towel to her head. She pushed his hand away and took the towel from him. When she tried to stand to walk out to the car, her legs gave way. In the end she let him pick her up and carry her. She was as light as a puppy.

In Accident and Emergency there were endless registration papers and a deposit that had to be paid upfront. Song lost his temper with an incompetent receptionist, then lost his temper with the nurse, who asked endless questions while Blue sat on a bench holding her bleeding head in her hands. In the end, Blue had beckoned him close.

'Please, Song,' she murmured in his ear. 'Don't shout any more. It makes my head hurt and it's embarrassing.'

Shamefaced, he'd apologized to the nurse, and to the receptionist, who wouldn't meet his eyes any more.

When they'd taken Blue to have her wound cleaned and stitched, Song rang Wolf. A woman answered the phone. She had a slightly breathy voice, and when Song asked for Wolf she giggled as she passed the phone over. Song told him what had happened, and Wolf was immediately frantic with worry. Song assured him that Blue would live, and that no, she had no brain damage as far as he could tell.

'Wolf,' Song said, 'Your friend sounds charming, but you've got to kick her out and get over to the hospital. I can't leave Blue on her own. I have to get back to the office.'

'OK, I'm on my way.' Song heard Wolf turn away from the phone and dismiss his companion. Her voice rose in protest. A door slammed. After a few moments, Wolf returned to the phone. 'What if the hospital calls the police?'

Song exhaled slowly. In theory he should have reported the attack on Blue. The investigation of an assault was a job for the police, but he was not inclined to involve them. For years Chen Dalei had been threatening to revoke Song's business licence. It was too much of a coincidence that the attack had happened on the same day that he had clashed with the detective. The man might be in disgrace, but he still had enough power to send a band of thugs around to trash the place.

'If the hospital brings them in, we can't do anything about it. Tell Blue it's OK to cooperate. But if the hospital doesn't call the police in . . .'

'. . . then we don't.' Wolf finished the sentence for him. 'We find them instead.'

*

An hour later, and for the second time that night, Song stood and stared around the devastation of the office. He glanced down and saw that the only thing still undamaged and lying in its appointed place was the cheap plastic doormat which greeted all who arrived in the office with the words '*Churu Pingan.*' May you enter and leave peacefully.

'Bastards,' he muttered. He prodded at the mess with his foot. Files had been pulled down from the shelves, paperwork ripped out and emptied on the floor. Invoices, unpaid bills, witness testimony, contact details, all littered the floor like confetti. He bent and, still cursing, started to pick up the papers one by one. But then he had nowhere to put the papers until he could clear space, so he started to do that. His rage poured into the task and he worked until he was sweating, but it was futile. At last he stood up, roaring with frustration.

He had borrowed his father's savings to set this place up. At last they were breaking even. He'd paid his father back *yuan* by *yuan*, he'd taken his father out to dinner the night they were even and ordered him lobster. He'd bought every stick of furniture in the place with cash that was hard earned. He'd invested in the computers and the listening equipment that he'd thought they could transfer to new premises. He paid Wolf and Blue decently because he needed their loyalty. This, the morass that lay around him, was the bread and butter of the agency. Without this, without Wolf's notes on the insurance scam he was investigating, without Blue's notes on her background checks, they had nothing. No one would pay them, and then how could he afford the deposit on a new office?

The gate squealed and Song stepped towards the window. He wanted the thugs to come back. He wanted to bury his fist in someone's face. Outside the rain was still hurtling down from the sky. He was mystified by the black and shiny creature who stood jigging impatiently in the rain, knocking on his door. It did not, at least, look threatening. He opened the door and a woman stepped past him, her face hidden under an oilskin. She removed the cloak from her head and shook the rain from it, and the water slashed onto the floor, soaking the pile of papers he had salvaged.

'What the fuck are you doing?' Song shouted.

The woman – in her thirties, thin, short hair framing a face that was bare of make-up or jewellery – stared around her, then looked at him, eyes wide.

'What the hell happened here?' she asked.

'Who the hell are you?'

'My name is Jin Dao.' She stepped towards him, holding out her business card and he found himself taking it. 'I'm delighted to meet you,' she said. 'So tell me what happened.'

Song looked at the card. It described her as a professor of law at Beijing University. In her jeans and T-shirt and wearing Wellington boots she didn't look like a professor of anything. He didn't want to talk to her or to anyone else, but Song found himself opening his mouth and speaking.

'They're demolishing the street.'

'You've been delaying?'

Song shrugged.

'And that?' she pointed to a patch on the floor that was unmistakably blood.

'They attacked my assistant, she's in the hospital.'

The woman frowned.

'It's unusual for them to go that far,' she said. 'Harassment is normal, and beatings, of course, if nothing else works, but it's usually a process that takes weeks. To progress so rapidly to physical harm . . . have you considered the possibility that there was another reason?'

How was it, Song wondered, that this woman could be in his office for less than five minutes and ask the very question that was on his mind?

'Tell me why you are in my office or get out,' he snapped. 'I've had a bad day, as you can see.'

She looked at the devastation around her. There was nothing to sit on, scarcely anywhere even to stand.

'We can't talk here,' she said. 'Is there somewhere quiet we can go?'

He gazed at her in disbelief.

'I'm not exactly in a position to take on any new clients.'

'No,' she said. 'It's about a former client of yours, Li Hetian.'

'I don't have a client called Li Hetian.'

'Well you don't now – ' she was matter-of-fact – 'because he fell off the top of the International Trade building.'

They walked through the rain. Song tried to shelter both of them under his umbrella, but it wasn't easy. Song avoided the biggest of the puddles while Jin walked straight through them in her boots.

'Li was never my client,' he told her.

'But he came to see you?' She turned towards him, rain dripping from her hood down over her face. 'I'm assuming he came to ask for your help.'

'He did,' Song agreed. 'But I threw him out.'

They walked in silence. He could feel her disapproval.

In a moment they had reached an empty cafe in the centre of a strip of three buildings that remained, like an island, in a sea of demolition.

'It's certainly quiet enough,' Jin murmured.

'Xiao Wei, you're still here,' Song said to the owner of the cafe, who had opened the door and was ushering them inside.

'Only just. We'll be packing up tomorrow. I don't want any trouble.'

Song nodded and cast a warning glance at Jin Dao. He didn't want to talk about what had happened to the office, although he knew that by the next day the whole neighbourhood would be buzzing with it. Wolf would not keep quiet. He had no sense of discretion. Some-times Song wanted to wire his jaw shut.

'We need somewhere to talk,' Song said, and Xiao Wei showed them into a small back room with a table and a bare lightbulb. There would not be much to pack, Song thought. They ordered beer and tea. Then Song ordered noodles, because he realized that he had not eaten for several hours.

'If you know Li came to see me, you must know who sent him,' Song said.

She didn't reply immediately. She fiddled with the teapot. Song could see that she didn't want to answer.

'I have a right to know,' he said. For some reason this made her smile, and he asked her why.

'Because I am drowning in other people's rights,' she said.

'I don't understand,' he said, irritably.

'Well, I'm a professor,' she replied. 'I teach at Beijing University. But my research is on vulnerable popula-tions.'

'You must be very busy.'

'I take on cases pro bono – in most cases my clients have no way of paying me. And most of the cases are in the countryside.'

'Are you what they call a "rights defender"?' Song asked.

'I suppose I am.' She met his eyes with a cool gaze. 'That's what some people call us. I don't like it much. It's a meaningless label. I don't suppose you like being

71

called a private detective much either, it must make people think you just follow unfaithful husbands.'

Song grunted, but he didn't say anything. He was thinking about her being a rights defender – simply a political activist by another name, everyone knew that. People were no longer 'pro-democracy' activists, instead bright young lawyers tried to argue with the Communist Party on the basis of its own constitution and laws. You had to be wary of people like that. Their aim was to stir up political trouble. And while Song was no friend of the Party, he had seen the bloodshed of a Communist backlash, and he had sworn then to avoid politics like the plague. It was a ridiculous resolution, of course. If you didn't touch anything that was tainted by politics, then you'd end up touching nothing.

'So who sent Li to me?'

Jin sighed.

'I'll tell you what I know. A week ago, I received a text message from my . . . source. It listed the name of a village, Yidong, and two names, Li Hetian and you, Private Detective Song Ren.'

'Who is your source?'

'His name is Tang Ning. He's a journalist for the *Economic Information News*.'

'I know him . . .' Song thought he should have realized; it made sense. He had met Tang Ning the year before when he was working on a case. He had liked the guy. The word 'journalist' covered a multitude of sins. Some of them were happy to live on bribes. Others, like Tang Ning, seemed to be fearless, taking on corporations and officials in fights they had no hope of winning. After their paths had crossed, Tang had approached the agency twice to help him dig up information, and twice Song had helped, each time against his better judgment. This was the way to get closed down. In the end, and in both cases, Tang's paper had refused to run the stories. But Tang had told Song that his reports would be circulated internally, among senior Party and government members, and that therefore ultimately they would have an impact. He had seemed to Song to be eternally optimistic, unfazed by failure, believing only that it heralded success just around the corner. Song tried to think back. Had he mentioned Detective Chen to Tang? Had he talked about his former father-in-law? He couldn't remember having done so. But if Tang Ning was an investigative reporter then he could easily have found out.

'How did Tang know about Li Hetian?'

'He visited Yidong six months ago, in the winter. There had been a whole series of mine disasters, and he wrote a report. But his text message was sent from Britain. He left three months ago to do a PhD in economics. By the time he left he had become disillusioned. He said he wanted a career change.'

'Did you tell him what happened to Li?'

Jin shook her head.

'I've been trying to get hold of him ever since he sent me the message but I can't reach him.'

Song rubbed his hands over his face.

'What's your interest in the case?' he asked. 'Why did you come and find me?'

'At first I didn't know what to do about his message. I wanted to ask for more information, but I couldn't reach Tang. When I began to see the name of Yidong circulating on the Internet, I realized that the Li Hetian in Tang Ning's message might be that Li, and when I asked some other sources they confirmed this. At that point I started asking around, trying to find you. I think Tang would only have sent me this message if he wanted me to look into the cover-up. We've worked together many times in the past. He'd only have suggested it if he thought Li Hetian needed my help. When I heard he was dead I felt ashamed. Are you sure there's nothing you can tell me?'

Song shook his head. He could have told her what he'd read on the petition, but he would not. He did not trust her, this woman who arrived in the middle of a rainstorm. He didn't know Tang Ning well, although he had liked him. He liked this woman well enough, but on this particular day he did not trust his own instincts. Name cards could be printed very cheaply. The names of mutual contacts could be discovered through third parties. He trusted no one.

'Then I'll have to go to Yidong,' she said. 'I want you to come with me.'

He watched her sipping her tea. She was so calm and so controlled. But even if she was who she said she was, she represented danger. There was a line that everyone knew about, an invisible line between political safety and political danger, like the borders of a country. The line twisted and faded, leaving everyone unsure where it lay, so that they stayed well back from it, afraid of stepping over by mistake. Song knew that the line was there, in this room, with him, and that it ran across the table like a ravine, dividing him from Jin Dao. He had already stepped over that line too many times.

'Well, will you come?' she repeated the question.

'Why do you need me? You can take care of yourself.'

'I can, but even I need help sometimes, and we both know that this is a sensitive matter. Tang Ning spoke highly of you, he spoke as though you cared . . .'

'. . . for what? For people's rights, like you?' He shook his head. 'No, you've got me wrong. Look, I'm sorry, but I scarcely know you.'

She stared at him, catching his eyes with her own and holding his gaze.

'I know you and your sort only too well,' she said, getting to her feet. She pulled on her waterproof and headed for the door.

He watched her leave, then lowered his head into his hands and closed his eyes. He saw the swaying child and heard her father's voice.

'*You're my last hope, please help . . .*'

He saw his former father-in-law's name written in the perfect calligraphy of Li Hetian, who had died of desperation. All that tomorrow promised was a visit from the police demanding the scrap of petition that he'd removed from the roof.

Everything he had was already in ruins. He got to his feet and went after her.

Nine

Yanhua couldn't sleep. As dusk fell, the search parties went and returned in waves while the women stayed in the houses with the children. They listened for the excitement that would mean that Fengfeng had been found and that it was over, and that she was safe and sound.

Lying side by side with her sister on the *kang* Yanhua clutched both of Meimei's hands and stared at the cracks in the ceiling, listening to the voices that whispered and wept and the shouts in the distance. The searches continued until the sky turned black, and torches could make so little impact on the night that the men didn't know where they were and they returned to the village. After that the rain came, turning their yards and their alleyways to mud. The shouts and the tears and the whispers were silenced by the roar of the rain, and at last Yanhua fell asleep.

The morning brought no relief. Homework or play was unthinkable. Yanhua and Meimei got their own breakfast, and the morning passed as rumour spread from household to household, adults gathering in the streets and alleys between the houses. When they got hungry at midday they found some leftover food and heated it up for themselves in a wok on the stove. They were still eating when their father reappeared.

'You're coming with me,' he said.

'Where are we going?'

He was not himself. Normally he would talk to them, he would explain. But today he herded them through the door. They found themselves, along with what appeared to be the entire population of the village, outside the offices of the Party Secretary. Yanhua was too short to see over the heads of the crowd. She could hear a man's voice and thought it was Chief Bo.

'I understand your concerns, and I'll reflect them to the higher levels . . .'

His voice was drowned out by a surge of shouts from the crowd.

'How long will that take?'

'This isn't the first time, you know what's happening . . .'

'What about the police? They're doing nothing.'

Yanhua elbowed her way into the crowd. She reached the front and saw that a small group of angry women had approached Chief Bo and were shaking their fingers at him and cursing him. At their knees two little girls shook their fingers too, and cursed. For some time, Yanhua watched, fascinated. She had never seen such a breakdown of the normal pattern of things. She had never seen such anger, she had never seen the villagers – usually a cliquish, squabbling lot – unite like this, nor had she seen Chief Bo look so much at a loss. She'd always seen him striding around like an emperor, his tummy pushed out in front of him. She'd overheard her mother telling her father how he filled that tummy with meat and alcohol over meals that lasted hours. But there he was, bowing his head in acknowledgement of their criticisms and assuring them he would launch an immediate investigation into Fengfeng's disappearance.

After some time, Yanhua got bored and began to look for Meimei, scanning the crowds. There were plenty of children – whole families had come together, no one was leaving a son or a daughter at home. She spotted her mother and her father, but she couldn't see her sister. She began to ask around.

'Have you seen Meimei? Have you seen my little sister?'

Yanhua elbowed her way through the crush of bodies, and eventually she found herself next to her mother.

'Mama,' Yanhua said urgently. 'Do you know where Meimei is?'

Her mother looked down at her.

'She's not with you?'

'No,' Yanhua wailed. 'I've looked for her everywhere. I thought she was with you.'

Her mother started to push through the crush towards her father. Yanhua kicked her feet into the dust and clasped her hands together impatiently.

A little boy came up to her. He was tiny, with a perpetually snotty nose and eyes prone to tears. Yanhua knew him well. He was always trying to hang around with the bigger kids.

'Your sister went to the amusement park,' he said.

'Meimei? You're sure?'

'They wouldn't take me with them.'

'Tell my mother I've gone to get her back!' she ordered him and turned and ran.

Yanhua set off down the path, as if she was going to school. But this time she was running as if her life depended on it. She was consumed by fury and by the need to reach Meimei before she was snatched up by the crocodile jaws that lurked in the amusement park.

When she stopped to catch her breath, she thought she heard children's voices. Thirty yards away, off the path, there was a small orchard, and the voices seemed to be coming from there so she decided to run in that direction to take a look. Sure enough, there were children darting among the stones and trees. Already she felt easier, and briefly she considered turning around and heading home. There were so many of them together, the sun was shining warmly, the tips of the trees were moving softly and slowly in a summer breeze, and even she couldn't believe that any of them were in danger. Meimei must be among them, she thought. When she shouted her sister's name, the herd of children ran in her direction, and one of them, a boy who often teased her, tapped her on the head as they swept by. But she could not see Meimei among them.

'Stop,' she shouted to the children, and because they were used to obeying her, they slowed and stopped and stood around while she addressed them.

'I thought Meimei was with you,' she said to them, and she thought that she might burst into tears as she looked from face to face.

'She is . . .' The children looked around, bemused.

'Did you go to the amusement park?' Yanhua demanded.

No one would look at her.

'Did you?'

'We sneaked in,' one boy said, the one who had swiped her on the head. 'Then we saw someone coming, and we got out of there.'

'Was Meimei with you?'

'Yes, she was . . .' a girl insisted, but the boy looked uncertain.

'Meimei! Meimei!' First one started to call, and then another, and another, all walking and running around, looking into the trees. But when there was only silence in response, and when the sky seemed to cloud overhead they drew closer to one another and hung their heads in silence.

Only Yanhua kept on running and shouting, returning to the path with desperation now driving her steps. She had to pass the mine. There were men milling around.

She looked for the young boy who'd asked whether they wanted to play. But all the men were so far off and so covered in dirt that she couldn't see their faces clearly enough to know whether he was among them.

She arrived at the gates of the amusement park. She stopped.

'It's just a poster, it's nothing,' she muttered to herself. 'You're being silly, there's nothing to be frightened of.'

If Meimei was inside, she must get her out and get her home.

Quaking, she approached the gates. They were swinging open. To her left, there was an unused ticket office. To her right was a gift shop, its windows painted with cartoon crocodiles. She peered inside. It was empty, except for a cardboard box that appeared to be full of stuffed crocodile toys. There was no one around, and for a moment she nearly turned and ran. Meimei was probably home by now, she thought. She must have missed her on the road. Then she remembered the way the boy had looked, his uncertainty that Meimei had been with them when they fled the amusement park, and her resolve stiffened.

She felt a drop of rain on her cheek, and when she looked up she saw thunderclouds gathering. Her chin quivered. She did not want to be here, and she most definitely did not want to be here in a thunderstorm. Nevertheless, she proceeded under the entrance arch, leaving ticket booth and gift shop behind her, and made her way further into the amusement park.

The path was shaded with plastic palm trees in garish colours, yellow and green and pink. On one side of the path there was a children's fairground, with a carousel, and a little train that would puff around a track, and bumper cars, except that all of it was immobile and rusting. On the other side of the path was an overgrown swamp, which terrified her. The path branched into a bridge over the swamp, but she kept going straight ahead, advancing deeper into the park. She didn't dare shout out Meimei's name here. She could hardly even bear to hear her own footfalls on the path, and she clung to the sensation that she was invisible. There were big cages which looked as though they were intended for large animals or birds. All of them were empty.

Then she saw her. Meimei was sitting on a swing, and next to her sat Stupid Girl. They were playing with one of the crocodile toys from the gift shop, but Stupid Girl kept glancing up, as though she was waiting for something. Yanhua was so excited that Meimei's name was nearly out of her mouth, but she bit it back. She wanted to run to her sister and slap her for running off, but instead she stopped dead. Something was terribly wrong. Her fear of this place overwhelmed her. In the distance, Yanhua heard the noise of a car.

At that moment, the sky darkened and the rain fell in a deluge over Yanhua and Meimei and Stupid Girl. Suddenly soaked, both of them stood, shrieking. Stupid Girl ran in one direction, towards a hut, shouting for Meimei to follow her. Meimei glanced at Stupid Girl, and then ran in the other direction, towards Yanhua –

who she could not see – and the shelter of the plastic palms. She was half blinded by the rain, so she didn't see Yanhua until her older sister reached her and grabbed her wrist and turned, pulling her startled sister behind her.

Yanhua could hear Stupid Girl shouting for Meimei by name and the noise of the car. Yanhua pushed Meimei, protesting, down into the foliage at the edge of the swamp, two or three metres from the edge of the road.

'Shut up!' she hissed in her sister's ear. She clamped a hand over Meimei's mouth.

Slowly, a white van approached, its wheels sending a sheet of water into the air on both sides. Meimei was struggling, but Yanhua held her down. She saw that Meimei was still clutching the stuffed crocodile. It blended into the leaves. Again she hissed, 'Shut up! Be quiet!'

They lay there, Yanhua convinced that at any moment a great jaw would snatch them from behind. Her eyes were glued to the road. As the van drew closer she couldn't believe what she was seeing. In the cab, turning her head this way and that to look all around, was Stupid Girl, and beside her, in the driving seat, was Yanhua's beloved Teacher Ding. For a moment she nearly stood up and waved. Then she dropped her head again into the leaves and moaned. She didn't understand what was going on. Why was Teacher Ding chasing Meimei? Her fear distorted everything, she couldn't think. She lay still until the van had passed, eyes wide open, gazing at the raindrops on the leaves. When she raised her head again the clouds had swathed the sky so darkly that it seemed like night, and Meimei sobbed beside her.

'Come on,' Yanhua said, 'let's go.'

But as they scrambled to their feet, Yanhua shivered and scanned the black path up ahead. They were still far from home.

Ten

BEIJING

First they took the expressway to the north of the city. When they exited onto small roads they found they were thick with coal trucks driving towards the city. The road started to rise up into the mountains, and Jin Dao gave him impatient instructions. 'No, no, you've missed the turning now . . . Yes, here, I said second exit, didn't I?'

The sky was blue, and Jin Dao rolled down her window so that the wind blustered through the car. She was wearing a T-shirt, loose linen shorts that ended just above neat knees, and her toes peeked out from flat leather sandals. From the corner of his eye he saw that she observed everything closely, frequently stretching her head out of the window to look behind them at something which had caught her interest. They toiled up mountainsides, stuck behind trucks which huffed and creaked. They made their way between terraced slopes, through vertiginous passes. They descended into the valley again and drove through cultivated fields.

On another day, on another mission, it would have

been a perfectly pleasant outing. But neither of them could enjoy it. For Song, the anger of the night before had transmuted into frustration and shame. All that he had worked for had gone, the agency was destroyed. Blue had been hurt, and all because he had failed to protect her. A man who had asked him for help had died. The police had not abandoned their pursuit of him and the missing scrap of petition. Every half an hour they called his mobile and he ignored it. Underlying all this was the sour memory of his meeting with his former father-in-law, and the foul image in his head of Psycho Wang and Lina.

He was largely absorbed in his own misery, but he knew, from the restless quality of Jin's silence, that she was not happy either.

When eventually Jin Dao admitted she was lost, it was already the middle of the afternoon.

'I'm starving,' she said first of all. Then, 'I think we should stop to eat, and ask the way.'

He didn't reply. He was too hungry to pick a row.

'Didn't you hear me?' She sounded irritated. 'I don't know where we are.'

'Nor do I,' he said. When he saw a hand-painted sign advertising peasant food, he followed the arrow along a dirt track and to a hut. There was a garden overgrown with herbs and vegetables, and a few wooden tables and chairs in the open air on a platform that overlooked the valley. When they got out of the car a woman appeared, dark-skinned, a bare-bottomed baby on her hip, a scruffy cat curling around her heels. She could provide them with food, she said, and with a room for the night too if they needed one. Jin Dao shook her head at that.

'I want to reach the county town tonight,' she said.

'Wherever it is,' Song added, and she pretended that she had not heard.

They sat down at a table. It was cool and pleasant. In the distance they heard the rumble of thunder, and a breeze moved briskly around them. Far below them, a silver river twisted and turned. Fruit trees grew on its shores. For the countryside, the summer was always a struggle between flooding and drought. The recent rains made this land look lush, although many had given up farming because of the lack of water. There were great reservoirs not far from here, but their waters were piped to Beijing to keep the capital from turning to dust.

An elderly man brought them a menu, and they shared a cold beer. When the food arrived, she fell upon it. In silence, they ate their way through a tomato omelette that was crisp and golden at its edges, sliced potatoes that had been deep-fried in oil and spices, and dark-green leaves that grew wild.

Once they had eaten, Song felt sufficiently collegial to share with Jin what he had read in the portion of petition that he had burnt. He remembered it almost verbatim.

'It said he and his wife decided not to surrender the body because it was the only evidence they had of murder. But they were afraid the body would start to decompose although the weather was cold. So they took the body to a friend's house where they could preserve it – that must have meant freezing it.'

'That must mean a meat-storage facility,' Jin said.

'And then he'd have needed a meat truck to get a frozen body all the way to the city from here,' Song said. 'He must have had good friends to help out with something like this.'

'If people had sympathy for him, they'd help him out,' she said. 'I've seen it before, even in extreme situations. We may think what he did was crazy, but to him it made sense, and probably it made sense to his family and friends too.'

'Is that what you do? You help people you have sympathy for? That's why you leave your libraries and your papers . . . ?'

She put her head on one side and looked at him seriously.

'No,' she said. 'I may have sympathy for them, but that's not the point. I do this because I believe the peasants need to be made aware of their legal rights and helped to demand them.'

'You're a revolutionary,' he said softly.

'Better that than a *counter*-revolutionary, but I don't care what they label me,' she shrugged. 'The law is above politics.'

'The law serves politics,' he told her bluntly. 'We both know that.'

'You're stuck in the past.'

He laughed bitterly.

'*I'm* stuck in the real world. I don't know where *you* are.'

She made an exasperated sound and looked away from him. The peasant woman approached to take away their dishes, then retreated.

'Look, if you feel sorry for someone and you give them a hand, I don't have any problem with that,' Song carried on. 'But tell a bunch of peasants to mobilize and demand their rights, and all you're doing is helping to get them beaten up while you run off back to your ivory tower.'

'Listen to yourself,' she protested, and he was surprised to see a small smile on her face. 'A big man like you, and you sound like a mouse . . . The peasants get beaten up anyway. I don't mobilize them, I just advise them what their rights are, so they can pursue a peaceful legal course. Things are changing . . .'

Song shook his head. 'I'm older than you, I've seen things . . .'

'You think I'm a baby? I'm not much younger than you. What is it you think I haven't seen?' She spat the words out with sudden fury. 'I was fourteen years old when my cousin lost his arm under a tank. I'm not interested in another uprising. That way lies suicide.'

'So,' Song said, after a moment, 'if not revolution, then peaceful evolution.'

'Call it what you want,' she said. 'The name is irrelevant.'

Song's mobile rang. It was Wolf. Song took the call and walked away from Jin along a path that followed the contour of the hill. Despite their argument he was finding it difficult to dislike her. Still, he didn't want her knowing all his business.

'How is she?'

'She's doing fine. She's going to have a scar, but her hair will cover it.'

'Good,' Song said, although he was less interested in Blue's scars than in who had hurt her and torn apart his office. He could not shake the thought that it had been ordered by Detective Chen. The sheer malice of it fitted with what he knew of the man. It occurred to him that perhaps there had been more to it. Had he mentioned the scrap of petition to his former father-in-law? Had Chen sent someone to find it? But there had been no systematic search of the agency, just destruction. He tried to concentrate on what Wolf was saying.

'She was worried that she wouldn't be allowed to go to England next week, but the doc said she'd be fine.'

'Good,' Song said again. 'What does she remember?'

'There were four of them. She thinks she's seen them around Anjialou before. One of them she definitely recognized. She thinks their main aim was to smash the place up. She got hit because she challenged them.'

'She what?'

'She's very brave,' Wolf said. 'She told them to stop.'

Song found himself smiling, despite everything, as Wolf continued speaking.

'I'm in the office, trying to find stuff, tidy it up.'

'Thank you,' Song said, although the idea of Wolf tidying anything up was not encouraging.

'The police from the local station came here this morning, they said they'd heard there was a break-in. Blue gave them a statement. They took a look around, gave me an earful for not calling them. Then an officer rang asking where you were, saying he was trying to get hold of you on your mobile . . .'

'He's rung me a dozen times this morning,' Song said, 'I'm not picking up. I know what he wants, and he's not getting it.'

They talked a little more about Blue, and about the office, and then Song ended the call. He walked a little further along the path and thought about Jin Dao. Peaceful evolution – working for the erosion of Communist rule and towards a Western-style democracy – was as bad as counter-revolution in the lexicon of the Party. Revolution, counter-revolution, rightists, leftists, peaceful evolution, a harmonious society, political reform, democratic dictatorship . . . He had long ago lost faith in all these words. When she was fourteen, he was eighteen. He'd seen it all too, the uprising, the backlash, the purge, lives lost and careers ruined. He'd been training for the national swimming team at the time, and the training camp was a virtual prison, but the news of the anti-government protests had reached them there too. He'd made the mistake of showing his support for the protesters and then, after the shootings, he'd been criticized in meeting after endless political meeting.

When he walked away from his swimming career, his coaches said he'd lost his competitive edge. It was true, actually, the desire to swim for his country had left him. No one talked about that time any more. Everything had changed, of course, people were living better. But a massacre and what it meant didn't just vanish. It had made its mark on all of them.

He thought about his mother. She'd had a label too. She was a 'reactionary element' for protesting that the Red Guard had hounded her friend, who was a musician, to suicide. Song could remember her standing there, one person in front of a mob, scolding them for their lack of common humanity. They had bundled her away, and his father had tried to cover Song's ears so that he did not hear her screams. But he had twisted his head and heard them anyway. His father had knelt and clasped him against the rough cotton of his jacket so that he could not run to her. They had pushed her out of a window, breaking her neck. The memory halted him and he stood with head bowed. After a while he looked up and gazed out across the valley. It was so peaceful. Rainclouds were casting shadows across distant hillsides. Far away he could see a settlement, a small town, its hard-edged industry softened in the hazy light. This land was so vast and so ancient. His life was small and fleeting in comparison.

He turned and walked back along the path. He could see her up ahead, talking to the peasant woman, handing over money, then gesturing this way and that, getting directions from the elderly man. By the time he got back to the car she was sitting in the passenger seat waiting for him. She didn't seem surprised to see him back. But then, he reflected ruefully, it was his car, where else could he have gone?

'We're a long way off our route, but I know which way to go now,' she said confidently. 'They know Yidong. It's just to the east of Wanmei County Town. He says that villagers from Yidong are causing trouble in Wanmei.'

Eleven

WANMEI COUNTY TOWN

The light was gone by the time they drove into Wanmei. Unlit cyclists and pedestrians emerged out of the gloom, cutting across the traffic or travelling in the wrong direction. Coal trucks were parked along the kerbs. With their cabs tipped forwards to afford access to their engines they looked like vast animals driven to their knees. Mechanics poked around with flashlights inside their great oily bellies. There had been rain here, and muddy puddles shone in the lights from streetside stalls.

'Idiot!' Jin Dao muttered, as Song swerved around an unlit vehicle, just managing to avoid a collision. She leaned out of the window and shouted 'Idiot!' at the driver as they passed.

'Would you like to tell me where we're going?' Song was weary and fed up. It seemed as though they had traversed most of northern China that day, zigzagging the length of the Great Wall and back, their journey punctuated by political spats which always boiled down to one thing: she thought him a moral coward, he thought her a dangerous idealist.

'Explain to me,' she'd challenged him, 'how a private detective does any good at all?'

'Do we have to do good?' he retorted. 'Can't we just make a living?'

'But you're like the secret police – you monitor people's private conversations, photograph people in their private lives and follow them around.'

'Only if we think they have something to hide.'

'That's what the secret police say!'

He stopped the car, pulling into the side of the road.

'If you compare me to the secret police one more time,' he said quietly, 'you can get out.'

Jin stared through the windshield. She gave a nod.

Song pulled out into the traffic.

'I'm sorry,' she said, some minutes later. 'Tang Ning must have sent Li Hetian to you because he thought you would help him. He must have known you were a good man.'

Song thought it was a backhanded compliment. The man he was supposed to help was lying dead in a police morgue, and they both knew it.

After a few moments she spoke again.

'Let's head to the local government headquarters. If there's trouble that's always where it is.'

Song pulled into the side of the road again so that she could get out and ask the way. When she climbed back in, he obeyed her instructions. After a few false starts they found themselves outside a monster of a building, all plate glass and polished marble, and illuminated by spotlights. It dwarfed everything around it, and was fenced off. Access to its vast forecourt was controlled by a uniformed guard at the gatehouse. Its windows were dark.

'Who's going to bother to protest outside an empty building?'

'Just park. We'll walk around the perimeter.' But even she sounded doubtful. 'You never know, it's summer, they may be camping out.'

Song parked, got out of the car, and locked it. Side by side they crossed the road and began the long trek around the perimeter, the Party and government headquarters looming over them.

'I wonder how many peasants were bled dry to build this thing,' she muttered. He noticed in the dark how her pale skin seemed almost luminous, and how the shadows threw the lines of her shoulders and of her throat into stark relief. She had slim legs and narrow hips and she walked, as she did everything else, fast and purposefully.

A beggar was lying on the corner, face down on the damp pavement, one hand extended palm upwards to receive alms. Jin Dao paused to dig in her pocket and brought out a note which she pressed into the woman's hand.

There was a row of fruit stalls, their owners lounging on deckchairs, taking advantage of the spotlights to do some late-night business. Jin Dao stopped to ask them whether they had any knowledge of protests outside the government headquarters. They directed Jin to the other side of the building.

It was as Jin had said, on the pavement at the rear, there was a makeshift camp. There were no tents, but the warmth of the summer night made shelter unnecessary. Instead there were small groups of men smoking and talking in urgent voices. Some were lying already asleep on bedding that had been unrolled directly onto the ground.

Song thought that Jin would scare the protesters off, but as she approached the men she seemed to shed her academic intensity.

'So many of you,' she remarked, strolling up to join one of the groups. 'But it's a good night to be outside, the rain has cleared the air.'

They shifted amicably to make space for her, and Song moved quietly to stand behind her.

'Are you all from Yidong?' she asked, shaking her head to refuse the offer of a cigarette.

There was no clear answer at first. They muttered and shifted awkwardly, exchanging anxious glances.

'I heard that the people of Yidong are bringing their grievances to the attention of the county government . . .'

'You heard right,' one man spoke up.

From his position slightly set apart from the group, Song could see that in the shadows was another group of men who were listening to the exchange. Whether they were with these men from Yidong, or were something altogether different, he could not tell, but he feared the worst. So many towns had established groups of *chengguan*, patrols of so-called city inspectors, who were often little better than gangs of thugs. Their job description was elastic enough that they were charged not only with getting rid of unlicensed vendors but anyone else who made the streets untidy.

'The police don't listen to us, the county government is trying to drive us away,' one man said glumly, stamping on the dog-end of a cigarette.

'What are your grievances?' Jin asked. She didn't push it, she just let the question hang there in the warm night air.

In the shadows shoulders flexed, hands went to pockets and to belts and came out armed. Song spun around.

'Run!' he shouted.

He grabbed Jin Dao by the arm. Not understanding, she turned, snapping at him to get his hands off her. Then her face froze as she saw them, and she let him pull her clear. 'Run!' he shouted again, and she ran, flanked by protesters, into an alleyway that led away from the government headquarters.

The attack happened so fast that some of the Yidong protesters were too surprised to flee. Now a handful of them cowered under blows and tried to retreat. Song hesitated, watching. This wasn't his battle. He didn't even know what the battle was about. He had resolved quietly to himself not to fight again, except in self-defence. He stepped away.

One of the protesters was on the ground, with his arms over his face, and they were kicking him as though they meant to reduce him to a pulp. Elsewhere, one of the thugs was bashing a protester's head against the pavement.

Song cursed. He waded in, hauled one thug off the protester's throat, then staggered as someone landed a vicious kick in the small of his back. Usually his size was his protection – no one wanted to take him on. But when he swivelled around, he came face to face with a man who could have been his twin. Tall, broad-shouldered, with a shaved head, the man stared at Song for a long moment, then drove his fist into Song's stomach. Song doubled over, pain searing through his guts. As Song went down on his knees, the man brought his fist up into Song's face, connecting with lip and nose. Song stared at the pavement. He spat bile and blood onto the ground. The anger that had simmered inside him for twenty-four hours boiled and became a mist of fury, and he lost himself. He was back in Beijing, these were the thugs who had clubbed Blue and trashed his office, and now he would trash them.

He jolted himself upright and at the man in one move. He felt the man's teeth against his fist, and when the man cried out and clutched at his bleeding mouth, he grabbed the man's arm just above his elbow, fingers clamping through skin to muscle, and twisted, jerking the man's arm up behind his back. He felt something break. The man screamed like a pig.

'Call them off,' Song hissed in his ear.

There was a sickening pause. The man moaned. Song forced his arm further. The man took a gulp of air.

'OK, get out of here,' he gasped.

'You heard him?' Song shouted. 'Get out of here.'

The thugs stared.

'Get the fuck out of here,' their leader yelled in a voice high with pain.

The street cleared.

Slowly, Song released the man's arm. He shoved him in the direction his men had gone, and the man ran, stumbling and sobbing, and cradling his arm to his chest. 'Fuck you!' He yelled over his shoulder, sobbing. 'Fuck your mother!'

Song turned full circle to check he was on his own. He was shaking. They were all gone, protesters and thugs. His stomach heaved and he squatted to retch into the gutter. He heard a voice, footsteps. She put her hand on his head. He closed his eyes. His guts churned. He waited for her to berate him for his violence. All he could feel was her hand that lay, light and cool, on his scalp. He vomited again, then sat back on his haunches. He thought he liked her speechless. He thought he might like to carry on squatting there by the side of the road and a pool of vomit. Then she took her hand away and he knew that it was time to go.

They returned to the car without speaking. He saw that she winced as she got into the car, and that there was blood on her knees.

'I fell,' she said, in answer to his glance. 'I'm fine.'

As he drove, she pulled her mobile phone from her pocket. When he glanced across he saw that she was checking images on the screen.

'Did you just take those?' he asked.

'Yes.' She held the mobile in front of his face, and he glimpsed a grainy shot of the fight before he pushed the phone away so that he could see the road.

'They're for my album,' she said.

They registered at a guest house and went to their rooms to wash. Afterwards they met in the lobby. The restaurant in the guest house had already closed, so they went outside in search of food.

'Thank you,' she said as they walked.

'For what?'

'For protecting the protesters.'

'You think I was fighting for human rights?' He burst out laughing.

'Weren't you?' She sounded offended.

'No. I lost it. I was out of my mind.'

She didn't say anything, and when he turned to look at her he thought she looked disappointed.

'How often do you lose it?'

'I don't. Not any more. Not until today. Fighting is like cigarettes, it's addictive. If I start I won't stop. I'm either going to kill someone or get killed.'

'Oh,' was all she said. She sounded wary, and who could blame her? He didn't know what he was doing, telling her things like that. He'd never told anyone else.

The only place they could find to eat was a restaurant underneath a karaoke lounge. They ate the mediocre food in silence, the beat working its way through the walls and the ceiling, drowning out the possibility of conversation. Once or twice they made helpless gestures about the fact that they couldn't communicate.

Once he had eaten, and the beer had calmed him, Song felt better.

'Come on,' he said, 'let's go and take a look upstairs.'

He pushed back his chair and made for the stairs, raising his eyebrows and beckoning her with his head. 'Come on.'

She looked at him as though he was mad.

'I haven't sung karaoke since I was a student.'

'Aha!' he said. 'You admit it.'

'And you?'

'I was never a student.'

Upstairs, the room was dimly lit. There were grimy booths with candles on the tables.

'I'm glad we can't see much,' Jin Dao shouted over the music, sliding into the booth. Song squeezed in opposite her. The booths had not been designed for people as big as him.

A waitress came to their table, and they pointed at the drinks list and mouthed their order.

A man was at the microphone, belting out a love song. His eyes were closed with emotion. His friends, gathered around a table, were cheering him on. Jin Dao turned to watch, smiling.

A group of girls got up to dance. They tried to pull the men to their feet, but they resisted. They weren't fashionably dressed like city girls, but they weren't as self-conscious either, Song thought, watching.

When the man finished singing, Jin Dao joined in the

applause and the cheering. The performer who followed was a woman so toe-curlingly bad that all they could do was laugh. When she left the stage to loud sarcastic cheers, Song leaned across the table.

'Why don't you go up there?' he said to her.

'You must be mad!'

'Go on,' he had to shout it over the music, 'I dare you. Don't tell me a brave human rights lawyer is too scared to sing a song in public.'

She glared at him. But she got to her feet.

He watched her walk to the stage, and was anxious for her. He shouldn't have goaded her. What if she was as bad as the last woman? What would he say to her then? He started to sweat.

There was no backing music for the song she chose, so she sang it a cappella. It was a politically dangerous song, and he knew she'd chosen it for him. Cui Jian, who wrote it, had been banned after he sang it with a red blindfold across his eyes. Red was the colour of the flag, and of the Party, and of the little red book. Song shook his head, laughing at her audacity.

She had a powerful voice that never missed the note, even without accompaniment, and she had the room in the palm of her hand. He felt goosebumps on the back of his neck. When she sang the second verse, she stepped down from the stage and brought the microphone over to stand directly in front of him. He glanced around, embarrassed. The other guests were cheering her on. She leaned in and sang to him. He wanted to look away from her, but he couldn't. He thought he would drown in her eyes.

Afterwards, on the way home, Jin Dao seemed preoccupied. Eventually, she linked her hand through his arm and began to speak.

'The work you do, following unfaithful husbands, I'm sorry I was rude about it. The work wouldn't exist if there wasn't a social need for it.'

'Then it's in the same category as prostitution . . . No one starts out happy and no one ends up happy.'

'If your client knows the truth doesn't that make them happy?'

'At least if you don't know, you can pretend. Life can go on. Most people just put up with it, it's the minority who come to me.'

'No,' she said, quite bluntly. 'You can't pretend, not if you care. Even if you tell yourself you're wrong, the doubt eats away at you, and you can't be happy.'

They walked along in silence. The town had closed up, and the shops and restaurants they passed were sealed with iron grilles. The air was still warm around them.

'You sound as though you're speaking from experience.'

For a while she didn't answer, and he thought he would rather she did not. He didn't want to know about her experience with other men.

'My source, Tang Ning, the man who sent Li Hetian

to you,' she said. 'I didn't tell you the whole truth. He's my husband. When he left to go and study in London it was a surprise to me. I thought he loved his job, but he said he had become disillusioned. He didn't tell me why, but I assumed it had something to do with his work. My approach is always to make things public. But although he's a journalist, he's also well connected. His uncle is the head of the Central Discipline Inspection Commission. Perhaps that's why he's not confrontational. When something's too sensitive to publish in a newspaper he believes it should be reported to the authorities secretly so they have a chance to deal with the problem without the public ever finding out about it.

'When he arrived in London at first he used to email me constantly. Then he told me he was moving. He wanted me to send him some papers concerning Yidong that he'd left behind, and he sent me his new address. He wouldn't tell me why, but he sounded alarmed about something. Well, I sent the papers. I wish that I'd read them before I sent them, but I was busy with something else and I just put them in an envelope and addressed it. After that I heard almost nothing from him. Then, about ten days ago, he sent me the message I told you about. Yidong cover-up. Li Hetian. Detective Song Ren. I didn't know what he meant by it. I tried to call him, but he didn't answer . . . of course I tried again and again, but now the phone is dead, and when I rang the landline at his old flat a new tenant answered.'

Song kept his gaze on the pavement under his feet.

He didn't want to lift his eyes to her. He thought she would see the disappointment on his face. He had always hated this part of his job, the documentation of infidelity. Now he hated this conversation. What did she want from him, reassurance that her husband still loved her?

'Have you contacted his family?'

'I don't want to worry them . . . They often went for weeks without speaking, so if they hadn't heard from him they wouldn't necessarily be alarmed.'

'It sounds as though the two of you were on good terms.'

She didn't respond, and when he glanced across at her he saw that she was walking with her head down, as if ashamed.

'We argued,' she said eventually. 'He wanted me to join him in London, but I didn't want to go. My work is here. He can't expect me just to give it up and run after him like some . . . little girl. You know, I've moved in with my mother temporarily, she lives on the campus at the university so it's convenient for both of us. I don't need to run off to England. He'll come back eventually.'

Song didn't reply. There didn't seem to be much to say. They walked side by side in silence, her warm hand still linked through his arm, and when they reached the hotel they went to their rooms, which were adjacent.

'Sleep well. I'll see you in the morning,' Song said, unlocking his door. Then he hesitated and turned towards her. For a moment they just stood there facing each other. She seemed to want to say something more to him. There were things he wanted to say to her too, but in the circumstances he could not. After a moment she reached out and touched his hand. She gave a little shake of her head and wished him goodnight. Then she unlocked her door and went into her room.

Later, lying awake on a mattress that was like a block of cement, he could still feel the fleeting touch of her fingers on the back of his hand. The sound of her voice came through the thin wall. He thought she must be speaking on the telephone. Her voice had a muted quality to it, as though she was trying to speak quietly, and he couldn't make out the words. When she stopped talking he expected her to go to bed, but instead he heard her door opening and then closing. He assumed that she was going to speak to Reception about something – where else could she be going? He lay awake and waited. When she didn't come back, he thought perhaps he had been right in the first place. He didn't know her and he shouldn't trust her.

Twelve

YIDONG VILLAGE

The storm had soaked them both so thoroughly that Meimei's hand kept slipping from Yanhua's grip. Splashing across the rough ground in the deluge Yanhua half-turned towards her, shouting over the hiss of the rain, 'Come on, hurry!' There was a flash of lightning above them and then, too soon, a crack of thunder. Yanhua knew they must get clear of this open ground. She yanked her sister's arm almost out of its socket, but then Meimei stopped altogether and started to cry.

'Where's my crocodile?' the little girl wailed, pulling her hand from Yanhua's and turning to face the way they had come.

'Don't you have it?' Yanhua stopped. She looked at her sister and the rain landed on their hair and splashed down their faces, half blinding them. Their clothes were drenched.

'I dropped it,' Meimei cried.

'We can't go back now,' Yanhua shouted. 'We've got to find a safe place.' Every instinct told her to pick up her sister and carry her, but she wasn't strong enough if the girl resisted. And anyway, where was this place of safety?

The little girl raised her arm to point.

'Look. There's someone coming.'

Yanhua looked and saw a light. In the storm, she found herself unable to judge the distance. She scanned the landscape. Sheets of rain worked across it, roaring with the force of the downpour. The land was unforgivingly bare except for the skeletal outline of the mine. She heard a dog barking in the distance and thought it must be tied up at the outhouse. But the barking grew louder and the light that Meimei had seen grew bigger. A cloaked figure appeared and moved towards them, a bedraggled dog slinking at his feet. He had a torch in his hand. Yanhua stared. The figure seemed to vanish behind patches of rain, re-emerging where she had not expected, then vanishing again. Now she saw that he carried a pick over his shoulder. Panic overwhelmed her.

She turned towards the mine again, and in a flash she knew that it would be dry in there, and safe. They would be safe from the lightning, and from this creature who was approaching, and from the dog. She moaned aloud at the thought. She saw again the broken bodies that had been pulled from the mine as if from the belly of hell itself. In the howling rain she heard again the keening of the women made widows. But her very fear made it an obvious refuge. Every child in the village was frightened of the mine. No one would think of looking there.

'Come on,' she cried, pulling on her sister's arm

again, and this time Meimei came with her. They set off at a run across the earth, their ragged shoes so heavy with mud that they could hardly lift them. When they reached the mine, and the younger child realized what her sister intended, she stopped dead in her tracks and wailed at the sky. Yanhua forced herself to remain calm. She was determined not to think about the coal-dark depths that awaited them. She hurried over to the metal cage that was waiting at the top of the shaft. She ran her wet hands carefully over the structure, finding the door, pulling back the bolt. Then she went back to Meimei and pushed her, still crying, towards the opening. They hurtled into it, and Yanhua fell against the lever that sent them plummeting down. They clung to each other as the metal cage shuddered, clanking and screaming, down through the darkness.

'You see?' Yanhua whispered, to still her terror, 'you see? It's dry.'

Meimei did not reply but Yanhua could hear her ragged, fearful breathing.

When the cage lurched to a halt they clung to each other.

'I can see a little bit,' Meimei said.

They could not see the source, but somewhere in the maze of narrow tunnels radiating from the bottom of the shaft there was light, trickling through to them. There was enough light to clamber out of the cage and know that there was ground underfoot. The air was fetid and water had found its way down from above so that a thin river trickled on the ground.

'What are we going to do?'

'Let's find the light,' Yanhua said.

They crept along a tunnel which seemed less dark than the rest and found, a few yards down, a small room hollowed from the ground. Inside, a single light-bulb glowed above a cheap poster that had been tacked to the wall: palm trees, a blue sea, beach. It seemed to be a control room, there was a panel of switches, and a chair.

They sat down, sharing the chair, still clinging to each other, their sopping clothing sticking to them. Now that they had stopped moving and the water was drying on them, they were shivering with cold.

'What are we going to do?' Meimei asked again.

Yanhua did not know. She tried to distract her sister.

'Tell me what happened in the amusement park.'

'When everyone else ran off I got frightened, but Stupid Girl found me and gave me sweets to cheer me up. She was very nice to me. She said she would look after me and we would have fun until someone came to find me.'

'That was nice of her,' Yanhua said.

Now that they had stopped running Yanhua couldn't think what it was that they were running from. She forced herself to think coldly over what had happened. There had been no threat in the amusement park except her own imagination. Her sister's disappearance, and then the crocodiles and the storm had panicked her, her terror had run wild. She had brought them here, to this subterranean maze, and all for nothing. Her parents would be going mad with worry. Her heart pounded and her head began to spin at the magnitude of what she had done. Yanhua clutched her little sister to her. She listened to her heart until it had slowed, and made herself breathe slowly, but a haze of fear had settled in her blood and would not be banished.

'We'll wait until the rain stops and then we'll go home,' she said, trying to keep her voice steady.

Suddenly they heard a noise – a roar and a clanking and the screaming of metal straining against metal.

'What is it?' Meimei asked in alarm.

'It's the cage,' Yanhua whispered. 'Someone's pulling it up to the surface.'

It was the hardest thing that Yanhua had ever done to leave the single lightbulb in the control room and run with Meimei further into the tunnel and into the darkness. They huddled on the ground in a corner behind what felt like a metal tub.

There was silence, and then the roar and scream of metal that told them the cage was descending once more. There was a loud noise as the cage came to rest, and the door banged open. There were footsteps and a man's voice uttered a muffled curse.

Yanhua closed her eyes and tried not to breathe. She listened intently but could barely hear Meimei breathing. She held her sister's hand tight. If he tried to snatch Meimei away he would take her too. She got ready to scream and fight.

All of a sudden, she was overtaken by a strange urge to stand up and announce herself, and ask him to take her away. If he left, she and Meimei would be all alone again down in this dark damp misery.

But who was there? She opened her eyes.

The footsteps receded, the door clanged shut, and the metal cage roared upwards once again, but fear had exhausted them. They had nowhere to go. The cage was at the surface. They would have to wait for the miners to come on shift. Yanhua was beyond despair. They huddled together, and eventually Yanhua felt Meimei's head heavy on her shoulder. The grip of her fingers relaxed. Yanhua's fortitude deserted her, and she felt tears coursing down her face. She closed her eyes. She drifted to sleep.

They were woken by an explosion. The vibrations tore them from each other, throwing them against the walls, pounding them with stones that fell from the roof. A great booming, clashing noise roared through the tunnels. It seemed to last for ever, then subsided as suddenly as it had arrived.

Thirteen

The next morning, when Song got out of bed, he saw that a folded sheet of paper had been slipped under his door. Yawning, he stooped, unfolded it and read:

> *Song Ren,*
> *I think you should return to Beijing now.*
> *Don't wait for me. I have matters to attend to. Don't*
> *worry about me. In case I do not see you for some time,*
> *I would like to inform you of the telephone number and*
> *the London address you were enquiring about . . .*

There followed a collection of numbers and words in English which Song could not read.

At the bottom the letter was signed, 'Your friend, Jin Dao.'

He gazed at the note, blinking. He shook his head in angry wonder. Who did she think she was? *I think you should return to Beijing now. Don't wait for me.* As though he was nothing more than her driver. Disappointed, he crushed the note and tossed it into the bin. He had not expected such arrogant behaviour.

He shaved, looking at himself in the mirror. Hurt eyes looked back at him. *Don't worry about me.* Why would he worry about her? A cool hand laid on his head, a song sung to him alone, let me tell you all about my husband, goodnight, fingers brushing his, and oh by the way I'm off. What was she playing at? He gathered his things together. As he ran his eyes over the room to make sure he hadn't left anything, he caught sight again of the bin. He thought that if he left her note there it would be thrown out with the trash, and somehow that didn't seem right. He bent and retrieved the crumpled paper, smoothing it out and folding it, and putting it into his wallet.

Just in case, he knocked on the door of her room, but there was no answer.

In the hotel lobby he settled his bill.

'What about Room 28?' he asked casually, as he put his wallet back in his pocket. 'I assume she paid when she left.'

The receptionist cast an eye at her computer screen.

'She settled her bill,' she confirmed.

'She had to leave early, right?' Song asked, with a smile, as though he was amused by the fact that his companion had had to get up so early.

'I don't know.' The girl didn't look up. 'It wasn't my shift.'

'Don't you note the time on the computer?'

This time she looked up at him and held his gaze. He got out his wallet again and slid a 50-*yuan* note across the counter. She slipped the note into her pocket and turned her face towards the computer screen.

'She checked out at twelve minutes to 4 a.m.'

'Did she ask for a taxi? Was she on her own?'

'None of that's on the computer.'

'Can I talk to whoever was on duty?'

'He's sleeping.'

Song took another fifty from his wallet and put it on the counter. She looked at it for a moment, weighing up the cash against the friendship of her colleague. She took the cash and dialled a number.

'Hey, I've got someone here asking about the woman who checked out of Room 28.' She whined, to let him know she was making the call under duress. 'I know, I know. I'm sorry. I don't have any choice. He just wants to know if she was on her own ... come on, I'm sorry, just tell me ... I ... you want me to tell him what?' She started to giggle.

Song lunged over the counter and seized the phone from her, and she gave a little shriek.

'Was the woman from Room 28 on her own when she checked out?' he demanded.

There was a brief, confused silence.

'Yes.' A young man's voice, wary but obedient, came down the line.

'Did you see us come in around midnight?'

'I saw her with a big man, if that's you.'

'And she left around 1 a.m., is that right?'

'That's right.'

'Was she alone then?'

'Yes, and alone when she came back at about 3 a.m., and when she left just before four. Every time except the first time, she was on her own.'

'Did you see anyone waiting for her outside?'

'No,' the voice was getting bored. 'I told you. She was on her own.'

'And she didn't say anything at any point about where she was going, or who she was going to meet, or why she had to leave so early?'

'No.'

'What about her mood? Did she seem frightened? Agitated?'

'I don't know. She looked serious, but she wasn't crying . . . she didn't look scared to me.'

For a moment Song hesitated. He didn't like to let go of the only informant he had, but he couldn't think of any question he could ask that would tell him anything more than he already knew. He thanked the man on the other end of the phone and hung up.

He drove past the Wanmei government headquarters, but where the protesters from Yidong had been camped out, the street was now clear. Every few yards plain-clothes security officers were posted and in the side streets there were minivans of police officers parked under the trees.

He took the road out of the county town and towards Yidong. *I think you should return to Beijing now. Don't wait for me.* Did she expect him to obey her? Was she trying to keep something from him? The road was lined with small industry, with shops selling car parts, and massage parlours, and not far from the road there were mines that Song guessed were privately run. He had once been to Datong and seen the gargantuan state-run mines that were like cities, with dormitories and hospitals and kindergartens all inside their soot-stained walls. These makeshift structures that pockmarked the landscape were too small, the state wouldn't bother with them.

He opened the windows and let the warm air blow through the car. He passed an amusement park, with posters advertising crocodiles.

What was it that Li Hetian had called down from the scaffolding? *There's no other way. Don't worry.* Then Jin Dao's note: *I have matters to attend to. Don't worry about me.* Could he have misread it? Had she been coerced? Had she meant him to read the opposite into it? But the hotel receptionist had insisted that there had been no one with her. If she'd been in trouble she could simply have come and knocked on his door and asked for help.

Song was not concentrating on driving. He heard a shout, and when he looked and saw the concrete bollard that had been rolled across the road, he hit the brakes. He brought the car to a squealing halt and leaned out of the window. A group of men stood by the side of the road. They waved him back in the direction he'd come.

'I'm going to Yidong, let me pass.'

'It's closed.' They waved him away again.

'How can a whole village be closed?'

He could see the village not far down the road.

'None of your fucking business.'

Song sat for a moment, but he had no options to consider. He watched the group of men. For the past few days, every way he turned he seemed to come up against groups of hired thugs. Who had the power to mobilize and finance this many men?

He did a U-turn. He drove back the way he'd come, looking for a turn-off that would take him across the plain to Yidong, but when he found a likely-looking road that too was blocked, and by men just as ugly.

He stopped outside a roadside cafe and went in. It was a filthy place with grimy walls, a grease-covered hob and a dog sniffing around the floor, but the table was covered in a disposable plastic cloth, and the woman who appeared to run the place looked decent enough, with her hair pulled back from her round face in a bun and wearing a cleanish apron. He sat down, ordered a bowl of hand-pulled noodles, and she brought him a pot of steaming tea with big black leaves that slowly sank to the bottom. He poured a little of the tea into his bowl to rinse it out, and tipped the residue onto the floor.

'They've closed the road to Yidong,' he said to the woman when she brought him the noodles, which were served in a clear soup with slices of pork and spring onion. She nodded, but her jaw clenched and her lips were set. He ate his lunch in silence with the dog sniffing around his feet. When he had finished he went to the counter to pay and told her that the noodles had tasted good, and this seemed to thaw her reserve. He thought he would try again.

'Why have they closed the road to Yidong?' he asked her.

'There's trouble at the mine. The foreman ordered it closed,' she said.

'What kind of trouble?'

'The villagers were out trying to clear the mine shaft when the foreman comes along and tells them all to go home. A fight broke out. The foreman doesn't want strangers seeing the chaos up there, so he's closed the village down.'

She had given him his change. She was expecting him to go. But he knew there must be more to the story. He pointed to a can of Coke in the fridge and got out his cash again.

'Why were they clearing the mine shaft?'

'There are two more children gone,' she said. 'They found a hairband belonging to one of the girls at the top there, so they thought they might be down there. Although why they'd be down a mine shaft when everyone knows they've gone the way of all the rest . . .'

'The way of all the rest?' Song murmured. It was an echo with just the hint of a question at its end.

'The same way as Li Hetian's daughter,' she responded.

A man walked into the cafe. He was well built and shirtless, with sun-darkened skin that stretched over the balloon of a belly. One of his trouser legs was rolled up above his knee. Song thought he recognized the man from the roadblock. The man gave him a suspicious look as though he recognized Song too. Song picked up his can of Coke from the counter and made to leave.

'Poor little treasure,' he heard the woman say behind him, 'and her husband fallen to his death as well. No wonder the mother swallowed poison.'

Walking outside, Song was blinded by the sudden light. For a moment he stood, disoriented, overwhelmed by the blast of sun and weakened by what he had been told. Children were going missing. And Li Hetian's wife had swallowed poison because he had not helped her husband.

Fourteen

BEIJING

Blue's convalescence was driving her up the wall. The doctor had told her to rest, but the sound of drilling coming from the flat next door meant that she couldn't concentrate on her novel. Her neighbour was renovating. He'd been at it for a week already and had warned her it would be at least another week before he finished. She turned on the television to drown out the noise, but the evening news irritated her more than ever, with its mixture of truths and half-truths and omissions. She had always known something was wrong with China Central Television news, but it was only after she'd started reading on the Internet that she had begun to get an idea of what she was missing. She switched to another channel and watched a dancing competition. Her eyes glazed over with boredom. And still the sound of the drill whined through her head.

She lay down on her bed and covered her ears with the pillows. She closed her eyes and thought about what had happened the night before. She couldn't think when she'd felt more miserable. She'd been so happy when Wolf turned up at the hospital, so pleased to see the look of concern in his eyes. He'd stroked her hair so gently and, for her at least, his touch had the thrill of electricity. Still, she'd been hurt that Song had rushed off like that, and she'd said as much to Wolf.

'Of course he cares about your welfare,' he said. 'After all, it was Song who told me to come to the hospital to look after you.'

She flinched as though he had slapped her.

'I'm so sorry I ruined your evening,' she snapped. 'Why don't you go back to bed so that you can give her a grade?'

'She's already . . .' Wolf's voice trailed off.

Blue looked at him stonily. 'She's already what?'

'Gone,' Wolf said. He stared at her. 'You know . . . ?'

'Of course I know about the blog,' Blue hissed at him.

She had refused to listen to his excuses – it was just a joke, it was all made up, it was just to please his mother – and told him to leave. When he tried to insist that he must stay with her and take her home, Blue had told the security staff at the hospital that Wolf was harassing her. In the end he had been escorted from the premises and she had made her own way home in a taxi.

She sat up in bed. It was too hot to lie there like that with pillows over her head. She had to get out. Usually, she would have turned to the office for comfort. But with the computers in pieces there was no comfort to be had there. She knew of a cyber cafe in the basement of an apartment block a short taxi ride away. She would never have chosen to use the computers there, jammed elbow to elbow with sweaty gaming boys. But it cost almost nothing, just three *yuan* an hour, and she had no alternative. She hailed a taxi and asked the driver to take her there.

Hungrily, she visited her favourite sites. There were pictures of a scuffle in Wanmei the night before, where protesters had been attacked by an official patrol. The pictures were grainy, lit in the gloomy orange light of the streetlamps as though whoever had taken them had used a mobile phone. Blue frowned at the screen. One of the combatants was big, with broad shoulders and a shaved head. He looked a lot like Song, but she couldn't be sure because the bad quality of the photographs would have made any identification impossible. The photographs were accompanied by text linking the protest to Yidong, Li Hetian and a document posted below the pictures.

Blue scrolled down. There was a scan of the document, presumably to prove its authenticity. It was dated five months before. At the top of the page, in warning characters, the document was labelled, 'Top Secret'. She had gorged herself on internet fare for months, but never had she seen a secret Party document appear online. This document appeared to be an internal report for the eyes of senior officials only.

Everyone knew that journalists had two jobs. One was to write for the newspapers. The second concerned news that was considered by the Party to be too sensitive to print publicly. The journalist still wrote the report, but it went upwards, to be read only by government and Party officials. Those reports were regarded as state secrets – and here was one right in front of her eyes. Nervously, she twisted to look around her at the ranks of heads bent over their screens. Could she be arrested just for reading? The computer would retain a memory of what material she had accessed, but she had given no one her name and each computer here would have hundreds of users in one day. She suspected that there were closed-circuit cameras around the hall, and she lowered her head, pulling her long hair across the large white dressing which covered her wound. She could not just get up and walk away. She hunched over her screen and started to read. There was a name written by hand at the top of the report. The scan had reproduced it only faintly, and she frowned, trying to make it out.

'Chen Dalei,' she mouthed the name softly, then sat back staring at the screen. Song's former father-in-law, father of the awful Lina. She could not believe her eyes. But there was no time to waste. She read on.

This report contains information gathered by reporter Tang Ning, staff reporter for the *Economic Information News* during a week-long investigation trip to Wanmei County Town. The reporter went to Yidong to probe a recent spate of mine accidents, in which nine men had died and several had become paralysed. This is a poor rural area, some 150 km east of Beijing. Traditional farming activities have shrunk as income from the land has dried up. Local officials are aggressively involved in the transformation of the countryside, and there are many small-scale local industries. These include mining, car-part manufacturing, tourism facilities and service industries. The local population is entirely dependent on the success of these projects. Their attitude to their local leaders, especially to Chief Bo, is ambivalent.

This reporter had been in Yidong for less than twenty-four hours when villagers started to speak to him about the abductions of children aged six to sixteen in the area between Yidong and Wanmei, the county town – Yidong village is 3.7 km west of Wanmei County Town. The area they described also included the village of Gaoling, 1.4 km to the north of Yidong, and Ruilin, 1.8 km to the south-east of Yidong. At the time of his visit, this reporter was told of six abductions:

Meng Lianhao, female, aged 11, Wanmei County Town

Fu Mingzhen, female, aged 13, Gaoling village

Cheng Xianyou, female, aged 9, Ruilin village

Hang Yu, male, aged 7, Ruilin village

Li Suxia, female, aged 6, Yidong village

Wu Bingbing, male, aged 6, Wanmei County Town

However, this reporter's sources also stressed that there might be more cases they had not heard of. There has been no press coverage of the abductions.

Gangs involved in the kidnap of children have been active throughout China's countryside. Where those gangs have been arrested, police have discovered that the children have been abducted for sale, either, in the case of girls, as wives to men in rural areas who cannot find a mate, or into prostitution. Babies and young boys are sold to childless couples, and older boys are sold as slave labour. These gangs take the children they have stolen far across provincial boundaries and sell to the highest bidder, with no care or concern about the lives they sell these children into.

In Yidong, villagers told this reporter that the pattern of disappearance was similar in most cases. Children set off for school or went out to play on their own and did not return. In each case search parties of concerned neighbours were formed, but the children were not found.

The families concerned reported their missing children to police forces in their locality but were not satisfied with the police response. Families' approaches to village and county level government and Party offices have so far failed to provoke action.

I was introduced to a man called Li Hetian and to his wife, Huang Xiuhong. They have lived all their lives in Yidong village. Their only child, a daughter, six-year-old Li Suxia, went missing three weeks ago, on 10 January, after she went out to play with older friends and became separated from the rest of the group. Extensive searches by villagers have turned up no clues as to her whereabouts. Her parents and other villagers say she was a good and obedient child who had never tried to run away.

Li says that some junior officers at the local police station are sympathetic to his plight and assure him that her abduction will be investigated, but that he has seen no evidence of any action taken by the police to find his daughter.

Among those peasants this reporter spoke to, there was a sense of injustice that it would be a mistake for the authorities to ignore. Many families have taken their children out of school in fear. Rumours circulate constantly about the possible existence of trafficking operations, and of the involvement of this or that village or county official. They are deeply suspicious of newcomers to the area, and particularly the population of miners, some of whom have been known to tease and harass teenage girls in the area.

In the spirit of building a harmonious society, this reporter recommends to the relevant police departments an urgent investigation . . .

All at once, the page dissolved. Blue stared. The server had gone down. She picked up her bag and stood up. She glanced around her nervously, but no one seemed to pay her any attention. Within moments she had left the building, head lowered against surveillance cameras.

Fifteen

Lina handed Doudou his school bag, and he struggled it over his shoulders.

'Are you sure you have everything?'

He looked like a comic-book turtle, she thought, with his bag on his back full of books and his great tummy in front of him. He'd been up until midnight the night before, completing his homework.

'I've got everything,' he confirmed. His voice was downbeat about everything these days.

When he was gone, Lina collected her bag and left the flat. The *ayi* was coming in later on so she could leave the washing-up for her.

In the lift she hit the button for the basement car park. She smiled as she saw her car waiting for her. It was lime-green, with a sheen fresh from the showroom, and she already loved it. She loved the remote-locking device which meant that she could click imperiously as she entered the car park and the car would leap into life. She loved her collection of stuffed animals that she had arranged on the back shelf. It meant that when she looked in the rear-view mirror all she saw was a jumble of fuzzy dogs and seals and polar bears.

But she could still use the mirror when she needed to apply make-up, so it wasn't wasted.

She pulled out of the car park and onto the road, failing to look either to left or right before she made the turn. She'd taken her test just the week before. Some people got nervous about their test, but she hadn't. She'd made the appropriate approach to the examiner through a friend of her father's, and she'd donated two hundred cigarettes as a gesture of respect. She'd only taken a few hours of driving lessons and they, as well as the test, had all been spent inside the walls of the driving instruction compound. The journey from the car showroom to her home had been her first experience on the open road and this would be her second.

Her instructor had told her that her reflexes were quick so she knew she didn't have to think too much about driving or worry about smashing the car up. Which was as well, because she had a lot on her mind: in particular, her father. He had rung her the night before and pleaded with her tearfully that she come out to see him this morning. Eventually she had given in. She thought she was probably being too swayed by pity. It would be safer to keep away from him. She had heard, the night before, that her father's Communist Party membership was to be officially revoked. That was always a prelude to a trial. First you had to be stripped naked of Party protection, and then the law could get its fangs into you. She thought that he might be kicked out of the sanatorium. Or removed by the police. It could happen any day now. Really, she shouldn't be going anywhere near him.

She saw a space in the fast lane and nipped in between two cars – they were moving more rapidly than she had thought and one of them had to brake hard. She saw another space and moved again, forcing another car to swerve out of her way honking angrily. Her female friends had told her to ignore male drivers. They said men just got angry when a woman got into a space before they did. But all this honking was making her nervous.

Poor Doudou, she knew her father had upset him. Doudou needed his own father, someone to spoil him. Her thoughts went to Wang Rong. He had been pursuing her for years, and she had gone out with him to humour her father. He liked to think of his former second-in-command looking after his daughter. It was a pity she didn't find Wang Rong at all attractive. His head was too small for his body. And he was very vulgar. Still, she couldn't see why Song had nicknamed him Psycho Wang. He seemed to know how to treat women properly. He'd taken her shopping at the Xinguang shopping mall, and he'd spent thousands of *yuan* on a new bag for her, and jewellery and even lingerie. She'd had to show her gratitude, of course, although in bed he'd treated her roughly. Then he'd gone to Europe on a business trip. Wang had told her he had some investments to make in England. She'd understood by this that he had cash which needed to be removed from the country. There were times her father had spoken like this, but he had used Wang to run his financial errands abroad. For a moment Lina imagined herself in London, sailing through the door of a grand department store, her arms full of carrier bags. Wang had not invited her, but he'd said he would bring her something nice from London. It would be worth sticking with him for a little while longer, just until she saw what he brought back.

When she'd arrived and parked at the sanatorium she called her father's mobile phone, but got no answer. She went to his room and tapped on his door, but again there was no answer. Afraid that he might have collapsed, she tried the handle and found the door unlocked. She opened the door and went inside. It was surprisingly tidy. The bed had been made, the desk cleared. His mobile phone was lying in the centre of the desk, and when she glanced at it she saw that it had registered her missed call. Her father would need the mobile phone, wherever he was. She snatched it up so that she could hand it over to him and they didn't have to come back to his room. And then she waited for a few minutes in case he was in the bathroom.

When he still did not return, Lina went back out into the corridor. There were nurses and cleaning staff around, but she didn't want to talk to them about her father.

Outside, gardeners were watering the lawn under a baking sun. Today the blue sky was obscured, however, by smog that was as thick as chalk in town and here was little better. She walked in the direction of the Slaughter Pavilion. He had seemed to enjoy sitting there the last time she saw him. She remembered Doudou reading aloud the inscription about the sacrificing of animals, and her father's hopeless remark – 'It's the right place for me.'

What had he meant? As she approached the red-roofed structure, she could see him – or someone like him – sitting and admiring the view. A few steps closer, she noticed that the figure was strangely slouched. She hurried on.

'Pa!' she called to him as she approached. He did not respond. His limbs were splayed in an unnatural way, his arms hanging behind him, head thrown back over the back of the bench. There was something lying on the ground, and she thought, ridiculously, that it looked like a gun.

She ran up the steps to the pavilion platform and then stopped short. At his temple there was a charcoal-black hole. It was just a hole, not much bigger than a coin. Surely it couldn't have done any damage. His head was in every other way still intact. He was just sleeping. Lina stared. Everything spun around her. The trees revolved, her father's body seemed to be on a carousel, dancing up and down as it circled her. When she extended her hand, that too seemed to drift away from her and she felt herself sway. Everything darkened, and she would have fainted, but a tiny spot of light remained at the corner of her vision, and she fought herself back to consciousness from there.

She stepped closer, and reached out her hand. Her lips quivered. She touched his shoulder, poised to scream and run if he should move in response. But he did not respond to her touch, and when she tried a second time, in case there was any life left to save, still there was only the heavy immobility of the dead.

Sixteen

YIDONG VILLAGE

For as long as she could remember, Yanhua had been digging. It seemed to her that days and nights must have passed like this, and that the thin trickle of light had waxed and waned, but she had carried on digging. She no longer thought of her hands as part of her body; they were tools with no feeling, their nerve endings battered by the sheer volume of stone and rock and earth that she had shifted. They were swollen and so coated in dirt that they could not now have served any purpose except to carry on digging. Her body was beyond hunger. For a while she'd thought she would scream because she could feel her insides clawing for food. Now it was the thirst that drove her crazy, that fogged her brain and made her shake. At first she had sobbed as she worked, but now even the tears had dried up. Meimei was curled behind her on the floor. The explosion had thrown her so hard against the tunnel wall that she had broken something in her shoulder. She'd screamed with pain and cried herself to sleep.

*

Yanhua reached out, as she had a thousand times. She grasped the sharp edges of a rock and pulled, as she had a thousand times. It moved against the earth and she prised it loose. Then, unexpectedly, as she removed the rock from its place, a breeze of fresh air brushed her face. Staring, discerning a glimmer of light, then roused to even greater effort, she seized rock after rock, and pulled them out from the earth, not caring when a small avalanche of loosened stones fell on her.

'Meimei,' she said, her voice hoarse. 'Meimei, come here, look at this.'

She carried on working until she was kneeling in earth and debris almost up to her waist, her hands scrabbling in the dirt. Twilight shone onto her face. She had managed to make an opening into the air. It was small, but she thought perhaps Meimei could squeeze through it.

She tried to call her sister over but she couldn't move her tongue in her dry mouth. She stumbled away from the opening, and felt her way to her sister, and shook her until she was awake. As she became conscious, the pain returned, and she cried out, kicking Yanhua away. But Yanhua pulled her to her feet and pushed her, still crying out in pain, into the gap between the stones. Gasping and clutching, Meimei had one arm outside. Yanhua shoved at her from behind, ignoring the girl's screams, the jagged edges of stones tearing at her clothing and her skin, until she was through.

It must have taken another half an hour for Yanhua to follow, although she had lost all sense of time. Her fevered mind told her she was some dirt-crawling insect, working her body between rock and earth, arms and legs in constant motion, in danger of getting crushed or stuck. At last her head emerged into open air and then the rest of her body found purchase and pushed, expelling itself into the open.

Yanhua lay for a few moments on the uneven ground, staring up at the stars. Nothing, not the darkest of nights, would ever be as dark again as the mine.

'Come on,' Meimei said, whispering and whimpering as though someone might hear them in this vast expanse of sky. 'Come on. I want to go home.'

The walk was a long one and when they reached the village it lay in silence. They staggered and stumbled to their house and bashed on the door, and tried to shout for their parents. Their startled father let them in, and when he saw them he fell on them in delight. Their voices woke their mother, and soon neighbours too had been woken and had joined the throng. Yanhua could not remember ever having had so many people gathered in their house at one time. The noise was immense. She was wrapped in blankets. Soon Meimei was wearing a makeshift sling, and had been fed some pain-killing medicine that had sent her to sleep. Her mother was dabbing at Yanhua's scratches with boiled water, tears of relief running down her face. Neighbours were bringing food and drink, great bowls of *zhou*, and cans of Coca-Cola. Yanhua thought she would never forget that first sip of water. It had tasted like nectar. Now, with so much poured in on top of it, she felt sick.

She could hear the questions ringing around the room: What happened? Where were they? Who abducted them? How did they escape?

She felt hot and then cold, as though her body was being boiled, then chilled, and seized and shaken. Dizzy with fever, she closed her eyes. She heard Teacher Ding's voice. He was asking what had happened. Was she all right? Would she be able to return to school?

She opened her eyes wide and stared around the room, seeking him out. But she couldn't see him anywhere.

'Teacher Ding?' she muttered.

'No, my treasure, he's not here,' her mother murmured to her. 'He went to the amusement park to look for you when the boy told me you'd gone there to look for Meimei. We were all so frightened . . .'

Yanhua flung her body against her mother, who tried to hold her still. She tried to scream, but no sound came out. She had put Meimei through all this for nothing. If only she had not thrown her sister to the ground, they would have been home hours ago. They would never have been caught in the storm, they would never have seen the apparition with the pick slung over his shoulder and the dog at his feet . . . but had she seen him? She had led her sister into danger. She was a bad daughter, a bad sister, a bad student. Yanhua wept, stricken with distress and regret.

Seventeen

Both roads to Yidong were still blocked, but the little that Song had learned in the cafe had only whetted his appetite for more information. He tried to improvise a cross-country route, but the development of industry between Wanmei and Yidong meant there was no clear run. A dirt road led him into a maze of workshops and warehouses, and a ditch finally brought the car to an abrupt halt.

He spent the afternoon in a repair shop having the car's undercarriage fixed. While half a dozen men worked on the car he paced up and down the yard, checking his mobile phone and checking it again for messages from Jin Dao. He realized he was becoming obsessive so he put his phone in his pocket. Six times it rang and each time he grabbed the phone. But each time when he checked the screen he recognized the number. It was the police – they sent text messages, too, telling him to report to the local station without delay, 'and immediately to hand in evidence seized from the scene of crime, or bear the consequences'. He ignored the messages and the calls, but the undefined threat made him even more uneasy about returning to Beijing. 'Consequences' were never good.

He tried calling Jin Dao's mobile a dozen times, but a recorded message kept telling him 'the subscriber has turned off the phone'. He couldn't understand why she hadn't called him, or why she wasn't answering. In his head, he went back over everything that had happened the night before. Had he offended her? He thought it possible that she had realized he was attracted to her, and that this was her way of rejecting him. She was married, after all – Song could not expect anything from her. He had taken the touch of her hand as encouragement, but perhaps she had meant it as apology – there was to be no more than that.

By early evening, when Wolf rang, Song had reached the end of his tether.

'I need you back here,' Wolf said.

'Give me another day,' Song said. 'The road to Yidong will be clear tomorrow.' Besides – although he was not about to tell Wolf this – he didn't want to go too far from Wanmei County Town, where he had last seen Jin Dao. He thought that she must be somewhere close by and that she might reappear as unexpectedly as she had disappeared.

'You have to come back now,' Wolf protested. 'I've done what I can, but you can pack your own clothes or they can be buried in the rubble, it's up to you.'

'Just one more day . . .'

'No, you don't understand, there is no one more day. We've got no electricity, no water. They knocked down everything up to Xiao Wei's tattoo parlour yesterday.'

'It's going to get knocked down whether I'm there or

not. Get the *ayi* to pack my clothes, just stick the papers from my room in a box.'

'Song, listen to me.' Wolf's voice was low and serious. 'Li Hetian was never a client. You did what you could. You get back here or you'll have no agency. We've both offended Blue. I . . . well . . . that's another matter. I'll deal with that. But she thinks you should be going after the thugs that hit her, not waltzing around the country on behalf of strangers . . .'

'It's all connected,' Song burst out. 'It's Chen Dalei . . . I challenged Chen Dalei over Yidong, and he sent thugs to beat up Blue . . . I'm sure of it . . . Yidong is where the answers are.'

There was a long silence.

'You're not making any sense, my friend,' Wolf said. 'And unless you come back to Beijing, I'm quitting.'

Back in Beijing three hours later, Song opened the door of the office and stepped inside. He'd brought a torch with him, and he shone it around the bare whitewashed walls. The agency no longer belonged to him. He felt it acutely. Even invaded and smashed, the agency had been his. His abandonment, his flight to Yidong, had severed the tie. Now, cleared by Wolf, drained of electricity and water, nothing but brick and plaster, it was a lifeless skeleton waiting for the blows that would reduce it to dust. The air was still and hot, undisturbed by fan or air conditioner.

He went through to his own quarters, kicked off his shoes and lay down on the bed in the dark. He thought of the morning that he had awoken on this bed to the text message from Li Hetian. Then he thought of Jin Dao, and the note that she'd put under his door while he slept in Wanmei. Where was she?

This would be the last time that he slept in this room. I am homeless, he realized.

Before he went to sleep, he composed a text message to Jin Dao. 'Please let me know where you are and whether you are safe. You told me not to worry, but I'm afraid that's impossible. I won't bother you again if you can reassure me.'

He pressed Send, although he suspected it was hopeless.

When he awoke in the morning, it was to the sound of shouting. He got out of bed and went to the window. Outside, a demolition team was gathering, picks and hammers resting against their shoulders, baggy vests hanging around scrawny torsos. He opened the door, still in his shorts.

'You've got to get out, mate,' the foreman told him.

Song considered arguing. He looked at the men, and they looked back at him without resentment or embarrassment. He would wager it was not they who had trashed the office.

'OK,' he said, turning back inside. 'Give me a hand with this stuff, will you?'

He turned back into the office. His mobile rang, and he snatched it out of his pocket. It was Blue. His heart sank but he took the call.

'Blue, how are you? I'm sorry I haven't been around.' While he spoke, the demolition team were moving around him and starting to pick up boxes.

'I need to see you now.'

The men were carrying the boxes out, like a swarm of ants with crumbs.

'When you say *now*?'

'I mean *now*,' she said firmly.

He told her he would meet her at the Starbucks in nearby Jiuxianqiao in half an hour.

He helped the demolition team lift his bed and his wardrobe out onto the street. He would call Wolf later to bring a van. By the time Song left to meet Blue the agency was falling brick by brick.

When he got there she had arrived already and was sitting in an armchair sipping a Frappucino. The white dressing on her head looked alarmingly large because the rest of her was so small. Song ordered himself a cup of green tea and went over to join her.

'Blue, how are you?'

'I'm OK,' she said, waving him to the armchair opposite hers. 'I'll get my stitches taken out in England. I leave tomorrow.'

'Blue, I'm sorry I haven't been around.'

'That's not important.'

Nevertheless, she seemed agitated, and it occurred to him that she might think that her job had disappeared along with the agency.

'Blue, while you're gone I'll be looking for new

offices. With any luck by the time you're back we'll be moved in. All you'll have to do is turn up to work . . .'

'Yes,' she cut him off. 'We can talk about that later. There's something I have to tell you now . . .' she paused to glance around her nervously, then leaned in towards him, indicating that he should do the same. 'The night before last someone posted online a secret document about abductions in Wanmei County. I saw it with my own eyes. It was posted just for a few moments, and then the server went down. I checked again today, and it's been deleted. It said that six children have gone missing there, and that Li Hetian's child was one of them . . .' She hesitated before continuing.

'The document was a report for internal circulation in the Communist Party, written by a reporter from the *Economic Information News*, Tang Ning, and it was passed to the relevant authorities more than five months ago. It was a scan of the original document, so I could see a name handwritten on the top. Song, it was your father-in-law's name, Chen Dalei. I think perhaps it means that the document had been passed to him. Would he really do nothing if he received something like this?'

She looked at him expectantly, but his head was bowed in thought. He could not think why Tang Ning would have sent his report to Chen Dalei. He remembered how Li Hetian's petition had also been addressed to Chen Dalei. After a moment he raised his head and glanced around the cafe. He wished she had not chosen such a public place to discuss this. There were groups of people sitting too close to them for comfort. He didn't like the look of the man who was sitting all on his own at the table behind theirs. He had a laptop out on the table, but that didn't mean anything.

'Let's go for a walk,' Song said.

The street was busy but they made their way to the canal where there were few pedestrians. The water was brown with detergent fuzz floating in patches on top and a disagreeable smell rose from it.

'Was there any indication who posted the document?' Song fired the question at her. He walked fast, his long legs eating up the ground. Blue had to scurry to keep pace.

'It was anonymous. But this document is classed as a state secret. The Ministry of State Security will investigate. They will trace it back. They can find out . . .'

'I was in Wanmei,' Song interrupted her. 'I was there with the wife of Tang Ning. She disappeared while I was there. It must have been her.'

'Did she show you this report?' Blue asked.

'I can't believe she even knew about it.' Unless she had been lying to him all along.

'But she must have known about the abductions?' Blue insisted breathlessly.

'I don't think so.' Unless she had been lying to him.

'Please,' Blue came to a halt. 'I need to catch my breath.'

Song stopped and stared at the cloudy water. After a moment Blue said, 'Whoever did this will go to jail.'

Song nodded.

'I don't know how she got hold of the document, and I don't know how she posted it online, but I think she's on the run,' Song said, thinking aloud. 'I think she's switched off her phone, or she's ditched it, so they can't track her signal. I think the reason she didn't tell me what she'd done was to protect me.'

'But you were with her in Wanmei. If she gets in trouble you'll be in trouble too, no matter whether you posted anything online or not,' Blue pointed out.

Song nodded, thinking about the fight outside the Party and government headquarters. 'You're right,' he told Blue.

'Did she know about your relationship to Chen Dalei?'

Song frowned. That was another thing he assumed that Jin Dao had not known. He had not discussed it with her. But Tang Ning had known, or he would not have sent Li Hetian to Song.

'I don't think so,' he replied to Blue. 'But I'm beginning to realize I don't know much about her.'

Song's mobile rang. For once, he answered without checking who was calling him. A woman's voice, shrill and fraught with emotion – it was Lina.

'Song, my father is dead.'

Song – his mind still with Jin Dao in Wanmei County – struggled for something to say.

'What happened?' he asked.

'Someone shot him.'

'Shot?' Song echoed, and he saw Blue flinch at the word.

'He was sitting in that pavilion. I went to find him. He was sitting there . . .' Lina's voice rose. 'Song, I don't know what to do. They'll have to drop the investigation, surely. They can't criticize him now. They'll have to investigate who killed him instead.'

'Surely it was suicide,' Song said without thinking. The man was about to be put on trial for corruption. He would be found guilty, it was a foregone conclusion. Others had committed suicide in his position.

'No, don't say that!' she wailed. He waited for her to stop crying. Song was aware that Blue was watching him and frowning. 'Please,' Lina sobbed. 'I want you to come and take Doudou. I can't cope.'

Song told her that he would be at her home in half an hour. When he had ended the call, he spoke to Blue.

'My former father-in-law is dead,' he said. He observed Blue's shock as she absorbed this information. 'I don't know how this fits . . .' He rubbed his forehead.

'I should stay,' Blue said. 'I shouldn't go to England.'

'No,' Song shook his head. He took her tiny hand in his huge palm, and squeezed it. 'Thank you for what you've done,' he said.

When Song went to Lina's apartment, he found Doudou there on his own. His mother, he said, was being interviewed by the police.

'She told me to pack some clothes and wait for you,'

the boy said, looking dazed. 'She told me she doesn't have time to look after me right now.'

Song looked at his son. He didn't want to let him down, but he didn't know where he himself was going to spend the night, let alone where Doudou would sleep.

'Come on,' he said. 'Let's go and see your aunt.'

That night they ate with Song's father and sister and his sister's husband at their flat. It was spacious and newly renovated, with three bedrooms and their own bathroom and kitchen, which Song's sister had not yet stopped exclaiming over. Only their father had lost more than he had gained. When he'd been moved out of his old hutong he'd lost his friends of fifty years. He endured the loss for the sake of his family and the new kitchen, and even he admitted to liking the fact that he didn't have to queue for the public toilet every morning.

Things were looking up for Song's sister. Her husband – who had cooked the evening meal – had just landed a job in an insurance company which was well paid and fairly secure. Her daughter, who was studious, had done well in her school exams. Her parents had high hopes for her. At dinner, aged fourteen, she wanted to discuss career options. Which was just as well, most other topics – frozen corpses, demolition and death by shooting among them – having been banned by Song for Doudou's sake in a hushed consultation with his sister.

'Uncle Song,' the fourteen-year-old said, peering through thick spectacles, 'what career do you think I should pursue?'

'You should go abroad,' her grandfather said. 'Learn about the world, observe its strengths and its weaknesses, then come back to China and help to build a great nation.'

'There's no need to go abroad these days,' Song's brother-in-law jumped in. 'We have everything here. I keep telling her she should study medicine. Every family needs a doctor.' There was a brief, embarrassed, silence. Everyone knew he was thinking about the money they had all spent on medical bills for Song's father.

'How about the law?' Song said, thinking again of Jin Dao.

'That's not a bad idea. Commercial law is going to be in high demand,' Song's brother-in-law said, pleased by the suggestion.

'I met a labour lawyer the other day,' Song said. 'A woman. There's a job you could do. She travels around the country . . .'

'Don't go filling her head with that stuff, we all know how those things end,' his sister said.

'What things?' the daughter asked, but they ignored her.

'Everyone's standard of living is improving,' his brother-in-law said. 'I don't know anyone who wants to pick fights with the higher-ups while they're getting richer.'

'She doesn't want to pick a fight,' Song said.

He helped his sister carry plates out.

'Who is she?' she asked him when they were alone in the kitchen.

'Who's who?'

'The lawyer. You're like a teenager. You can't stop talking about her.'

He shook his head.

'You misunderstood. She's married, she's nothing to me. The only reason I keep talking about her is because she's got herself in political trouble.'

His sister gazed at him and shook her head slowly.

'Are you in trouble?' she asked him.

'I don't know.' He started to stash the bowls in the dishwasher. 'I think I might be. I guess I'll find out soon enough.'

'Remember what happened to Mama,' she hissed at him. 'We all have to keep our heads down. We're all doing fine. I don't need human rights, do you? I just need my family to be healthy, and my kid to go to school, and for there to be food on the table. Look, we have a microwave, we have a flat-screen television. I know these are only material things, but it means something. We're not starving . . .'

Song's mobile rang, and when he saw that it was Blue, he took the call, miming apology to his sister.

'Your friend has been detained,' she said. 'It's online. I don't want to say any more.'

Song closed his eyes.

'Baba.' Doudou was at the kitchen door. 'Is anything wrong?'

He shook his head, waved the boy away.

'Blue,' he said. 'I have an address for her husband in London. I want you to take it with you, and find him and tell him what has happened to his wife.'

Eighteen

Pulling her suitcase behind her, Blue emerged from the Arrivals gate at Heathrow and scanned the crowd. She looked for Robin's red hair and spotted her waving furiously. Blue hurried over, and the two women stood for a moment not knowing how to greet each other.

'Well, welcome to England!' Robin said, and they hugged. She held Blue at arm's length and said, 'What happened to your head?'

Blue felt too embarrassed to say she had been assaulted, so instead she said, 'I fell over.'

Robin led Blue to the car park, where they located Robin's car and loaded Blue's small suitcase into the boot.

'I wasn't sure we'd see each other again,' Robin said when they were sitting in the car.

'I know,' Blue said. She had not slept on the flight and she was finding it difficult to think in English. But she knew what Robin meant. They had met the year before when Robin came to Beijing to investigate the murder of a British businessman. Blue had been Robin's interpreter – if that sounded like a straightforward job, it had not been. Robin's investigation had led Blue deeper into danger than either of them had expected. They had parted suddenly, unable to say goodbye let alone plan for a reunion. But they had spoken on the telephone and established a rapport by email that was better than the one they'd had in person. When Robin and Finney had decided to get married they had invited Blue to be there, sending her tickets so that she had no reason to refuse. Now here she was. To Blue it seemed incredible.

As Robin drove out of the airport, Blue gazed out of the window. Everything surprised her. First the speed of the traffic, because it was faster than in Beijing. Then the traffic jam on the way into London because it was just like Beijing. She tried to concentrate on what Robin was saying.

'I'm afraid it won't be a traditional English wedding. We're trying to work out how to keep my mother and father apart – we're thinking either water cannon or an electrified fence. My sisters will take sides, so that could be ugly. And of course Finney has no family at all because he is an orphan, so he's making up his numbers with his police colleagues. It's going to be a strange mixture. I'm just hoping they don't all turn up in uniform.'

Blue smiled, but she was at sea. She had forgotten how fast and idiomatic Robin's conversation was, and the thought of a wedding ceremony full of police officers blew her mind. She took refuge in the view from the window.

Closer to the city the first sight of residential areas disappointed her because the houses looked old and stained. She had expected brighter, newer structures. Cars parked nose to tail along the roadside surprised her because that was just like Beijing. It was true that in London she could not see cars left on the pavement, as they were at home. Still, she had expected something more from the West, a better solution to the car-parking problem.

'Here,' Robin passed a map to her, stabbing her finger at Earl's Court. 'That's where we are.' Blue looked out of the window, expecting a palace. But there were more of these narrow streets, old weathered facades crammed hard against each other, and shops that looked like convenience stores. She tried to follow their route, but she had never seen a map like this that showed every little thing. Maps in Beijing had mysterious blank patches wherever there was a military or Party compound.

She let the map fall to her lap and looked out of the window. She didn't understand why a developer hadn't just knocked all the old houses down and built something new. If they built upwards they wouldn't be so crowded.

Hordes of people walked along the pavements, and people of so many colours. It was considerably cooler than Beijing, and she was surprised at how few clothes they wore, shorts and vests, as though they were boiling hot.

'There are so many foreigners,' she commented to Robin.

'I'm not quite sure what constitutes a foreigner in London,' Robin smiled.

In China, the word 'foreigner' had always conjured up anyone who was not Chinese. Here Blue understood that she must qualify as the foreigner, but she would not stand out as she had feared, not on these streets. She learned to look at the white plaques on the sides of houses, and saw that they were on Fulham Palace Road. Then Robin drove along what she told Blue was the South Circular – a sort of ring road – until they had reached Streatham, where there was a patch of green on the map that called itself a common and looked like a park.

Eventually, Blue found herself at the bottom of the steps that led up to Robin's door. This door, too, disappointed her. Or rather the neighbourhood disappointed her, with its thin, dark, houses that were accessed direct from the street. There was nothing – no wall, no gate – between privacy and the man on the street except this modest front door. She had expected more evidence of wealth in this city; she had expected foreigners to live in homes that reflected their place in the world.

When Robin opened the door two beautiful children appeared. Inside, the house seemed to open up. There were white walls, polished floorboards, a chaos of coats and shoes and school bags. No, Robin protested, she didn't have to remove her shoes, but Blue could not bring herself to walk the dirt of the street into the house so she removed them anyway. The children disappeared, flitting away giggling, before Blue could greet them properly and give them the gifts she had brought for them.

She followed Robin down a staircase and into a large room with light pouring through a window which led onto a garden. The children were down here, the girl with brown curls and the boy with lighter, straight hair. They were bursting with anticipation, their eyes going from Blue's head to her toes in an instant. A black dog, leggy and shaggy, like nothing she had ever seen before, rose, stretching, from a basket and approached her, and one of the children, the boy, rushed over and, laughing, pulled the dog away by his collar.

'You are William?' Blue asked. 'You're so big, not like the photos.' The boy nodded, grinning and turning red.

'And I'm Hannah,' said the girl, who came up to them with her hand extended. Blue thought as she shook the small hand that when she looked into the girl's confident eyes it was as though she was looking into Robin's.

'You look like your mummy,' Blue said to Hannah.

'She's like her in every way,' a voice behind her said.

When she turned, startled, Blue saw that a man was walking down the stairs. He was tall, with unruly grey hair, and he had already loosened his tie, so that he looked like a film that Blue had seen in which there were British schoolboys in scruffy uniforms.

'Finney!' Blue exclaimed, smiling shyly, extending her hand. 'I would like to congratulate you on your wedding.'

That evening, when the children had gone to bed laden with gifts from Blue – she had brought them paper cuts of animals, and calligraphy brushes, and traditional Chinese jackets – the three of them sat and ate together at the kitchen table. Robin placed a bowl of salad leaves on the table, drizzled oil and vinegar on top, and passed Blue long wooden utensils, with which she understood that she should help herself. Bowls of Italian pasta in sauce followed, all handed from one to the next of them in turn. She watched Robin, picking up her fork and spearing a piece of pasta as Robin did. Blue took a mouthful. The taste of cheese nearly made her gag. She swallowed, then washed it down with a mouthful of the red wine that Finney had poured into her glass. The flavour was new to her. She took another mouthful of the pasta, and another sip. Taken in turns like this, the food was palatable, and so was the wine.

'Please tell me about your wedding preparations,' she said to Robin, laying her fork on her plate as she had observed Finney do.

Robin told her that there would be purple tulips on the tables, and she would wear a silver dress. Again she warned that it would not be a traditional wedding. 'I mean, look at us,' she said now, 'we're living together, I've got children by another man. I can't dress up in virginal white. My family is a disaster when it comes to marriage. I'm only giving it a go because Finney is such a stickler for convention.'

'Except that *you* asked *me*,' Finney put in.

Robin smiled and patted his hand. 'A minor detail.'

In her exhaustion, Blue was losing her grasp on the conversation. But she was excited and pleased to be here in this alternative universe. Robin was an attentive hostess. Before dinner she had noticed Blue's eyes go greedily to the laptop on the kitchen table and had urged her to treat it as her own. Blue was feeling a little light-headed.

'I don't think it's true that you're doing this only for him,' she said earnestly to Robin. 'When you emailed me to say that you were getting married you seemed very happy.'

They both smiled at that, and Robin asked Blue whether she had a boyfriend.

'No,' Blue said firmly. 'I'm short, and I'm not rich. It's hard to find the right man.'

'What is the right man?' Finney asked.

She thought about Wolf.

'The right man would not disappoint me,' she said.

'It's difficult here too,' Robin said. 'A lot of people try Internet dating.'

Blue nodded. She didn't feel up to explaining that she had tried that, but that every Chinese site had asked her to state her height and she had seen no point in lying. She had met with a few of the men who responded, but it soon became clear to her that they were all either short or ugly or penniless. That wouldn't have ruled them out, but they all seemed grimly focused on marriage. None of them seemed interested in her, only in the fact of her short stature, which meant that she must be not only available, but desperate for a husband, any husband, no matter whether he was kind to her or had anything in common with her.

'What are your plans?' Finney asked. 'Are there things you want to see?'

She nodded. She had a long list, from Big Ben and the Houses of Parliament to Buckingham Palace.

'I also have work to do,' she told them. 'I must find a missing person. In Beijing a woman has been arrested. Her husband is in London, and I must find him and tell him what has happened. He lives in Fountain House.'

'Fountain House,' Robin echoed, as though she was not sure where that was.

Blue saw that the smile had left Finney's face and had been replaced by an expression of concern, and she remembered through her jet-lagged haze that this man was a police officer. She didn't know what that meant in this country. He had such a nice smile, but she wasn't sure whether she could trust him.

'That's a tall order in a strange city,' was all he said.

'I have his address,' she said defensively. 'I'm sure I can find my own way. It's important that I find him. His wife needs him.'

She was going to tell them about the abductions, but

she came to an abrupt halt. That was all a world away. Robin might understand, but Finney would not. She picked up her fork and stuffed pasta into her mouth.

Silence had fallen over the table. The temperature had fallen as the evening drew in, and Blue shivered.

'I'd advise you to think twice before getting involved,' Finney said gently. 'These things are always best left to the professionals, whatever country you're in.' When Blue glanced up at him she saw that his face was watchful and grave.

Nineteen

BEIJING

Song drove into the car park at Babaoshan Cemetery.
You clever bastard, he addressed his dead father-in-law.
Babaoshan's hallowed grounds were the resting place of
revolutionary martyrs. Detective Chen hardly seemed a
reputable candidate but he appeared to have pulled off
one last, post-mortem, coup.

The cemetery was nestled in the hillside eight miles
west of Tiananmen, and he had calculated the timing so
that he arrived early. He wanted to watch the mourners
arrive. If Psycho Wang was among them he would turn
around and leave. He couldn't bear to be in the same
room as the man. He sat in the car and waited and
watched, his thoughts on Jin Dao. Blue would have
arrived in England by now, he thought. It was a long
shot getting her to look for Tang Ning. No matter how
well connected Jin Dao's husband was, how much could
he do for her if she was accused of subversion?

Song dug his mobile out of his pocket and dialled
Zhou Caishi, who was the only one of his former police
colleagues he'd kept in touch with. Zhou was surprised

to hear from him – they hadn't seen each other for nearly a year – but agreed to meet Song the next day for dinner. Small groups of mourners were gathering before walking along the paths that led to the rooms where funerals were held. Detective Chen's was one of several that morning. Stalls were doing a busy trade in wreaths.

He saw Lina and Doudou emerging from a black limousine – she had demanded their son back again before the funeral so that he would be seen to arrive with her. His ex-wife carried a wreath. She was in a short black dress, their son in a navy-blue shirt and dark trousers. Song got out of the car and went over to greet them. Doudou looked gloomily up at him. He looked uncomfortably hot in his formal clothes.

Lina was highly agitated. 'The official in charge of the cemetery rang me this morning and tried to cancel the funeral,' she told Song angrily. 'He said my father couldn't be put to rest here because he was under investigation. I spent more than an hour on the telephone to my father's friends. I begged them, I reminded them of the favours my father had done for them. I told them I've kept quiet about their ties to my father so far, but I might change my mind if he suffers indignity. I told them he deserves an honourable funeral . . .'

'Did the cemetery contact you to agree that the funeral could go ahead?'

'We're here aren't we? And Daddy's body's here. What are they going to do about it?'

Song gazed at her in disbelief, but no one could reason with her when she was like this, so he kept silent.

She grabbed Song's wrist.

'I want you to investigate.' She lowered her voice.

He had been expecting this.

'The police are investigating,' he replied quietly.

'The police will protect them,' she hissed.

'Protect who?' Song glanced at Doudou, who was listening miserably. People were walking past. They would overhear. She was making a laughing stock of herself.

'My father had no reason to kill himself.'

'He had every reason.'

Suspended, investigated by the Central Discipline Inspection Commission, about to be stripped of his Communist Party membership, the evidence of corruption by all accounts piling up against him. He'd been allowed to stay at home, but no one – not Detective Chen himself, not his daughter, not his few remaining friends – could have been under any illusion. The axe was about to fall. If he'd been lucky, it would have been jail rather than execution.

'One of his enemies killed him,' Lina went on. 'Someone who was afraid he would name them as part of a plea bargain.'

In fact she wasn't the only one who had questions about whether her father had committed suicide. In the absence of Blue, Song had been teaching himself to navigate cyberspace, and he'd seen plenty of frenzied speculation that Chen had been murdered by former cronies who he'd threatened to bring down with him. But Song didn't intend to discuss that with Lina now.

'Come on,' he said, 'we should go in.'

Inside, the coffin had been placed at the front of the memorial hall, but carelessly, as though someone had put it down there because they were not sure what else to do with it. There were no wreaths except for the one Lina carried. She walked up to the casket and opened the lid. She bowed, lowering her face close to her father's, then beckoned Doudou over and indicated that he should bow, which he did. Song scrutinized his late father-in-law's cold face. It was good to see the man was dead.

They took their seats in the empty room. Lina twisted in her chair.

'Nobody's here,' she hissed bitterly. 'None of them have come, none of the people he helped.'

They sat and waited, but still no one came. Song reflected that even the friends Lina thought she had mobilized must have been scared off. After five minutes an official entered the room.

'We need the room,' he announced loudly. 'Someone else is booked in here.'

Lina stared at him.

'But . . .' she started to say.

'We need the room,' he repeated firmly.

There was silence as Lina digested this.

'Why don't you just say a few words?' Song suggested to his ex-wife.

She got to her feet and went to stand next to her father's coffin. She started to speak to the empty room about her father's philanthropy, but after a few words her voice trailed off. She turned to glance at her father, then shrugged, and indicated with a jerk of her head that they should leave.

As they made their way back to the car, an official approached her.

'You're going to have to find somewhere else to put your father,' he told her. 'We can't have him here.'

Afterwards, Song accompanied Lina and Doudou to their car.

'We're going to my father's house,' Lina told him. She looked pale, and Song felt an unexpected surge of pity for her. She should not have had to go through such humiliation. 'I need to sort some of his papers,' Lina said, apparently determined to carry on as though nothing had happened. 'And then I've invited two officials from the Central Discipline Inspection Commission to come to the house. I want to show my respect for their work.' She sounded like an echo of her father. 'Will you come back with us?' she asked. 'I've got so many things to discuss with you.'

He almost said no, but then he saw Doudou's face. He didn't want to be alone with his mother, not after what had happened.

'I'll follow on behind you,' Song said. 'Doudou, do you want to come with me or your mother?'

He hadn't intended it as a competition, but there it was. Doudou chose to ride with Song.

Song followed Lina through the gates to Manhattan, the residential compound where her father had set up home, driving past guards who saluted them. The Manhattan villa had been an unwise extravagance, it had drawn attention to Detective Chen. Police officers were public servants. A detective's monthly salary was a few thousand *yuan*, which would stretch to a modest flat, not this Spanish-style hacienda. Song had never been here before. Even Lina had known to keep her distance. For all her whining and her slavish devotion to her father, she was not stupid. She knew that when the storm broke, she would be deluged. His assets would be seized, along with the gifts he'd showered on her. She invested what cash she had in Doudou's name or sent it abroad, and she'd hidden valuable jade and jewellery.

They climbed the steps and Lina opened the heavy front door by inputting a code on a keypad. Inside, the three of them stood in the silent hallway. Even when Chen Dalei had lived here it had been too big for him. Now the silence echoed noisily with the hum of air-conditioners turned up to maximum, as though the house was being chilled ready for the return of a corpse. Here was Chen Dalei's taste, in the gilt banisters, and the marble staircase, and the statuettes of naked women in classical Greek poses. It all looked dusty.

Doudou turned immediately into a sitting room to the right of the hallway and settled himself in front of a large plasma flat-screen television. Lina beckoned Song into her father's study. She sat there behind Chen's desk in a leather chair as though she had been born to it.

'My father talked about something in the weeks before he died,' Lina said. 'I want to know whether he mentioned it to you.'

She waited with a conspiratorial expression. Song said, 'I don't have a clue what you're talking about.'

She breathed in sharply, and he thought that she was the only woman he knew who could hiss just by taking a breath.

'The panic room?' she said pointedly. 'I know he talked about it to you that day we went to the countryside.'

'Ah that,' Song said. 'I assumed he made it up.'

She frowned at him.

'My father didn't make things up,' she said. 'What I want to know is where it is.'

Song gazed at her. Had the old man trusted anyone? Not his daughter, clearly.

'I don't know where it is,' he said. 'And if I were you, I'd let whatever's in there lie.'

She turned angrily away from him, and he left the room. He glanced into the sitting room and saw Doudou stretched out on a leather sofa watching cartoons.

Song decided to tour the house. He went briefly into the basement, where there were two small, boxlike rooms for the *ayis* and a tiny bathroom. There was a small room just off the garage, also, where the driver had a bed. Returning to the ground floor, he discovered a kitchen, where both *ayis* were preparing food. He was surprised to find them still at work. Outside the kitchen was a back door that led into the garden. There was an oak-panelled dining room as well as the sitting room where Doudou was lounging and the study. As he moved around the house, he tapped the wood panelling, wondering if this might give him a clue as to the whereabouts of the panic room – if such a place existed – but one knock sounded much like another. Upstairs, there were five bedrooms leading off an L-shaped corridor. In the master bedroom, Chen Dalei's clothes were still in the closets, and the smell of him hung in the air. The bathroom was a revelation. There was a jacuzzi, a massage shower, a sauna and a steam room. There was black satin women's underwear folded on the edge of the bath, as though the *ayi* had found it in the bathroom and not known what else to do with it. Song opened the cabinets. Next to the bed he found an assortment of sex toys – he suspected that these too had been tidied away by the maid – and a small package of something that he suspected was amyl nitrate.

When he returned to his starting point, he found Doudou still slumped in front of the television and Lina shredding documents in her father's study. The phone rang, and he gathered from her end of the conversation that the guards were telling her that the visitors were on the way. Lina seemed immediately flustered. She issued information to Song as though he was a member of her staff.

'Mr Wen and Mr Guo are senior members of the Commission. They are both dealing with my father's case. We need to show them great courtesy and explain the situation to them clearly.'

'In general,' Song said, 'people have given up asking me to attend meetings like this.'

'Can you be polite? You know how important this is to me and to Doudou.'

The two men arrived and were ushered inside by Lina. The men, both formally dressed in dark suits and ties, their faces giving nothing away, looked ill at ease. Stiffly, they expressed their condolences. Lina guided them towards the sitting room, where Song saw that Detective Chen's maid had laid the table for a meal.

Song watched Doudou being introduced to the officials, saw him take his place reluctantly at table. Surely Lina could have spared her son this.

They sat, avoiding each other's eyes, as the maid brought out food, delicately arranged on the plate and decorated with tiny flower sculptures cut from radishes and carrots. They started to eat, Lina making a show of taking the choicest morsels and placing them on the plates of her guests.

'My son misses his grandfather terribly,' Lina said, dabbing at her eyes. 'Grandfather was honourable, wasn't he, Doudou darling? He was an upright man, a patriotic man. Isn't that so, Doudou?'

Lina seized her son's wrist and squeezed it hard, digging her long nails into his fat arm. The boy muttered something under his breath.

So this was Doudou's role, Song thought angrily. Did Lina think nothing of using him like this?

The men continued to eat in a businesslike fashion as though they had a lot of food to get through and not much time. Lina continued to prod Doudou to speak in support of his grandfather but she had failed to prepare him and he refused to play along, shaking his head and screwing up his face and pulling away from her.

The maid poured French wine. Lina raised her glass.

'I want to express my appreciation of the work of the Commission and of the Public Security Bureau,' she said. 'Because of their work we can have complete faith in our public servants. The Commission is thorough and incorruptible in its pursuit of those who would defraud the people or betray their trust.'

She raised her glass. The men, apparently unmoved by her speech, also raised their glasses. They emptied the wine efficiently into their mouths.

Song touched his lips to the wine. He had consumed wine only once before in his life and had found it sour and unpleasant.

'I know I'm among old friends,' Lina said. 'I feel I can speak openly with you. My father warned me that he had many enemies who would stop at nothing to keep him quiet. My father was an honourable man who never took so much as a penny from the masses, but he knew many men who had a different attitude, men who took advantage of our country's great opening and reform to enrich themselves. He told me, "Lina, I can ruin these men a hundred times over with what I have on them, not only in my head but on paper."'

Song watched his ex-wife. Her eyes swam with tears, the pale skin at the base of her throat seemed to flutter with emotion. She was botching it. Her father could have pulled it off but she was an amateur. In Lina's voice the words sounded like the threat they were.

He saw the two officials exchange a stone-cold glance. He couldn't let her do this to herself or to Doudou.

'I'm afraid my wife is excessively stressed with grief for her father,' he said, pushing back his chair and standing up. 'I promised her doctor that I wouldn't let her become distraught, it will put too much strain on her heart. Please finish your meal while I take her upstairs.'

The two men glanced at each other again, but they rose courteously from their chairs and wished Lina goodnight.

'I'm fine,' she muttered to him, and she shook his hand from her shoulder. For a moment he thought she was going to fight. She glared at him. Then a calculating gleam appeared in her eyes and she crumpled against his arm.

'It's true,' she said. 'My doctor has told me that my grief is damaging my health. Please excuse me.'

She made a pathetic exit but outside in the corridor she was spitting with rage.

'Why did you do that?' she hissed. 'It was going so well.'

'I saved your neck. This way they pity you for your grief instead of resenting you for your threats.'

She began to climb the stairs and he followed her up, afraid that if he left her alone she would return to the dining room.

They reached a guest bedroom. The four-poster bed was made up with embroidered sheets. Lina sat down on the side of the bed and berated him.

'Why do you always have to ruin things?'

'You can't corrupt these people, don't you see? You were making a fool of yourself.'

'There's no such thing as an official who can't be bought or threatened,' she scoffed. 'You're so old-fashioned, no one believes in right and wrong any more. Look what your ridiculous naivety has achieved for you. You're a failure, you have nothing.'

She shouted curses after him as he left. He had learned long ago that he could not reach her.

Song paused at the bottom of the stairs. He could still hear Lina spitting mad. He could hear Doudou's voice from the dining room and he went to listen at the door.

'I don't know, I didn't see . . .' he heard Doudou say miserably. 'I don't know anything about my mother's financial affairs.'

'I'm sure your grandfather showed you all sorts of things, secret places he kept special things?'

'My grandfather never showed me anything.' Doudou sounded on the edge of tears.

'Has your mother been going through your grandfather's documents?'

'She doesn't care about my grandfather's papers. I saw her shredding them.'

There was a moment's silence. Song ran his hand over his face.

'We've heard your grandfather has a room made of steel which he can lock and that the door is hidden. That must be fun to play in, isn't it?'

'I don't know what you're talking about,' Doudou said. 'I never play here.'

Song took a deep breath and walked into the dining room. Doudou was standing in front of the officials looking distressed.

'Doudou,' he said, 'go and watch TV.'

'Can't I go home? Where's Mama?'

'Your mother's upstairs resting. Go on, turn that TV on.'

When the boy had left the room, Song took a seat at the table.

'I heard what you were asking him but I'm afraid you've been mistaken. My grandfather used to joke about having a secure room and about what he kept in there. He had a cruel sense of humour.'

Mr Wen, the more senior of the two men, spoke first.

'If you haven't seen it, you can't say for sure that it's not here.'

'That's true,' Song acknowledged. 'I'm telling you my understanding of the situation.'

'The maid would know,' the younger man said.

They called the *ayi*, and she stood before them wide-eyed. She was a middle-aged woman, hair short and curled, in a uniform of white tunic and black trousers.

'How long have you worked for Detective Chen?' The elder bureaucrat commenced the interrogation.

Song heard a movement outside the door and thought that Lina must have come down to listen.

'Three years.'

'Do you work on your own?'

'There's a cleaning girl who works under me.'

'You manage the house for Detective Chen?'

'Yes.'

'You know the house well.'

'Yes.'

'Is there a secret room in this house?' the senior bureaucrat asked.

The woman looked nervously from man to man.

'A hidden room,' the younger man clarified.

'I don't know,' she said.

'What do you mean, you don't know? This is the house you manage. You must have seen it if there is one.'

'If it's hidden, how could I see it?'

The two men shook their heads in disgust and dismissed the maid, then got up from the table. Mr Wen turned to Song.

'Things are not right here. If you are not involved, I advise you to stay clear of the lot of them. That daughter of his is trouble. You made the right decision to seek a divorce. Why are you still hanging around with her? You can only harm yourself.'

Song nodded, as though he was grateful for the advice, murmuring, 'You're right, of course you're right.' As they opened the door to leave, Song half expected Lina to fall into the room. But if she had been eavesdropping, she had got out of the way in time. There was no sign of her.

Song walked the two men to their cars as a gesture of respect.

When they had gone he went back inside and found Doudou watching a soap opera on the vast flat-screen TV. He sat down next to his son on the overstuffed leather sofa. It felt strange but comforting to be sitting there with his son. Song let himself be soothed by the sound of the television. His mind was elsewhere. The remains of Detective Chen were to be reduced to ashes but the malignant presence of the man remained.

Song could not shake the thought that Detective Chen had committed suicide. Lina had not been able to come up with any evidence for her claim that he'd been murdered. The timing of his death could be coincidental, but suppose that Detective Chen had been made aware that Tang Ning's secret report had been posted online. He would have known, then, that questions would be asked about why he had seen this months ago and done nothing. If he was found guilty of a cover-up his jail sentence for corruption would have turned into a death sentence in front of his eyes. In that case, suicide might have been his best option. Meanwhile, Jin Dao would rot in prison for exposing a crime he had covered up.

'Baba,' Doudou was elbowing him. 'They were buried alive!'

The soap opera had ended and a chat show had begun. The hosts, a man and a woman, were as beautiful as each other. The guests were two men who had dug themselves out of a coal mine days after the rescue teams had given up on them. They had drunk their urine and eaten coal – cue a melodramatic grimace from the hostess – and kept each other going with jokes.

'I thought of my wife and how ugly she was and how she wouldn't be able to find another husband,' one of them said to guffaws of laughter, 'so for her sake, I had to get out of there.'

The men – wiry peasants with strong regional accents – were treated like national heroes by the middle-class audience, none of whom had been down a mine in their lives.

'They're so brave,' Doudou said.

'You'll have the chance to be brave at some point in your life,' Song said. Then he thought, and what do I advise you? To seize it or to pass it by? He thought of Jin Dao. She had known what she was doing, he was sure of it.

'If you were the host what questions would you ask?' Song said to his son.

'Me? I couldn't be a TV host, I'm too fat.'

'Just pretend. You've been on a diet, I've had you swimming up and down a pool for the last ten years, you haven't an ounce of fat on you, you've graduated from college, and you're offered a job as TV host...' Song hesitated for a moment. Doudou was looking at him as though he was mad. 'OK. Forget the chat show. They're sitting here on this sofa. They've been trapped underground in a mine. What would you ask them?'

Doudou struggled with the question for a few minutes. Then he said, 'I'd ask them why they chose such a dangerous job in the first place.'

'Right,' Song clapped his hands in approval.

'And I'd ask them why the mine collapsed,' Doudou hazarded, encouraged by his father's praise.

'Exactly.'

'And I'd ask why don't they sue the mine owner.'

'Hah!' Song pounded his son on the back. 'We have a lawyer in the family.'

His son leaned against him, and for a moment they just sat there like that.

'And did they ask any of those questions?' Song asked his son eventually.

'No.'

And why not? Song wanted to ask his son. But he didn't. He thought that his son didn't understand the nature of the situation in which he lived. He was too young, he had seen too little. And if he didn't know, then why alarm him?

'They just asked easy questions,' Doudou said, 'all about drinking pee and eating coal. Maybe they didn't want to get anyone into trouble.'

'Maybe,' Song said. Exhaustion washed over him. He thought of Jin Dao in a police cell. He was powerless to help her, and resentful of the fact that she had chosen her course of action without telling him. The fact that she had been trying to protect him only made it worse. But if Jin Dao was right about Tang Ning's connections high in the Party hierarchy, it was possible that he could mobilize support for her, assuming Blue could find him.

He sighed. It occurred to him that Lina had fallen silent.

'Your mother's asleep and I don't want to disturb her,' he told Doudou. 'So we'll all stay here tonight. Go upstairs and pick a room.'

In the middle of the night, Song awoke. He lay there uneasily, disorientated in the strange room. What had awakened him? He could not remember any noise. Still, he swung his legs out of bed and went to check on Doudou. He did not like to think of the boy wandering the endless corridors.

Doudou was fast asleep, lying on his back and snoring like a man four times his age. But as he returned to his room Song heard a noise from the corridor. This time it was unmistakable, a soft knocking sound. He stopped and listened and then, barefoot, he made his way silently to the bend in the corridor. Beyond this was the master bedroom, and the bathroom with its jacuzzi and sauna. He was aware that he was unarmed and virtually naked. He stood with his back to the wall and peered around the corner. The corridor was lit by a yellow glow from lamps mounted on the wall every metre.

Lina was squatting in the corridor. She had abandoned her high heels, but she was still dressed in the black dress she had worn to the funeral and then to the dinner. In front of her on the ground was a toolbox. As Song watched, she took a screwdriver from the box and stood up. Now he could see that she had found the panic room. Or at least, she had found the door to the panic room. In front of her, just next to the door to Chen Dalei's bedroom, a section of wood panelling had slid open to reveal a sheer metal door.

Lina approached the door and tried to insert the screwdriver between the door and its frame, but no matter how she tried, there was not sufficient space.

Song moved closer.

'What on earth are you doing?'

Startled, she leaped backwards and flourished the screwdriver at him.

'Don't you dare spy on me!' she shouted. 'This is my house . . .'

'You invited me here,' Song reminded her. He turned towards the panic-room door, running his hands over it. Behind him, she was rattling around in the toolbox. Suddenly she hurtled into the door next to him and bashed it with a hammer. He seized her wrist.

'What are you doing?' he asked again. 'Have you gone mad?'

'Wouldn't you go mad?' she turned on him, spitting. 'My father has ruined my life, and now he's died on me without telling me how to save myself.'

She burst into tears and turned, running down the corridor away from him. He heard a door slam and assumed she had returned to her bed.

Song bent to pick up the toolbox, then he stood and

ran his hand over the metal door again. It was a beautiful thing, sleek and seamless and unyielding. In the doorframe at chest height there was a slot so narrow that Song thought Lina must have missed it. He guessed that it was designed for a card, and that it might open the door. He tried running the blade of a knife into the slot, but the door did not budge. Chen was dead, and he would keep his secrets.

Twenty

LONDON

Blue waited for the bus Robin had assured her would take her to Croydon. Robin had offered to come with her, but Blue had insisted that she would go on her own. After the difficult conversation at the dinner table the night before, she had no intention of involving Robin or Finney in her search for Tang Ning. It was hotter today, and Blue sheltered under the roof at the bus stop.

When the bus came, it was full, and Blue – who had met few foreigners – spent forty minutes rammed up close against half a dozen of them. There were old ladies clutching sticks and complaining about the heat, young mothers manoeuvring buggies on board and teenagers who spoke loudly and made her nervous. When she eventually got a seat, Blue looked out of the window.

Everywhere, she was surprised by the age of things and the shabbiness of them, although she had begun to understand almost unconsciously that some of these narrow houses were not, as she had at first assumed, slums. Intuitively she began to readjust her aesthetic judgement, to register the differences between Regency,

Victorian, Georgian and Edwardian without knowing the names of any of them. But soon the landscape changed. There were grey blocks of flats and what looked to her eyes like government buildings. There were large car parks and pubs.

It is surprising how fast we adapt, she thought. Yesterday I was a woman in a crowd on a Beijing street and today I am something else entirely. She had lived in envy of those who had the opportunity to go abroad. Now here it was, the world outside. The door had opened, she had passed through, and nothing was as she expected.

When she got off the bus she was surprised by beggars with white skin. She was embarrassed to be stopped in the street by a religious fanatic and even more embarrassed not to understand what he was saying until she had been listening politely for several minutes. Fascinated by what everything cost, she stopped and looked in estate agents' windows in an effort to try to compare Beijing prices with London prices per square metre.

Tang Ning's address, 1521 Fountain House, sounded elegant but when she asked the way no one seemed to have heard of it. Raynley Road got a bit more of a response, and after an hour of walking she reached her destination. She stood and looked up at Fountain House and knew that this was a slum. There were broken windows and sheets rigged up as curtains.

'I thought Song said Tang Ning was well connected,'

Blue murmured to herself. 'Why would he choose to live here if he didn't have to?'

Nevertheless, there was no point in turning around and heading back across the city, although the prospect was more attractive than the pungent stairwell which greeted her when she approached.

She stopped off two or three times on gloomy corridors, trying to understand the numbering system. Eventually, on the fifteenth floor, she found the right flat.

Blue rang the bell and waited, with growing impatience, listening for footsteps on the other side of the door. Someone had spray-painted graffiti, using the spyhole in the door as part of the pornographic design. She wrinkled her nose. There was a foul stench which she had thought was part and parcel of the corridor, but which seemed to be at its strongest by this door.

Still no one came and, without really thinking about what she was doing, she tried the door handle. She was surprised when the door swung open on its hinges. For a moment she stood there hesitating.

Then she stepped inside. Immediately the smell was worse, as strong as sewage. It was all that she could do not to retch. She always carried a small tub of tiger balm in her bag – a habit inherited from her mother, who used it for every conceivable ache – and she rubbed some around her nose. It masked the smell a little.

Despite the sunshine outside, the flat was dark except for an electric light that burned in a kitchen no bigger than a cupboard. A pan and a plate lay unwashed in the sink.

Trash, including vegetable peel and a piece of meat, perhaps chicken, were rotting in a plastic bag. Blue thought she had found the source of the rancid smell. Her stomach turned when she saw flies gorging on the meat. They were in the air, too, and on the tiles around the sink. She did not want to spend a moment longer in there. She turned and ventured further, into a small sitting room. There were papers all over the floor, as though someone had upended a file. Force of habit made her bend to pick some of them up, and as she did so she glanced at them, but the putrid smell meant that she couldn't concentrate on anything. A mobile phone lay on the floor and she picked it up. Had Tang Ning abandoned the flat? If so, he must have done so in a hurry.

She went through into the bedroom. Or rather, she stopped on the threshold of the bedroom, turned to stone by what she saw. Half on, half off the bed lay a dark, gnarled, shape that was at once inhuman and human. It was on its back, with its legs hanging over the side of the bed as though, being pursued, it had stumbled backwards onto the bed. Its torso was twisted, arms flung to the side. There were gaping orifices where eyes might have been, and nose and mouth, and each of these heaved and crawled.

Nausea engulfed her.

Flies and maggots had gathered in patches on the

chest, and around the throat. They were in the air. One of them landed in her hair, others flew towards her face, fluttering tiny wings around her nose and eyes.

Her stomach heaved and, clutching her mouth she fled, gagging, for the front door and stood retching in the hallway.

Further down the corridor a woman came out of her front door. At once the odour hit her too, and she moaned and swore loudly. A group of youths emerged from the stairwell and howled, waving their arms around them and clutching at their mouths.

'I smell Chinese fucking takeaway,' one of them shouted, and the others howled with vicious laughter. Two of the youths peeled off and turned back, defeated by the smell, but that only seemed to goad the others to advance towards Blue, and the smell made them wild. They were jeering, shouting things she could not – and did not want to – understand.

For a moment she stared, paralysed. She had stepped into a nightmare, into a surreal symmetry. She was standing in the agency again, and the thugs were advancing on her, but this time they had white skin and they were armed with beer bottles not with wooden clubs. Carelessly, without breaking his stride, the youth in the lead smashed his bottle against the wall and raised the lethal remainder in his hand, waving it at her.

'Come on, you know you want it,' he shouted, and his friends collapsed in helpless laughter. For a moment that slowed them down.

Blue looked around her for an escape route. The

woman who had come to her door was still there, standing watching in her doorway, her dressing gown clutched over her mouth and nose like a mask. Blue ran towards her, but she could see the fear on the woman's face too. When she was a moment from safety the woman spun back inside and flung the door shut in her face. Literally, in her face. Blue felt the slam of the wood against her cheek. For a moment she leaned into the door as though it might give under her feather weight. Then, as the voices closed in behind her, she turned and ran for her life.

Twenty-one

For his meeting with Inspector Zhou Caishi, Song chose a restaurant with tables set one by one in private booths. They were protected from public view by pots of tall bamboo that formed walls around them. A mynah bird sang in a cage that hung above the table.

'This is very nice,' Zhou said, looking around him as he arrived. He had a round face and spectacles. When he smiled, he beamed. 'But it's not necessary, you know, we're old friends.' He sat down opposite Song. 'If you need anything you only have to ask.'

Song smiled tightly. His shoulders were hunched and tense. He would not immediately broach the subject of Jin Dao, or Zhou would get up and leave. Zhou was a senior police officer these days, and Jin's was a major political crime.

Song could count on one hand the officers with whom he was still on speaking terms. He had walked out on it all, police career and marriage, in a red haze of anger, and he'd lost most of his colleagues at the same time. For a while he'd stayed in touch with a couple of friends, hoping they would be useful sources for the cases that were beginning to come his way. But they assumed that anyone in business on their own was rich. They wanted cash in hand, and wads of it, even for information that proved worthless. In time, Song dropped them too. Only Zhou Caishi remained, and until now Song had never asked him for information.

Song ordered food and beer and attempted small talk. But even the small talk soon advanced onto dangerous ground. They had both worked under Chen Dalei and neither of them pretended to be sorry to see him dead.

'They won't let it go,' Song said, picking up a sliver of mushroom with his chopsticks. 'Lina has had investigators sniffing around the house. I think the Central Discipline Inspection Commission intends to issue a denunciation of his crimes.'

Zhou nodded, chewing. When he had swallowed, he said, 'I've heard they've put a figure to his crimes. Seven million *yuan* in bribes, nineteen million *yuan* in public assets redirected for his own use and a further 160,000 *yuan* in cash siphoned off. It's a pity they can't try him, of course, but a denunciation will work just as well. People will assume he killed himself because he was guilty. They will feel that the Party achieved the proper result and has purged itself of corrupt elements.'

Song wished there was a way of protecting Doudou from the fallout of all this. If he was a rich man he would have sent his son abroad.

'Chen was certainly guilty,' Song said. 'We both saw

the way he operated. But Psycho Wang seems to manage to escape unscathed. How come they never executed him?'

Zhou smiled.

'He's a slippery character. He left the police force at the right time and set up in business on his own. He's just a gangster, but he kept his ties with Chen and he always had a good eye for an investment. I'm sure between them they both lined their pockets. I heard he fled when he realized how much trouble Chen was in. He's in London or Paris or somewhere. Apparently he's putting money into property there.'

'They're welcome to him,' Song said, thinking of Psycho Wang standing looking like a thug underneath Big Ben. It was the only British landmark Song knew.

'Did you know,' Zhou said quietly, and with the air of a man imparting an amusing if politically risqué anecdote, 'that Chen had recently been put in charge of petition work for Beijing and Hebei?'

Song stared at him. He thought of Tang Ning's report, addressed to Chen Dalei, and of Li Hetian's petition, also addressed to Chen Dalei.

'Isn't it extraordinary?' Zhou smiled, enjoying Song's reaction, 'that the Minister should choose a man like him, with absolutely no interest in justice, to do that work?'

'What did the work consist of?' Song asked.

'I hear the leaders are fearful of peasant unrest, there have been too many disturbances. So they've ordered local police forces to take peasant grievances more seriously and to pay attention to petitions. Wherever any other part of the government received petitions pertaining to police work, they were forwarded to Chen Dalei, and it was his job to order further investigations if local police forces failed. I think it's one aspect of his career that the leadership won't want to advertise.'

Zhou started to pick at the food again, and Song was glad to be allowed to think. Tang Ning had clearly known to whom his report should be addressed. But how had Li Hetian known? As far as he could tell, Li Hetian had written his petition some time after Tang Ning had written his report. After all, Tang Ning only wrote about the disappearance of Li's child, not about a body. Somehow his daughter's body must have found its way back to Li, or been discovered, after Tang Ning had left Yidong.

Zhou leaned back in his chair with the look of a man who had eaten all he possibly could. He looked as though, in a few minutes, he might say it was time for him to go home to bed. Song tried to gather himself. He must put Chen and Li and Tang out of his mind until later when he could try to work out what it all meant. For the moment he must concentrate on what he had come here for.

He leaned forward, placing his elbows carefully in spaces between plates and bowls. Song had ordered in a state of such nervous anticipation that the food had just kept on coming, dish after dish. A plate of asparagus nestled up against beef with orange peel, and spiced lamb kebabs were wedged in between a steamed garoupa and deep-fried squid rings. He trusted Zhou and knew him to be a decent man. Their friendship had always been based on the understanding that they shared similar views. The difference between them was that Song had not been able to remain silent, whereas Zhou had kept very quiet indeed. Song was encouraged by Zhou's frank remarks about Chen. But now, about to introduce Jin Dao's name, Song felt exposed.

'I would like to discuss something with you. It's quite sensitive.'

Zhou's eyes flickered to the waitress, but she'd served them everything they'd ordered and was flitting around the table in the next booth.

'What is it?'

'There's a law professor at Beijing University who's been detained. I wondered if you knew anything of her situation. Her name is Jin Dao, Professor Jin Dao.'

Zhou's jaw had tensed, his lips were working nervously, and when he spoke it was in a voice so hushed that Song had to strain to hear.

'I'm aware of the case,' he muttered. 'We're under strict instructions not to discuss it.'

'I'm not a journalist,' Song replied in a low, urgent voice. 'I'm not going to make trouble for you. I'm asking simply in the capacity of a friend. Professor Jin's so-called crime was to post on the Internet a confidential document about the abduction of children in Wanmei County.'

'It was marked "top secret",' Zhou pointed out grimly. 'Making it public was a serious crime.'

'Its content was a report delivered to the authorities six months ago, on which they failed to act. Since then more children have gone missing. Did they tell you this when they told you not to discuss it?'

Zhou shook his head fiercely.

A waitress arrived to fill their glasses with beer and they both fell silent as long as she was in earshot.

'They should be thanking her not arresting her,' Song added for good measure, when the waitress had gone.

'But she's shamed the Party,' Zhou said between clenched teeth. 'That's her crime. She's exposed their inaction and she'll bear the consequences . . .' He broke off and shifted uncomfortably in his chair, and for a moment Song thought that he had lost him. But Zhou continued speaking, whispering. 'They've got her, you know, the State Security Bureau has her. The document was scanned into a computer inside the Wanmei County government, it wasn't hard for them to trace. It seems that she broke into the offices. The scan was still there on the computer, and she'd used an account that could be traced back to her. She must have had an accomplice but they don't know who it was. The police were alerted nationwide. When she used her ID to check in to a guest house in Harbin, they got her. She's being held in Banbuqiao Prison.'

'What will happen to her?'

'If she's lucky they won't try her, the police will send her off to re-education through labour, that would be less than four years. But the political climate's not good. It's too easy to put material on the Internet. It's become a battleground, propaganda versus grassroots campaigning. They have an important message to send . . .'

'. . . and she's the message,' Song finished his sentence for him.

They sat in silence. Song thought that Jin Dao's detention was potentially extremely hazardous for him. She had taken a decision not to involve him in posting the secret document, but the police knew she had an accomplice. Would they think it was him?

'What's your interest in this woman?' Zhou asked.

'It's nothing,' Song shook his head. 'She's a friend of a friend, nothing more. And I think perhaps the incident involving the frozen child is linked. Li Hetian was from Yidong.'

'What kind of man would freeze his child's corpse?' Zhou shuddered.

'I believe he froze her because he was trying to preserve evidence of murder.' Song looked at Zhou. 'The police have her body now. The forensic pathologist must have done a post-mortem.'

But Zhou had had enough. He interrupted.

'You know, Song, I admired you for leaving the way you did.' He spoke in an agitated way. 'I wish I'd had the guts to do the same, but I have my wife and son to consider, and I'm not the sort who can become an entrepreneur overnight.'

'Of course,' Song murmured. He gestured to the waitress for the bill. When he had paid, he tried again, leaning across the table towards his friend.

'Is there anything you can tell me, anything at all,

about the condition of the child's body? Anything that would point to murder?'

Zhou shook his head.

'Well,' Song tried to hide his disappointment. 'Thank you for meeting me. If there's anything I can do for you, just . . .'

Zhou cut him off.

'Thank you for dinner. But please don't contact me again,' he said, and got to his feet.

Twenty-two

LONDON

For all she knew, she was running for her life. At the other end of the corridor was a stairwell that was a twin to the one she had climbed to get to Tang Ning's flat. She flung herself down the dark steps, her feet barely able to keep up with the momentum of her body. Above her, she heard shouting and the sound of smashing glass. Footsteps started down the stairs behind her, then the sound of a body falling, thumping onto the concrete, an exclamation of pain, more laughter and drunken voices raised in argument. Down she ran, and down, and down.

At the bottom she paused an instant to catch her breath and then she kept on running. The exit brought her to a path and then to the street. She hesitated, glancing up and down, but she didn't recognize the road either way, so she turned left and kept on running. She passed bus stops and shops and pubs and people, some of whom stopped and turned to watch as she passed them by. She heard sirens and came to a halt for a moment, bending double to heave great breaths, and lifting her head to watch as two police cars raced past. Had the woman who'd slammed the door in her face called the police?

She ran another half mile or so and then, when she dared to stop and look behind she couldn't see them coming after her. She slowed to a walk. Her legs felt weak, as though they might give out on her. Her heart was pounding. She looked around her and was entirely lost. She was walking through a street market. Stalls were piled high with apples and bananas and with cabbages and onions, and vendors were shouting out their prices. She could have been in her home town, except that the stall holders all had white skin. Again she struggled to place herself, to rise above the surreal symmetry that confused and disoriented her, and to plant her feet firmly on the ground. Her head was so full of what she had seen that morning, of dead eye sockets alive with insect life, of a smashed bottle raised in her face, that there was no room for anything else.

She walked and walked, not knowing where she was going, not knowing how she would ever get back or where she would get back to. She was so distracted that twice she walked bang into people, oblivious even when they shouted after her. Buses passed her in both directions, but the destinations on the front meant nothing to her. More than anything, she wanted to go home. When she started to fantasize about a bus that advertised Anjialou on the front she knew that she needed to eat and drink or she would pass out.

She looked around. There was a fast food restaurant, a KFC, which looked identical to the ones Wolf had sometimes dragged her to. She knew what to order in there. She went in, and first of all she went to the bathroom, where she washed her hands again and again, and washed her face where the flies had brushed against her, drying herself with paper towels. Out in the restaurant itself, she pointed with a shaking finger at the picture of a chicken meal and a drink. She paid, fumbling with coins and notes, and took her tray as far from the window as possible, in case the gang of youths was still looking for her.

For several minutes she sat huddled over her tray, staring at it. Slowly she brought familiar food to her mouth and bit into it. Then she caught sight of the meat. The grease oozed out from under the skin, the white flesh was shredded where her teeth had torn through it. She moaned, clutching her mouth, and rushed to the bathroom, where she burst into a stall and fell onto her knees, her head in the toilet bowl, bringing up everything that was in her stomach.

She knelt, her whole body shuddering, her forehead resting against the cool tiled wall. She heard voices outside. Someone rattled the door.

'Is everything all right in there? Come on out now, can't stay in there all day.'

Blue got to her feet. She wiped her mouth. Outside the stall a stern-faced waitress was holding her bag out to her.

'Think yourself lucky no one nicked it,' she said. 'Get yourself home, you can't be sick in here.'

Blue's legs felt weak, but she walked out of the restaurant. Outside, on the street, there was a bench. She sat down. The wound on her forehead was throbbing but she felt very calm. She tried to think, tried to sort out what she had seen and what it meant. Her first reaction had been wrong, she could see that now. When she'd encountered first the body and then the gang, she'd jumped to the conclusion that the gang was guilty of the murder of the body. But now she thought that she had experienced nothing more than a coincidence. Tang Ning had taken up residence in a rundown slum where a drunken gang wandered the corridors. That did not mean the gang was responsible for his death. If the body was indeed that of Tang Ning . . .

She tried to make herself remember what had happened from the moment that she walked into the flat. What had she seen? There had been the smell . . . the kitchen, the rotting meat, the unwashed crockery . . . the small sitting room, with the papers scattered around as though someone had been searching for something . . . the phone . . . She had picked it up . . . what then? Her face creased in concentration. She grabbed her bag and pulled out its contents, piling them on the bench beside her: purse, brush, tin of tiger balm, a packet of paper handkerchiefs, the toothbrush from the plane . . . her mobile phone . . . and then a second mobile phone. She dropped it as though it had burnt her fingers. She stared at it. She must have slipped it into her bag instinctively, just as she would have slipped her own phone into her bag if it was in her hand and she wanted her hands free.

She bit her lip. She had removed evidence from a murder scene. If a murderer's fingerprints had been on the phone they were now overlaid with her own ... panic overwhelmed her. Would she be sought for murder? Surely they would know that she could not have had anything to do with the corpse – there would be immigration records that showed she'd entered the country only the day before ... the corpse had been dead for ... days, weeks, she had no way of knowing. She had seen nothing like it before in her life. How did the police operate here? Would they lock her up anyway until they were sure? They would want to know why she was there. They would want to know how she'd got the address. Finney would be apoplectic with rage that she'd embarrassed him, a police officer.

The mobile phone lay there on the bench. She could not take her eyes off it. It condemned her and it fascinated her. What secrets were locked inside it? Tentatively, she pressed Menu, but the screen remained dark. She tried the power switch, nothing happened. The phone was dead.

When she let herself in with the key Robin had given her and bent to remove her shoes, she found the house full of people and noise. Even the hallway was full of children she'd never seen before. Hannah detached herself from the squirming mass of purple and told her proudly, 'These are my cousins, and this is my bridesmaid's dress. This is the back.' She did a slow twirl. 'This is the side, and this is the front.'

'It's beautiful,' Blue told her with a weak smile. She turned away. She knew she was disappointing Hannah, and that she should stay and admire her, but her head was hurting so much. She needed to lie down. She started to climb the stairs. But somehow, above all the noise, Robin had heard her voice and was calling her downstairs to the kitchen. Reluctantly, Blue turned around and made her way through the children and down the stairs, only to find that the kitchen too was full of people talking and laughing and shouting across the room. There was an open bottle on the table, and everyone had a glass in their hand.

'Blue,' Robin greeted her. Blue could see how happy her friend was. 'I want to introduce you to everyone. Did you have a good day?'

Blue struggled to reply. The room had fallen silent. Everyone seemed to be looking at her and waiting for her response.

'Are you all right?' Robin asked. 'Sit down, have something to eat. There's bread, and salmon . . .'

'I'm sorry,' Blue whispered. 'My head . . . I have a headache . . . I would like to rest.'

Immediately there were expressions of sympathy, then conversation resumed, and Blue was able to slip out of the room and back up the stairs, through the barricade of children and up the next flight of stairs.

'She always takes her shoes off when she comes in, I don't know why,' she heard Hannah say to her cousins.

She lay down on the bed which was not hers and closed her eyes. The sound of voices drifted up to her. She longed for silence. After a few minutes she heard footsteps on the stairs, and then a knock at the door.

'Come in,' she said, although even the effort of speaking made her head hurt.

Robin came in and sat on the edge of the bed. She had a glass of water in her hand, and a small packet.

'I brought you paracetamol,' Robin said.

Obediently, Blue sat up and took the tablet from Robin, swallowing it down with water.

'Thank you,' she said. She lay down again, hoping that Robin would now leave her alone. She didn't know what to say to her.

'I'm sorry about the noise,' Robin said. 'I'm afraid my family talks a lot when we're not arguing. We don't all get together that often, and tomorrow it won't be the same, it won't be so relaxed. I'll tell them to keep it down.'

'No,' Blue said. 'Don't worry about that.'

Robin frowned down at her.

'Did anything go wrong today? You look awful.'

Blue gazed up at her. She had a strong urge to tell Robin what had happened, but she was so ashamed. She had run away. She had run from the police. Worse, she had pocketed evidence. What would Finney say? Her eyes welled with tears.

'Robin!' a female voice called up the stairs. 'Robin, you've got to hear this . . .'

'Blue . . . ?'

'You should go,' Blue managed a smile. 'I just need to sleep.'

Blue woke at four in the morning and was immediately alert. The pain in her head had faded and the house was quiet. For some time she lay awake. Once more she ran through what she had seen. Now that she was rested, her head was clearer. She discounted the gang who had threatened her. She did not know whether or not they would have hurt her, but her instinct was that the body on the bed in Tang Ning's apartment had not been killed with a broken beer bottle or as the result of random violence.

After a little while she needed to go to the bathroom. On the landing, as she returned to her room, she saw that a mobile phone was lying on a chest, and that it had been plugged into a charger. She knelt. The phone was already fully charged, so she thought it was all right to unplug it and leave it lying on the chest. The charger she took to her room and found that it fitted the phone she had taken from Tang Ning's flat. Now, when she pressed her finger on the keypad, the phone sprang to life.

She could not be sure that the phone belonged to Tang Ning, or that the body on the bed was Tang Ning's. She could not be sure of anything. But when she opened up the Inbox, then she knew. Interspersed with other messages, there were communications from Jin Dao.

Blue started to flick through the Inbox, and then the Sent Messages file, but separated out like this she could get no sense of dialogue, or the chronology of that dialogue. She thought of the laptop Robin had said she could use and quietly ran downstairs to the kitchen. She had forgotten the dog. When she switched on the light it uncurled itself from its basket and got to its feet, stretching. It walked towards her. It was nearly as big as she was. Blue stepped backwards, nervous. Her neighbours had dogs, yappy things that nipped at her ankles in the lift. The dog pushed its nose into her hand. What had they called it? Ziggy, that was it.

'Ziggy,' she whispered, patting him tentatively. 'Good dog.'

She lunged for the laptop, and turned quickly, closing the door behind her. She stood for a moment, listening to the dog whine, then hurried back up the stairs.

When she had returned to her room, she opened a file and started to make notes, collating the material from the Inbox and Sent Messages files so that instead of isolated messages she had a flow of conversation.

Two weeks before, Tang Ning had sent a message to someone called Wu Dan.

> *Tang Ning* – Hey, little brother, I saw a ghost eating dinner with you last night. You know who I'm talking about. What's he doing here?
>
> *Wu Dan to Tang Ning* – You're mistaken, I don't know any ghosts. Only benevolent spirits. Do you want to meet for lunch tomorrow New World restaurant 12.30?

Tang Ning to Wu Dan – The man I'm talking about is no friendly spirit. You should take care. I'll see you for lunch.

Then, two days later:

Tang Ning to Wu Dan – Friend Wu, what's going on? I'm being followed. My room has been searched.
Tang Ning to Jin Dao – Call me. I need your urgent help.

A day later:

Tang Ning to Jin Dao – Yidong cover-up. Li Hetian. Private Detective Song Ren.

Then, over the next few days, there was a series of increasingly panicked messages both from Jin Dao and from Wu Dan. And silence from Tang Ning.

Jin Dao to Tang Ning – Don't understand your message. What's going on?
Wu Dan to Tang Ning – Ring me. I want to talk to you.
Jin Dao to Tang Ning – Why did you send me names Song, Li?
Wu Dan to Tang Ning – Where are you? Why don't you answer your phone?
Jin Dao to Tang Ning – Li dead. Going to Yidong with Song. I beg you to call me.
Jin Dao to Tang Ning – Husband, I am going to need your help. Please call me.
Wu Dan to Tang Ning – Please forgive me. Let me know that you're all right.

Jin Dao's messages had ceased on the day that she had disappeared from Wanmei County.

Blue stared at the messages. There was too much that was not said, too much she couldn't fathom. She saw his fingers keying the words, 'I saw a ghost eating dinner with you . . .' She saw Tang Ning as she had last seen him, a rotting, crawling corpse. She thought perhaps the last thing he had done was to send that message about Yidong to Jin Dao. It was a hurried message, as though he was desperate to give her a clue although he knew he had very little time. He must have intended to send her a second message containing more information. Instead someone had come to the flat. Under attack he'd let his phone fall to the floor . . .

She noticed that the icon in the bottom right-hand corner of the screen was indicating that the computer had made a WiFi Internet connection. She checked her email and found a message from Wolf:

I've spent all day looking at offices for rent. What do you think? Haidian District? Dongcheng District? Are communal washrooms OK? At 3 metres along the corridor? At 20 metres along the corridor? What is more important, light or heat? Is 100 square metres big enough? I don't trust any of the estate agents I meet. They invent all sorts of fees on top of the rent. Song is no use to me. I'm left to make the decisions. I wish you were here. Even if you didn't know what to choose either, I wouldn't be on my own, and you would make me laugh. How is your head?

How is London? I haven't heard from you, and I know I offended you before you left.

Blue read the note with a sense of rising panic. How could Wolf be thinking about office space at a time like this? She hit Reply.

Tell Song to be careful. I went to find the man, but he's dead.

Twenty-three

Song never read the *People's Daily*, so when Wolf tossed that day's edition onto the table in front of him, he knew there was a reason. Since the demolition this was what the agency had come to – a table in a coffee shop.

'They've gone public. Front page, at the bottom,' Wolf instructed him, turning away to order a drink at the counter. Song picked up the newspaper and found the article. It was titled 'Party and Government Organs Launch Urgent Investigation into Child Abduction in Wanmei County'. Song read closely. This was the first time the police had officially admitted that there was anything to investigate. The Minister of Public Security, the paper reported, would send an investigation team first to Wanmei County and then to the affected villages. He had also issued emergency instructions to police forces nationwide ordering them to respond quickly to all reports of child abduction. The paper made no mention of Li Hetian. It quoted 'a local resident' as saying, 'This is very quick action on the part of the central authorities. We are very moved by their concern.'

Song drew in his breath sharply.

'She's left them no choice,' he muttered to Wolf. 'She'll pay dearly for this.'

'It's bad,' Wolf agreed. 'You have to keep out of this. There's more.' He took the newspaper from Song and searched through it, then replaced it in front of him. 'Here.'

Song bent over the newspaper.

This was a smaller piece, titled 'Deceased Police Official Accused of Corruption'. The article stated that Detective Chen Dalei, who had 'died at his own hand' days earlier, was the subject of an investigation by the Central Discipline Inspection Commission. The Commission had issued a report accusing him of corruption. Song noticed that the figures Zhou had quoted – seven million *yuan* in bribes, nineteen million *yuan* in public assets redirected for his own use and a further 160,000 *yuan* in cash siphoned off – were accurate. Zhou must, he thought, be well informed.

Song threw the paper down on the table angrily. 'Corruption is one thing, but what's his involvement in Yidong? The man had blood on his hands.'

Wolf grunted impatiently. He pulled out a sheaf of papers and placed them on top of the newspaper. Song glanced at them. They were property details, photographs of empty office space, floor plans, prices, agencies. He swept them off the newspaper and onto the table, then he started to read the two reports again. Wolf watched him with ill-disguised irritation. He snatched the newspaper from Song's hands and handed him a brochure in its place.

'Do you know what this is?' Wolf challenged him.

Song gazed blankly at the flyer.

'I've set up some viewings this afternoon,' Wolf persisted. 'The locations aren't as good as Anjialou, they're further out of town, but we can't expect to afford anything closer in.'

Song had picked up one of the leaflets and was leaning back in his chair, gazing at it.

'I leave it up to you,' he said, letting the brochure fall back onto the table with the rest of the pile.

'Don't do that, Song,' Wolf pleaded. 'This is your business, you need to approve the location.'

'All right then, I'll approve the premises when you've found them,' Song said, standing up. 'I appoint you Director of Office Relocation. Show me three offices at the end of the week and I'll pick one. And I need to see the accounts also by the end of the week, including all outstanding payments.'

He headed for the exit. When Wolf caught up with him, he was getting into his car.

Wolf grabbed the car door and addressed him angrily. 'You can't do anything for any of them, not the dead girl or her peasant father or the lawyer. So what are your priorities, Song?'

'That's exactly what I'm asking myself,' Song said, looking up at him as he lowered his tall frame into the driver's seat and pulled the car door from Wolf's grasp.

Song paused for a moment underneath the red lanterns which hung outside a seafood restaurant. He watched the opposite pavement where a few young men and women were trickling through the gates of Beijing University – it was the summer break, and most had gone home for the holiday.

Song crossed the road and walked through the gate, nodding at the guard as if he did this every day. It helped that Song wore spectacles on his long face. In spite of his shaved head he looked almost professorial. Also, Song had perfected a stride – not too hurried, not too slow – that made him appear so much at home that he could gain access almost anywhere in the city.

Inside, he took his bearings. Ahead of him was a lawn and beyond that a lotus pond. Paths led off in every direction. Windows exposed empty classrooms. He'd been here before in his early days on the police force. A tedious case, the theft of some computer equipment, but it meant he knew the layout of the place. Many of the buildings were pre-Revolution, with tiled curved roofs and peeling red lacquered woodwork. Elsewhere, even the red-brick buildings from the fifties had been weathered into an earthen tone that sat well with the foliage of shrubs and trees. There were areas of the campus where tumbledown cottages and old Republican-era houses were the perfect settings for secret meetings – the history of Beijing University was one of periodic blood-soaked dissent – and for liaisons of every kind.

He set off to his right, and soon he came to basketball courts, where T-shirted youngsters were playing, yelling encouragement at each other. Song felt an urge to join them; these days his muscles were heavy with neglect. He made his way past a canteen, past dormitories and modern lecture halls, and to the law department. This was a long shot.

Inside, strolling casually along the ground-floor corridor, he knocked on each office door. Most rooms were empty or locked. Inside one, a whitewashed and neon-lit room no bigger than a cupboard, he found an elderly man who was surrounded by books.

'Excuse me,' Song said, 'I'm looking for Professor Jin Dao.'

The elderly man looked up at him, startled.

'Don't you know?' he said. 'She isn't here. I don't think she'll be here in the near future.'

'Do you know where I can find her? I've tried her mobile phone but I'm getting no answer.'

'I'm afraid,' he said, 'that it's a difficult situation . . . I can't help you.'

Song smiled sheepishly. He indicated his briefcase. 'Last week she bought a gift for her mother and asked me to deliver it to her here. It's a book that her mother had been searching for, she was very pleased to find it and insistent that I should deliver it today. It's her mother's birthday. Professor Jin is a good customer, I don't want to disappoint her.'

The gentleman frowned in indecision.

'Professor Jin told me that her mother also lives on campus,' Song said helpfully.

The man scratched his head, looked up at Song again as if to reassure himself, then nodded.

'I can tell you where to find her,' he said. 'I see no harm in that.'

When Jin Dao's mother opened the door of her flat to him, all expectations of her frailty vanished. Her hair was grey and cut short, framing eyes that were fierce like her daughter's. Her chin was raised defiantly, also like her daughter's. She stood and waited for Song to explain himself. The sound of voices came from inside the flat.

'I'm a . . . a friend of your dau . . . of Jin Dao.' He found himself stammering under her intense gaze. 'I . . . I wanted to know if there is any news . . . I mean news of her.'

'Who are you? How do you know her?' She frowned up at him, trying to make up her mind whether to let him in. He knew that if he lied she would know and she would turn him away.

'I'm a private detective . . .'

'A private detective?' she sounded appalled.

'I helped Tang Ning with an investigation,' he hurried to reassure her, speaking in a low voice. He didn't like to discuss these things in a public corridor. If it became known that he had been with Jin Dao in Wanmei he too would be detained. They were looking for an accomplice. He would do. 'Tang Ning introduced me to Jin Dao . . .'

Again she interrupted him.

'You've seen Tang Ning?'

'No, he's still in England. The introduction to Jin Dao was done by text message . . . your daughter asked me to go to Yidong with her to investigate reports of abduction there. We'd only been in Wanmei a few hours when she disappeared.'

'You were with her?' She looked confused.

'For part of the time. She also spent some time on her own there. I didn't know anything about the document she posted.'

She considered this, then nodded, opened the door wider and indicated that he should come in.

He stepped inside and stooped down to remove his shoes. Glancing towards the voices, he saw that the sitting room was full of people.

'These are her friends,' Jin Dao's mother said, closing the door behind him. 'They've come to discuss what they can do to help her. We were informed this morning that she's been charged with subversion . . .'

'She's been charged?' he interrupted her.

'We heard this morning,' she repeated. 'We're all very upset. I'd hoped they wouldn't take revenge like this. I hoped that things had changed.'

Her telephone rang and she excused herself, indicating that he should join the others in the sitting room, but he stayed where he was, gathering his thoughts. He'd known that it might come to this, he'd known she might be charged with subversion. Now that it had happened it put both her situation and his in a grim light. It was unthinkable that she would be found innocent, such things simply didn't happen. As for him, he'd been with her in Wanmei County, he was guilty by association. The man he'd beaten up outside the Party and government headquarters could identify him. His name was in the guest-house register. He had driven his car repeatedly up and down the road to Yidong trying to get through the roadblock.

He edged into the room where her friends had gathered. He shouldn't have come. Such a gathering would surely alert the police. Outside the flat he had looked out for surveillance and seen none. Now he thought that either he had been mistaken, or possibly that things had changed. Blue had spent a great deal of time persuading him that the State Security Bureau had so much technology at their command that they no longer needed physically to follow people, unless it was to intimidate them. Looking around the room, he wondered how many emails this gathering of academics had sent that day, how many mobile phone calls they had made, how many SMS messages they had sent – and how many of those had been monitored. Quietly he slipped his own mobile phone out of his pocket and turned it off. Later he would change the SIM card so that the police could not trace its signal.

The most outspoken members of the group had taken up sofa space, while others perched on stools or leaned against walls. One or two of them cast sharp glances in his direction. He was a stranger, and if he was in their position he would be wondering if he was spying on them. No one challenged him, however. Perhaps they thought that the secret police would not employ anyone so tall or conspicuous.

What seemed like a crowd in this cramped space was actually eleven people, some young students but mostly slightly older academics, probably teaching staff. He cast his eye around the room. The walls were lined with books and there were pot plants on windowsills. A computer held pride of place on the desk. He wondered whether it was where Jin Dao had worked. He imagined her sitting there, looking out at the willows beyond the window.

He listened in to the discussion. They were going to gather signatures on a petition calling for Jin Dao's release and post it online. Song didn't speak but he thought that it could do no harm. Handwritten petitions from peasants ended up in the Party's trash. But petitions signed by academics at the country's most famous university and posted online would at least attract some attention from academics abroad, who in turn might put pressure on their governments to raise the case with the Chinese government. Dissidents had been released in the past because of such pressure, but usually only after they had already served many years in detention.

He saw that some of her friends were holding sheets

of paper, and he looked over the shoulder of the young woman next to him to get a better look. It was a photocopied sheet, and he recognized Jin Dao's writing instantly from the note she had left him, which he had read and reread. He tapped his neighbour on the shoulder and nodded at the sheet. She passed it to him.

My days are tedious but I am not ill-treated. I am fed bland food – gritty steamed bread, endless watery porridge – as if they believe that my thoughts will become more bland as a result. I am constantly questioned about my 'crimes', sometimes for eight or ten hours at a time. They want me to sign a confession, declaring that I have undermined the stability of the state through the publication of a secret document. I have insisted that I will sign only a statement that I have penned in my own hand and of which every word is my own. At first they were happy with this. When they read what I had written they changed their minds.

I have requested repeatedly that my husband, Tang Ning, be informed of my situation and that he be allowed to appoint a lawyer to work on my behalf. So far, my interrogators have countered that since I am a lawyer I am quite capable of defending myself and should save my own money. I plead with anyone who reads this to contact my husband, who may still be unaware of my situation. If anyone can help me, it is he. For ten years we have stood side by side. I know he will come to my aid now.

Song looked up from the letter. Jin Dao's friends were still debating how to go about publicizing her plight. He saw that her mother was in the kitchen and went to join her. She was preparing tea and snacks, placing bowls of dried fruit and melon seeds on a tray.

'How did you get this?' he asked her, raising the letter for her to see.

'I think,' she said, smiling slightly, 'that my daughter must have persuaded one of her guards to help her. We were allowed to take clean clothes to the police station for her, and some books and toiletries. Then, a few hours later, we were called to remove a package of clothes that she said she didn't want – the police thought this was a troublesome business, they said they weren't a laundry and that it mustn't happen again, but they went along with it. Inside, we found this letter.'

'Has anyone seen her?'

She shook her head.

'Because the charges relate to state secrets they're not letting anyone in.'

'Have you tried to contact Tang Ning's parents?' he asked.

'Of course, but they can't reach him either.'

'Your daughter said her husband is the nephew of the Commissioner Tang. Can he help protect her?'

'We've tried to contact him but he's so senior that he has secretaries to answer his phone, and he hasn't returned our calls. I think it likely he's heard what's happened and wants to stay out of it. It can only damage him. These people cling to their status even when the lives of those they love are at stake.'

'Could you go to see him? Where does he live?'

'He has a house in Grain Store Hutong just north of Jingshan Houjie, but if he won't return our calls he won't let us in. He'll have guards and alarm systems.'

Song didn't tell her that he had asked Blue to look for Tang Ning in London. He didn't want to raise her hopes.

'I have to go,' he told her. He was afraid that if he stayed in one place too long the police would find him.

'Will you sign our petition before you go?' she asked.

He looked at the group of young people, still engaged in animated discussion.

'No, I don't think I can,' he said.

'You're afraid, are you?' she asked, with disdain. For a moment he thought he was back in the car with Jin Dao and that she was branding him a moral coward.

'I'm nobody,' he said. 'My name has no weight to it.'

She scrutinized his face for a long moment and then nodded. She opened the door for him.

'I'll try to find some other way to help her,' he said as he left.

Twenty-four

LONDON

The household woke up with the creaks of floorboards and the patter of children's feet and distant laughter. Blue longed to stay hiding in her room. The memory of the corpse was like a black ball of horror that she carried with her. The thought of deceiving Robin was unbearable. If she went down to the kitchen she would have to talk about the wedding and pretend that nothing unusual had happened. Or she could ruin Robin's wedding day by telling her everything. Either course of action seemed intolerable.

Someone knocked on the door.

'Good morning,' Robin's voice called softly. 'I've brought you breakfast in bed. It's an English tradition.'

Blue stared at the door. If Robin came in she didn't know what she would say.

'Blue? Are you awake?'

Blue ran her tongue over her lips. She had to come clean, there was really no choice. A man was lying dead and rotting. A wedding was nothing in comparison, Robin would understand. The police would interrogate her, of course, they would be hostile, and Finney might ask her to leave. He would be very angry with her. But she would just have to face these inconveniences. Telling Robin what had happened was the right thing to do.

'Yes,' she said. 'I'm awake.'

She heard William's voice rise in a wail.

'I'll just leave the tray out here then,' Robin said through the door. She sounded cheerful. 'We're all going to leave at ten. Finney says he won't marry me if I'm late.'

Blue bit her lip.

'Robin, come in please,' she said, standing up.

But it was too late. She heard Robin's footsteps running down the stairs in the direction of the children's voices.

Blue went to the door and opened it. Outside, lying on the floorboards, was a tray, and on that a teapot and a plate of toast and jam. Lying beside the tray was a newspaper. Blue bent to pick it up. Full of apprehension, she scanned the front page. A bomb had gone off in Baghdad. That was the lead story. There was a large photograph of a government minister who had resigned. She laid the newspaper on the bed and returned to the hall to pick up the tray. She had eaten nothing for nearly twenty-four hours and she was so hungry that her stomach hurt. At first she just ate. Then, when the pain of hunger had gone, and warmth spread through her limbs and her brain had settled itself, she looked again at the paper, slowly turning its pages, searching the headlines. There it was, deep

inside the newspaper. 'Decomposing Corpse Discovered, Police Seek Witness'.

> The decomposing corpse of a man was discovered
> yesterday in a flat in Croydon after a neighbour
> raised the alarm. Police said they suspected foul play
> and that the body could have lain in the apartment
> for up to two weeks.
>
> A tenant in a neighbouring flat called the police
> after noticing a foul smell. Mrs Elizabeth Smart said
> she was alerted to the smell after hearing noises in
> the corridor.
>
> Detective Andy Reynolds said the police were
> eager to hear from anyone who might be able to help
> identify the body, which appeared to be of an east
> Asian man, probably in his thirties. The police were
> also eager to interview a young woman of east Asian
> appearance who was seen by several witnesses, both
> at the scene of the crime and subsequently running
> through the neighbourhood.
>
> 'We're talking to people who saw this girl,' Det.
> Reynolds said, 'and we hope to issue a photofit
> image later today. Witnesses have described her as
> about five feet tall, with long black hair reaching
> almost to her waist, and with features and complex-
> ion that would fit with an east Asian background.
>
> 'Clearly the initial crime happened some time ago,
> so we are seeking this individual as a witness, not
> necessarily as someone connected with any criminal
> act. She should be reassured on that point, and we
> urge her to come forward.'

Blue read and then reread the article. It didn't mention the name Tang Ning, but surely the police had
looked at the papers in the flat. She seemed to remember

that the research paper she had picked up had his name at the top of it. Perhaps, she thought, they were being cautious. The police could not assume the corpse was that of Tang Ning, and nor should she, she told herself. For a moment that calmed her. She had walked in on a coincidence, it was nothing to do with her. Even if she handed herself in to the police, there was nothing she could tell them that they did not know. But that happy thought lasted only for an instant. This was Tang Ning's flat. Tang Ning had dropped out of sight two weeks ago. Two weeks ago, he had stopped returning messages, he had stopped turning up at class. She knew that the body could belong to no one else.

She picked up the mobile phone, went once more to Sent Messages.

Tang Ning – Hey, little brother, I saw a ghost eating dinner with you last night. You know who I'm talking about. What is he doing here?

Wu Dan to Tang Ning – You're mistaken, I don't know any ghosts. Only benevolent spirits. Do you want to meet for lunch tomorrow New World restaurant 12.30?

Tang Ning to Wu Dan – This is no friendly spirit that I'm talking about . . .

She flicked through the messages that Wu Dan had sent after they had met for lunch. When Tang Ning didn't respond, Wu Dan's messages had become increasingly alarmed. He must have been a good friend, Blue thought, to be so concerned. And indeed, Tang Ning had called him 'little brother'. There could be no danger in contacting him. Blue closed her eyes and tried to talk herself out of what she was about to do. She had already broken every rule. She had fled the police sirens, she had removed vital evidence from a crime scene. And now she was about to act on the basis of that stolen evidence.

She called up Wu Dan's number on Tang Ning's phone, but she knew better than to dial from Tang Ning's phone. Instead, she dialled the number on her own mobile. A male voice answered in English, but instinctively she spoke to him in Chinese.

'Hello, is that Wu Dan?'

'It is, who's this?' He answered in clear standard Chinese. She could tell just from the way that he talked that he was from the mainland, not from Taiwan or Singapore or Hong Kong.

'My name is Blue Tang. I've just come from Beijing. Tang Ning gave me your number.'

She hoped that the fact she had the same surname as Tang Ning meant that Wu Dan would think she had some close relationship with him, although of course it was a sheer coincidence. Wu Dan didn't reply, so Blue hurried to fill the silence. 'I emailed him a week ago to say that I was coming to London, and he gave me your name in case he was out of town . . .'

There was a long silence on the other end of the line.

'Tang Ning told you to look me up?'

'Yes,' Blue lied.

'And he told you he had plans to go out of town?'

Wu Dan's voice was full of hope. Blue lowered her head, squeezing her eyes shut. It was an awful lie.

'I'm here for a wedding,' she said, trying to reassure him further. 'Tang Ning asked me to bring a gift for you, some Longjing tea to remind you of home. He gave me your number so that if he was out of town I could give it to you directly.'

'So he did tell you he was going away? Where did he say he was going? When will he be back?'

'I can tell you when I see you. I will wait for you at St Patrick's Church in Streatham at eleven fifteen,' she said.

'I don't . . .'

'Please,' she said urgently. 'I'll see you there.' And then she cut the call.

Somehow she showered. Somehow she put on her pale blue dress. She rarely wore dresses, and she had bought this one specially, in a sale in Beijing. It was an imported dress, although it said on the label it had been made in China. She had wanted a foreign dress so she wouldn't look out of place in England. Somehow she smiled at herself in the mirror, although she could tell that the eyes smiling back at her were hiding a terrible secret. Somehow she emerged from her cocoon and made her way downstairs. Somehow she had conversations about the arrangements for the day ahead. Somehow, when Robin appeared in her cream and silver dress, Blue exclaimed at how beautiful she looked. Actually that wasn't so hard. Her friend was radiant. Blue climbed into the car with everyone else and drove to the church. As she gazed out of the window at the leafy streets, she wondered whether she had imagined the discovery of the corpse the day before. It seemed to belong to a different world.

When they had parked the car and got out, Blue said to Robin: 'I'm going to get some fresh air out here for a few minutes.'

'That's a good idea, it's still early. Oh, and Blue, don't worry, people will talk to you, weddings are like that.'

'Of course,' Blue said. The fear of loneliness hadn't crossed her mind.

'Just don't miss it!' Robin called cheerfully over her shoulder as she went into the church.

Guests started to arrive. Blue had expected Finney's police friends to pull up in black limousines with shaded windows and to step out in uniform, but nobody did. She recognized Robin's sisters from the gathering in the kitchen the night before – there was one with golden ringlets, another with lots of children and a husband with a kind smile. Some of them cast her curious glances, or smiled at her, but she was almost oblivious. She scanned the street for Wu Dan. She was sure he would come, not to pick up a present – although she had placed in her bag a packet of Longjing tea that she'd brought from Beijing to give to Robin – but because he so badly wanted to hear what Tang Ning had said about going away. This certainty that Wu Dan would show up kept Blue outside the church long after most of the guests had gone inside. The street was almost empty. She looked up and down, unwilling to believe that he would not come. Behind her, the strains of music sounded.

'Excuse me,' someone said to her.

She wheeled around, but it was a man who'd stepped out from the church.

'Are you here for the wedding?' he asked.

She nodded.

'Then you'd better come inside or you'll miss it. Wouldn't want that, would we?'

With one last glance around, she went inside. She took her seat just as Robin started to walk down the aisle on the arm of her mother. Hannah and William walked with Robin, Hannah in purple, and William in jeans and running shoes – he'd refused to dress up. Finney was waiting for them at the front of the church. Blue thought he looked as handsome as a film star, and the smile that he gave Robin as she approached made Blue feel weak at the knees. This was why she had come to England, she told herself desperately, to wallow in the romance of Robin's wedding. There was nothing more she could do. The police had found Tang Ning's body, they would investigate. That was an end of it.

She achieved a state of suspended animation. For some time she did as she had ordered herself and did not think of Tang Ning or of his corpse. She didn't follow what was said, but afterwards she retained a visual record of Robin and Finney placing rings on each other's fingers, of the children beaming up at their parents, of Finney and Robin laughing at something, and of them kissing, and then the sound of applause and even cheers.

Afterwards, when the guests poured out onto the lawn, there were photographs, and Blue found herself pulled into picture after picture, standing next to people she didn't know.

'Blue! It *is* you, isn't it?'

She turned, surprised. It was Sal, a journalist friend of Robin's. Blue had been his interpreter once when he came to Beijing, and it was Sal who had given Blue's name to Robin. She should have expected that she would see him here. She smiled, surrendering awkwardly to a bear hug. He was no thinner, she thought, as she found herself jammed against his tummy.

'A truly delightful surprise!' he said, releasing her. His black hair still flopped over his face, but there were streaks of grey that she didn't remember.

'Are you here on your own?' she asked. Over dinner in Beijing Sal had told her stories about a whole series of girlfriends. She hadn't really wanted to hear, but he had told her anyway, and in the end she'd enjoyed them. They were tales of glamorous scandal, of enraged husbands and Sal making quick getaways in the middle of the night. She'd wondered, at the time, whether all these stories might lead to an unwanted advance, but they had not. Mainly he had seemed to want to make her laugh and to break through her reserve.

'I'm not on my own any longer,' he said, taking her arm.

*

The reception was at Blueberry Lodge, a hotel five miles away, but Sal gave her a lift. There was a buffet meal, and speeches that made everyone smile. Robin talked about how she'd met Finney, and how he'd done his best to get her locked up. Finney talked about how the children had set tests for him to judge whether he was an adequate father. Movingly, he spoke of how it had been growing up without a family, then finding this one. Then there was music from a band.

Sal made her dance. He wouldn't take no for an answer.

'I never studied dancing,' she protested.

'Not one person in this room has learned to dance,' he told her. 'You need to understand that the British like to make fools of themselves. Look at them. Far too much stuff to shake, but they're shaking it anyway. Come on. Have a drink and then you'll dance.'

She didn't have any alcohol to drink, just some fruit juice. But once she'd started dancing she couldn't stop. Sal made her laugh until she wanted to cry. He danced like a maniac, and she knew he was doing it to keep her happy, to make her feel as though she was at home.

Eventually, they sat down. Sal ordered a beer. He'd already drunk so many. Blue remembered this too now, the way he had drunk and drunk every evening until he staggered to his room. And then, she guessed, he had drunk more inside his room.

He signalled that he was going to the bathroom, and Blue nodded. She watched Robin dancing with Finney.

She had her head on his shoulder. William and Hannah were prancing around with their cousins. She felt happy. She'd made the right decision. Everything had worked out as well as it could, she'd been right not to tell Robin what had happened. Tomorrow was time enough, but she wouldn't think about that now.

'Blue?' Her name was spoken right by her ear.

She twisted around and found herself eyeball to eyeball with a man. He was Chinese, she'd have said in his early thirties, with spectacles, and hair that reached to his collar. He had an open, intelligent face, and he seemed to be trying to smile at her, but anxiety vibrated from him.

'I'm Wu Dan.' He extended his hand and when she took it she found that it was clammy. She released his hand quickly, and nervously he wiped it on his trousers.

'I don't understand,' she had to shout over the music. 'Why didn't you meet me this morning?'

'I wasn't on time this morning. When I got to the church everyone was leaving, so I followed the cars. Then I sat in the car park for a long time. I don't want to interrupt the party, but you said you had news of my friend Tang Ning.'

Blue gazed at him. There was something about him that reminded her of Wolf, and she was immediately filled with pity for this man whose friend had died so horribly. The thin facade of normality that she had hidden behind all day crumbled. The music she had danced to moments ago now sounded to her like a clamouring noise. The candlelight abruptly lost its romance. She was ashamed that she had allowed herself to forget Tang Ning's death, even for a moment.

She could see beads of sweat on Wu Dan's forehead.

'I need to go outside,' he said to her, 'it's too hot in here. Will you come with me?'

Blue looked around the room. Sal had returned from the bathroom, but he was engaged in conversation at the bar. Robin and Finney were absorbed in each other on the dance floor. Everywhere else small groups of friends and family were gathered around tables. Nobody would miss her.

Twenty-five

As he drew near to the heart of the city the new high-rise blocks retreated. There were cheap clothing outlets, restaurants, and shops which sold funerary urns and the everyday items – blankets, towels – that the dead needed to take with them into the next world. Closer in yet, the peaceful streets which circled the Forbidden City and Coal Hill had almost entirely escaped demolition, partly in deference to tourists, and partly because even the leaders who had given the orders to tear down most of the city knew that some remnant of tradition must be preserved if only for their own enjoyment. It was the most peaceful area of the city, but Song approached it in a state of distracted despair. He would not have attempted this otherwise. The country's leaders were there to be feared and avoided, not to be approached in their own homes and asked for favours.

Commissioner Tang's house was on Grain Store Hutong in a maze of alleys behind Coal Hill, which was in turn behind the Forbidden City. Song approached on foot. There was no point in driving into these alleys:

some cars never made it out. Several of the houses bore small plaques by the front door saying that this was the family of a revolutionary martyr. Tang had surrounded himself with reliable neighbours, old Beijing families, military men. Elderly men and women sat in the narrow streets on stools or in worn armchairs. Freed of vehicular traffic, they had turned this, their only space, into garden. There were pot plants by front doors, explosions of green and pink and red in the grey and dusty surroundings. He approached a group of men engaged in a game of chess and asked where Commissioner Tang lived. Only one of them answered him, and that with a jerk of the head in the direction of a high wall. The rest of them pretended studiously that they had not heard the question. But after he had turned his back he could hear them debating what his purpose had been in asking.

On top of the wall there was a metre of wire fencing that Song guessed was electrified. The house behind the wall was all but invisible from the street. This was how the politically powerful of Beijing lived, in mansions that were shielded from the eyes of those they ruled. The local residents knew about their powerful neighbour, of course, even if they didn't choose to acknowledge him. It would be a mutually beneficial arrangement. They wouldn't go opening karaoke parlours on his doorstep, and he would protect them from demolition.

Song approached the great iron gate with the sense that he was about to enter a lion's den. To enter here and plead for someone who had been charged with subversion was dangerous and impudent. To enter here as someone who was himself sought in connection with the same crime went beyond that to sheer idiocy.

At head height there was a slit in the metal, and through the slit a pair of eyes, a barked question. Commissioner Tang ranked high enough that he would be guarded by People's Liberation Army soldiers. There was no point in trying to get smart with them. They had been trained for this.

'What's your business?'

'I've come to see Commissioner Tang.'

On the far side of the door voices conferred.

'You have no appointment. Move on.'

Song leaned in so that his mouth was close to the opening, and spoke quietly.

'Tell the Commissioner that my name is Song Ren, and that I'm a friend of his nephew.'

Song waited. He glanced upwards and saw a closed-circuit camera pointing directly at him. There was silence from the other side of the gate.

Footsteps departed. The guard would go inside to report the unusual visitor, Song thought. He would be taken inside or he would be taken away, one or the other.

'I might see you yet,' he murmured to Jin Dao in his head, 'I might end up in the next cell along from you.'

His mobile rang, and he snatched it out of his pocket. He knew it would be Wolf. There was no one else who had his new number.

'Song, I've just seen a message from Blue,' Wolf sounded distraught. 'I'm sorry, I only just logged on. I . . .'

'Never mind,' Song's tone was abrupt. He already regretted taking the call. He had no way of knowing how widely his name had been circulated in connection with Jin Dao's arrest. If the Commissioner's men tried to grab him, he might have to make a run for it. He should be focusing, not dealing with office politics.

'The man she went to find is dead,' Wolf said.

'What?'

'The man you sent her to find is dead,' Wolf said again, exasperated. 'She said you must be careful.'

'The man I sent her . . .' Suddenly Song understood. He ended the call. For a moment he stood there staring at the dead phone. The man he had sent her to find . . . Tang Ning . . . was dead. Then he realized a second thing: Tang Ning was dead and here he was demanding an audience with Tang Ning's uncle. This was the wrong time. Either the Commissioner did not know that his nephew was dead – murdered, if Song interpreted correctly Blue's instructions that he should be careful – in which case Song would not be the one to break it to him. Or else he knew, in which case his mood was entirely unpredictable. Song turned to go.

Behind him a bolt screamed as it was drawn back and the gate clanked noisily open.

'Come on!' one of the soldiers shouted, and Song found himself turning back again.

Song walked through the gate. He found two stern-faced soldiers waiting for him and others watching from the window of the gatehouse. They said nothing to him as they escorted him through a courtyard where several vehicles were parked, then through a small formal garden and along an ornamental tiled path that was edged with tall bamboo.

But he observed these things with only half an eye. His mind was full of what Wolf had told him. Jin Dao's husband was dead and at that his heart leapt guiltily. But Jin Dao's husband was dead and he had been her best hope of freedom.

They arrived at the side door of a brick-built Western-style house. They went into the gloomy interior. Song guessed that it had been built before the Revolution and seized from whatever foreigner or rich Chinese had owned it after 1949. He glanced up and saw that there were several satellite dishes fixed to the roof of the second storey. Inside, he was led along a dark, wood-panelled corridor that was carpeted in thick dark-red wool. There had been a time when everything was red, carpets and curtains and bed-covers, as though the use of any other colour would be counter-revolutionary. The carpet seemed to be a memory of that time.

The guard pushed open a heavy oak door and waved Song in. Song had seen Commissioner Tang many times on news broadcasts at political gatherings, one of the handful of identically suited, identically coiffed engineers who ran the country. They even wore the same colour ties. For the first time Song saw Commissioner Tang in the flesh and on his own. He was sitting at his desk, head bowed. He did not look up when Song entered, and Song saw the grey roots where his black hair was parted around a bald spot at the centre of his skull.

Song waited. He knew that Commissioner Tang was putting him in his place. He would have expected nothing less. He glanced around the room, which was furnished with a heavy desk and fatly upholstered chairs that were pushed back against the panelled walls. Incongruously, in these 1930s surroundings, there was a large flat-screen television mounted on the wall, just as there was in Chen Dalei's villa.

Eventually Commissioner Tang sighed and looked up. His face was broad and open, his spectacles rectangular and modern.

'Why have you come here?' Commissioner Tang challenged him.

'I'm a friend of your nephew, Tang Ning,' Song said. He waited, but there was no response, not even the nod of a head, so he continued. 'His wife, Jin Dao, has been arrested for exposing a case of child abduction, which was the right thing to do. Her family has tried to contact you without success. I'm here on their behalf to pass on their best wishes and to ask respectfully whether there is any possibility that you might intercede on her behalf.'

'You're here for her?' Commissioner Tang seemed surprised. 'Not to plead for your father-in-law's good name?'

Song was momentarily speechless. He had not

mentioned Chen Dalei at the door. Commissioner Tang must have worked fast to find out about the connection. In his concern for Jin Dao he had never stopped to consider the fact that this was the man who had held his father-in-law's fate in his hands, and who now held his reputation.

'His good name is of no interest to me. Nor to him, I should think, at this point.'

Commissioner Tang gazed at him.

'Your wife has been aggressive in her attempts to clear her dead father's name.'

'My *former* wife ... we divorced years ago. Where her father's concerned, she's deluded.'

'I've seen reports that you have reconciled ...'

'Reconciled? Never!'

'You spent the night at Chen Dalei's villa.'

Involuntarily, Song took a step backwards. He'd thought he had the advantage of surprise but it was quite the opposite. Commissioner Tang had the upper hand. Song had known, of course, that Lina would be under surveillance. He should have kept away from her and away from Doudou.

'I've tried to provide my son with moral support. I've put up with Lina out of sympathy but nothing more ...'

'Her father killed himself because of this, do you know that?'

Song stared.

'When my nephew's report about the Yidong abductions appeared on the Internet we sent an officer to the sanatorium to question Chen Dalei immediately about his role. He denied involvement but he must have known it would all come out, as it will, and that he would be executed. The next morning he took a gun and killed himself. If Jin Dao hadn't posted my nephew's report, your former father-in-law would still be alive.'

'It's nothing to me,' Song said again. He was glad that Doudou wasn't there to hear him say it.

Commissioner Tang gazed at Song.

'You continue to support Jin Dao's action in making public a state secret?'

'It was a report her own husband had written! Your own nephew . . . did he show you the report? He must have shown it to you when he wrote it.'

Commissioner Tang flinched. After a moment he returned angrily to the subject of Jin Dao's actions, ignoring Song's question.

'Posting a report like that, which revealed so-called facts that haven't yet been verified. I think it entirely possible that the whole thing has been blown out of proportion. The countryside is full of rumours. Children sometimes disappear because they want to . . . The injuries on the frozen child's corpse—' he halted.

'The injuries on the corpse?' Song prompted.

'Never mind. That's both irrelevant and none of your business. The fact is, the court will say that Jin Dao humiliated China. Subversion is subversion. You either plot to undermine the stability of China or you don't.'

'She doesn't.' Song's voice was gruff. 'She was continuing the work your nephew had started. He tried to bring the abductions to the attention of the authorities and they failed to act. She took the only step available to her.'

'And where is *he*, where is my nephew?' Commissioner Tang challenged Song. 'Why isn't *he* here arguing on behalf of his wife? *You've* taken a risk, coming here. If she was continuing his work, where is *he*?'

Song hesitated.

'He's . . . in England,' he said. 'That's the only reason he's not here, of course.'

Commissioner Tang stared at him for a long moment. Then he nodded his head.

'I've tried to contact my nephew. In this situation, he should come back,' he said. 'If it was my wife who had been arrested, I would come back. And so would you. I'm proud of the work he's done, and he's been cautious. He's never been a whistleblower. He's alerted the Party to problems, and we've dealt with them. Of course, he's always enjoyed the advantage of my name. But now I'm disappointed . . . I don't understand . . .' he broke off, shaking his head. 'Maybe I do him a disservice. Maybe he's on a plane . . .'

Commissioner Tang got to his feet and walked around the desk until he stood in front of Song. He was a smaller man than Song and some fifteen years older.

'Jin Dao's a firebrand but I'm fond of her. We need more like her. However, my hands are tied. If I intercede on her behalf then questions will be raised about my political reliability, and I have many things left to do.

She knew what she was doing. She'll take the consequences.'

'But the consequence is years of jail time . . . If you're sympathetic then others of high rank will be sympathetic too. You can't be the only reasonable man among the leadership . . .' He broke off.

'I'm not prepared to discuss this,' Commissioner Tang said sharply. 'I told you that I'm keeping informed about the case. I know that you yourself are being sought in connection with the case. Your position is dangerous. You should not have come. You should be grateful that I'm allowing you to leave rather than turning you over to the police.'

The soldiers came and accompanied him from the building. When he was out on the street once more the great iron gate was eased shut behind him. He walked rapidly back towards the main road where he could lose himself among the crowds. His long legs carried him quickly away from Commissioner Tang's residence. He trusted no one, and Commissioner Tang himself had described the ambiguity of his position. There was no reason for Commissioner Tang to let him get away.

Again his phone rang.

'A police officer has been ringing me, trying to find you . . .'

'You know my situation!' All Song's frustrations exploded over Wolf's head. 'They've been trying to get hold of me ever since that first day. Why bother me with something that I know already?'

'No,' Wolf said, rushing to calm him down. 'It's not that. One police officer in particular, Inspector Zhou. He said that he has information for you. He wants to meet you. There's a late-night cafe on the corner of Dongsi West and Dongsi South, he'll be there until midnight tonight. I . . .'

Song turned the phone off, and Wolf's voice disappeared. What was Wolf thinking? All the police had to do was wait until Zhou had made his call to Wolf, then see what number Wolf dialled next and trace his mobile signal. For all he knew, they now had his new mobile number. He stopped in a doorway, dismantled his phone, slid the SIM card out of his phone and put a new one in place, slotting his phone back together. Now even Wolf didn't know his number.

But he couldn't let it be. It was clear that Commissioner Tang had seen the pathology report on the frozen child's corpse. Why had he refused to discuss it? If Zhou Caishi had also seen the pathology report might he have changed his mind about sharing information? Song made his way to the area where the cafe was located. Stopping some distance away, he could see Zhou Caishi at a table near the window. Still he didn't go in. He walked the streets surrounding the cafe, looking out for plainclothes police. He remembered the days when State Security Bureau agents had been issued with bags with the words 'Beijing Tourism' printed on them in English. The bags had been particularly uncool but in those days it hadn't mattered much and the agents had happily toted them around. Inside, a camera was concealed, its lens discreetly set into the fake leather cloth. These days technology had moved on but Song could still usually spot them at a hundred paces.

Eventually, he was sufficiently reassured to make his way into the cafe. Zhou, looking uncomfortable, nodded in recognition. Song ordered himself a cup of black tea at the counter and went to sit at Zhou's table.

'Thank you for contacting me,' Song said, nursing the tea between his hands. 'After the other evening I was afraid that I had lost your friendship.'

'Let's keep this quick,' Zhou muttered, leaning across the table. 'I have two things to tell you. The first is that they're determined to find the person who helped Jin Dao, and they have your name from the hotel register. Your name and description has been circulated nation-wide. I don't know why I'm bothering to tell you this since you didn't see fit to tell me the other day that you were in Wanmei with her. That puts me in a very difficult situation.'

Song nodded.

'I apologize,' he said. 'I had nothing to do with the posting of the document, but it would be hard to convince the State Security Bureau of that fact.'

Zhou shook his head. 'I don't want to know the details. I want to tell you that you should leave Beijing. In fact you should avoid any urban centre where the police will be well organized. I should not be telling you this . . .' His eyes flickered to the street outside. 'I should be going,' he muttered, 'my wife will be wondering where I am.'

Song prompted him gently, 'You said there were two things.'

Zhou heaved a breath, and when he spoke again it was in a voice so low that Song had to strain to hear.

'You asked me about the condition of the child's body,' Zhou said. 'And your question has haunted me. I've now seen the pathology report . . . and the child's body suffered massive trauma consistent with blows from a blunt instrument. Her neck was broken, and several ribs, and her left arm.'

He broke off and glanced outside, then turned back to Song. 'The pathologist states that there are marks on her skin at her ankles and wrists which suggest the use of restraints.'

'You mean that she was tied up?'

Zhou nodded, glancing nervously behind him.

'And that the evidence doesn't specifically point to abduction. It could equally as well have been her parents who beat her . . .'

This time, something that he saw in the street alarmed Zhou. He moaned. He didn't stop to bid Song farewell. He got to his feet and made for the door, breaking into a run as soon as his feet hit the pavement outside.

Song stayed where he was for a few minutes, watching through the window. He could not see what had alarmed Zhou and he thought that if this was a trap then they would have come for him by now. Nevertheless, after a decent period of time had elapsed, he got to his feet and left, and as soon as he had left the cafe he too moved swiftly away. Zhou was right, he must leave Beijing. He thought that Wanmei County might be the one place that they would not look for him. Whether that was true or not, he would make his way to Yidong the next day.

Twenty-six

LONDON

Head bowed against the rain, Blue followed Wu Dan, who was striding across the car park. Some of the wedding guests were leaving, running to their cars, holding jackets as makeshift shelters over their heads. They called to each other and laughed.

'Where are we going?' Blue shouted, but Wu Dan didn't seem to hear her, so she hurried after him. He stopped by a small silver car and opened the door for her.

'We can talk in here,' he said.

Eager to get out of the rain, she climbed straight into the passenger seat. When Wu Dan got into the car, started the engine and pulled straight out of the parking space, she was alarmed.

'What are you doing? Where are we going?'

'There's no need to be frightened,' Wu Dan said. But her fear seemed to infect him too. He shouted at her, 'Don't be frightened!'

'I don't want to go anywhere,' Blue protested. 'I thought we were just going to talk.'

'Don't get upset, please don't get upset,' Wu Dan pleaded.

When they stopped at a traffic light Blue tried the door, but it was locked. She tried winding the window down so that she could shout out to a passer-by, but he had locked the windows too.

'Let me out!' she demanded.

'I can't,' he yelled. She thought he looked as though he was about to cry.

She watched from the window, desperate for clues as to where they were going, but they passed through street after street, mile after mile of identical Victorian terraced houses, streetlights illuminating empty pavements slick with rain, water running in the gutters. Blue shivered. She had misunderstood, she had thought him a friend, she'd thought it safe to contact him. But Tang Ning had let a murderer into his flat, and it must have been someone he thought of as a friend. She had misunderstood, and it would cost her her life. Blue sank into the passenger seat. She no longer challenged Wu Dan. She waited for a chance to escape. How could she ever have thought that Wu Dan looked like Wolf?

They drove into a wooded area where the road narrowed and he pulled off into a clearing between the trees. Frantically Blue twisted in her seat, hoping she would see someone who might help. She had not expected to find this rural landscape in what must surely still be London. He turned the key, killing the engine.

Again Blue tried the door, again she found it locked.

'I just want to talk to you,' Wu Dan cried, banging his hands on the wheel. 'I need to know how you found me.'

He turned and seized her arm and she pulled away from him, shaking her head, mute with fear.

For a long moment he gazed at her. Then he shook his head as though he was ashamed. He seemed to regain control of himself.

'I just want to talk to you,' he repeated, but quietly this time.

Still Blue said nothing, and after a while he started to speak.

'Tang Ning was a friend of my older brother,' he said. He was calmer now, but his fingers pulled at the rubber cover on the steering wheel, shredding it into tiny pieces that fell onto his lap and onto the floor. 'They went to high school together, and I tagged along when they hung out. He used to call me his little brother. I didn't see him for years until I was having lunch just over two weeks ago and he was in the restaurant. After that we met only once. So you see I'm surprised that you found me.'

'Just over two weeks ago, that was the lunch when he saw you with the ghost,' Blue said.

His eyes seemed to double in size, and his previous distress returned.

'How do you know about that?'

When Blue refused to answer, he screamed the question again, 'How do you know about that?'

'I found his phone,' she whispered.

He sat there, breathing heavily.

'It was you who found him,' he whimpered.

'Yes, it was me.' There seemed little point in denying it. She would rather tell him than have him scream at her again. She couldn't see how it would hurt to tell him, she thought he was more likely to do her harm if she refused to speak. 'I just went to look for him to tell him that his wife's in prison. He didn't answer, and the door to his flat was open so I went inside,' she said quietly. 'I picked up his phone. I saw your messages. I thought you seemed concerned about him. Later I thought I'd try to speak to you, I don't know why.'

He nodded, thinking.

'Where's the phone now?'

For a moment she didn't answer and her mind raced. She thought a lie might yet save her.

'I gave it to the police,' she said.

'So they know it all.' His voice was dead. 'They must be looking for me now.'

Blue stayed silent.

'I suppose they can track my mobile-phone signal if they really want to,' he said, thinking aloud. 'They probably know where I am right now.'

He pulled his phone out of his pocket and switched it off. Then he turned towards her and attempted a watery smile.

'I've scared you,' he said.

He turned the key and the engine came back to life. He reversed back onto the road. Blue stared straight ahead. He did a U-turn in the road so that they were driving once again in the direction of the city. Still Blue stayed silent.

'I didn't kill him, if that's what you think,' he glanced at her. 'I arrange things for rich men who come to London. I help them find places to live, put their children in school, I introduce them to people who can help them do business here. That day I was with a client, someone who's here to invest. I didn't even know Tang Ning was in the restaurant. The next day I received his text message. I didn't take it seriously. That night, when I was drunk, I joked about it with my client, I told him that my friend Tang thought he was a ghost.'

Wu Dan fell silent, and Blue thought that he would say no more. They had re-entered the city and the car was nosing slowly through the streets again. She didn't recognize anything. She thought they were taking a different route. It looked more rundown. A gang of youths wandered drunkenly down the centre of the road, and as she thought of the gang outside Tang Ning's flat her muscles tensed.

'Of course my client didn't think it was funny,' Wu Dan resumed. 'I knew I shouldn't have told him. He told me he wanted to see this man for himself, he told me I should invite my friend Tang to lunch so that he could see him for himself. I didn't like the way he was speaking, but my client has lots of money to spend. I'd been showing him property, houses worth millions of pounds, and he'd found one he liked. I didn't want to offend him. We chose the table carefully so that Tang couldn't see him, but he could see Tang. At lunch Tang became very upset. He told me he had come across my client in the course of his work and that he was a crook. Of course I laughed. I said all my clients could be described as crooks. He spoke about a child-trafficking operation, he said he had documents in his possession which would prove my client's involvement in kidnapping tiny children. I thought Tang had gone mad. He was always seeing conspiracies everywhere he looked, and I was sure it was another one of those . . .' his voice trailed off.

'Did you tell your client what he'd said?' Blue asked.

'When I had the text from Tang Ning saying he was being followed and his flat had been searched I guessed he was being paranoid.'

Either Wu Dan hadn't heard her question, or he hadn't wanted to answer, Blue thought. She stared out of the window. Her mind was racing. If Wu Dan had told his client that Tang Ning said he had proof of his client's complicity in the kidnappings, then the client would have felt threatened by Tang Ning. She suspected that whatever Tang Ning had by way of documentation of the client's complicity, it couldn't have been good enough evidence for a court or he'd have passed it on to the police in Wanmei. But then, perhaps he had. Perhaps they had ignored it.

This street looked more familiar. She examined each building they passed. Suddenly she thought that she could see Blueberry Lodge up ahead. Wu Dan pulled into the side of the road. Blueberry Lodge was still a couple of hundred metres away. She fixed her eyes on it.

'I'm going to go away. There's no way I can get involved with the police,' Wu Dan said. She could see he was getting agitated again. He couldn't sit still. He turned towards her and spoke urgently. 'You've got to tell the police I had nothing to do with it. You've got to tell them I didn't know what Wang would do.'

She nodded, not trusting herself to speak. Her eyes were still fixed on Blueberry Lodge.

He leaned across her and she braced herself, but he just flicked a switch to unlock the door, then grasped the handle and pushed the door open for her. She scrambled out of the car without a word and started walking, then running, towards the hotel. There was silence all around her. There was no traffic on the road, and she could not see a soul. She wanted her feet to fly across the ground but her fear had made her legs stiff and unwilling. She could not hear the car behind her. What was going through his mind? Was he realizing only now that he had given her a name? Wang – it belonged to millions of men, hundreds of thousands of rich men, thousands of rich men visiting England, but it was a name nonetheless, and he hadn't meant to give her a name for the client.

She remembered the spyhole on Tang Ning's door. He would have looked through it. If he had seen the man he called a 'ghost', he would not have let him in. But an old friend he was expecting ... was that how

Wang had gained access to Tang's flat? Had Wu Dan helped Wang get access to Tang Ning and left before the attack?

Behind her she heard the engine roar. Had he changed his mind? The car shot past her. She came to a halt, peering into the darkness, trying to make out the number plate, but it was gone. She started to walk again towards the hotel.

When she arrived there, the lights in the hall were off. She stood, staring around her in the lobby. A lamp was still shining at the desk but there were no staff in evidence. She had no idea how to go about getting back to Robin's house.

Suddenly Robin was there, still in her silver dress, her face pale and tired. She was barefoot and she carried her shoes in her hand.

'Where have you been?' she exclaimed. 'We couldn't find you anywhere. Sal's driving around the streets and Finney's gone back home in case . . .' She broke off. 'My God, Blue, what happened to you?'

Blue seized her friend's hand.

'I'm so sorry I frightened you,' she said. 'But now I need to talk to the police.'

Twenty-seven

WANMEI COUNTY TOWN

Song had talked his way into many hospitals, and this one presented no particular difficulty. It was smaller and grimier than its equivalent in the capital, but its population of pyjama-clad patients shuffled through corridors and public areas as they did in Beijing, and grey-coated physicians moved with purpose. He was not challenged as he made his way up the concrete stairs to the wards. No one – not the nurses, not the visitors, nor the patients who wandered the corridors trailing their IV drips – paid him any attention. When he stopped and asked the way, explaining that a female relative had swallowed poison, he was pointed further and further into the belly of the hospital, until he felt able to use her name.

'I'm looking for Huang Xiuhong,' he said to a nurse whose head was bent over a clipboard. She looked up. She had grey hair cut into a short bob and eyes that were immediately impatient.

'She's in there,' she nodded towards the entrance to a ward. 'What do you want with her? There's an investigation team from Beijing coming to see her tomorrow, and we've had orders that no one's to visit her before then.'

Song's heart rose. He had raced here to make it before the arrival of the official delegation, but without precise information about their schedule he hadn't been sure he would make it in time. The weekend, he thought, worked in his favour.

'I'm doing preparatory work for the investigation team,' Song lied. He continued to speak, trying to impress upon the nurse that he knew the details of the case. 'She took poison after the death of her daughter and her husband, but there are many details we need from her. I'm supposed to prepare her for the range of questioning tomorrow, make clear to her what will be needed so that the investigation team doesn't waste its time.' The nurse looked coolly at him, and he added for good measure, 'The team is made up of very senior officials. It's sensible to please them rather than to annoy them.'

'I'll need to see your ID,' she said. 'They didn't tell me you were coming.'

'I didn't want to disrupt your work too much,' Song murmured, handing her a card.

'Du Minghui, Team Leader, Preparatory Team, Special Investigative Branch of the Ministry of Public Security,' she read. She looked up at him, and he could see that she was beginning to be impressed.

'I need to phone the hospital director about this,' she said. Silently, Song cursed.

She tried, and he could see her standing at the nursing station, the telephone receiver held to her ear. But eventually she had to turn back to him and report that the hospital director wasn't available.

'Well, there's no harm in you seeing her,' she said. 'I doubt she'll be able to speak to you anyway.'

She dipped her head to indicate that he should follow her. She entered the ward, and Song tried not to look at each bed as they passed. Bad enough that he should trespass on Li Hetian's wife, but he had no reason to invade these women's misery. Still, as he walked behind the nurse he drew an impression of glazed eyes, of enduring pain, of shifting discomfort, of the smells of illness and of medicine. The nurse came to a halt by a bed in which there lay a skeletally thin woman under a flimsy blanket. He let his eyes go to her face. He would have thought her sixty years old, just as he had overestimated her husband's age. Neither of them could have been more than about forty. Hardship and poverty would have aged her even without the poison that she had drunk. Only her hair was still dark and thick. Her skin was like fine leather, drawn tight over her cheekbones and gathered in wrinkles around her mouth, as though she had once spent time smiling. Her upper teeth were prominent and untidy.

She was awake, or at least she seemed to be awake. Her eyes stared at the ceiling, they didn't move towards him although he stood right over her. There were tubes that disappeared into her nose and into her wrist, and other tubes that emerged from the blankets carrying yellow liquids. Song was disappointed. He doubted she could answer any of his questions in this state.

'We saved her life,' the nurse said, 'but her internal organs are damaged. If she lives she'll be in constant pain. We can't do anything for her mental state except to give her tranquillizers, that's why there's no point in you seeing her. We had no choice. As soon as she regained consciousness she became hysterical.'

Huang's hands lay like bunches of twigs at her side.

'Will she be sedated tomorrow when the investigation team comes to visit her?' he asked. 'I need to prepare them for what they'll find here. They're expecting answers to their questions. She's no good to them like this.' Or to me, he thought.

'Well would they rather question a vegetable or a maniac who screams at them that she wants to die and tries to tear the tubes out of her body?'

'Can she hear us?' Song asked.

'Probably. But I don't know whether she can make sense of us . . .' Her tone softened. 'She's a pathetic creature. She's done such damage to herself but I'd probably have done the same myself.'

She turned away from Song in answer to a summons and left him at the woman's bedside.

He glanced around. Who was there to attend to her? The ward nurses would do what was medically necessary and no more. Her husband was dead, and her child. Did she have family who came to tend to her? Perhaps this shell of a body didn't need tending. The tubes probably took care of food and the other end as well.

He took Huang's fragile hand in his. He did not dare exert pressure in case it fell to dust.

'I'm so sorry,' he murmured. 'I could have done more. I don't know if I could have prevented this . . . I couldn't have prevented what happened to your daughter . . . but this . . . Your husband came to see me . . . I was there when he died. I tried to help, but it was too late . . . There's no excuse . . .'

He lowered his head. When he looked up again he found that her eyes had moved and were seeking out his face.

'Can you hear what I'm saying?' he asked.

She did not respond, unless there was a flicker of movement in her fingers. He bent, leaning on the bed so that his mouth was close to her ear.

'I want to find out what happened to your daughter, but there are some things I don't understand,' he said, desperate for some reaction. 'Her name appeared on a list of children who were abducted but you were in possession of her body. How did it get back to you? And why did it bear those marks as though she'd been beaten? Why did you freeze it?'

He straightened up and watched her face but there was no response. Her eyes had left his and were staring once more at the ceiling. He waited by her bedside until she slept and then he left.

The nurse who had shown him to Huang's bedside was in the corridor talking to a young man. When she saw him, she broke off and beckoned him over.

'This is Teacher Ding,' she indicated the man. 'The

school that Huang Xiuhong's little girl went to has been collecting money for her mother's treatment, and Teacher Ding has come here to take care of the paperwork. And this is . . . Mr Du, a member of the preparatory team for the special investigation team at the Ministry of Public Security.'

She nodded at both of them smartly, turned on her heel and left them together. The teacher shifted from foot to foot shyly. He was much shorter than Song and half his width. Song found himself bending slightly at the knees to talk to him, as he did with Blue, much to her disgust.

'I'm honoured to meet you,' the teacher said awkwardly. 'I had no idea that an investigation team was looking into this.'

'The central government will praise the school for raising funds for the child's mother,' Song said, to change the subject.

'Teachers and parents have been very moved by her plight,' Teacher Ding said. 'I was asked to coordinate the money-raising efforts. But it's not enough . . . I've just been to the Accounts office and the bill is huge. I can't see how they arrived at it. The amount we've collected doesn't begin to cover it.'

'Doesn't she have family to settle the bills?'

'Her brother, Huang Jianmin, came to see her,' the teacher said. 'But his family has no money and he left when the accountant told him how much her treatment had cost. They can't keep her here for much longer unless the bill is paid.'

'What will happen to her if it's not paid?'

'I don't know.' Teacher Ding scratched his head. 'I expect the hospital will ask her family to take her away . . . but if they haven't paid the outstanding fees, they won't let the family take her.' He concluded with a small giggle of confusion, 'It's a conundrum.'

'Did you know the child?' Song asked.

'She was too young to be in my class. But I know the family. I helped Li Hetian to write a petition to the authorities about his daughter's disappearance.'

'I've seen that petition,' Song said. 'The calligraphy is exquisite.'

Teacher Ding reddened with pride.

'Li Hetian didn't know how to write, at least, not a document of that length. So he asked me to help him.'

Song thought for a moment, then sighed.

'There's one point the investigation team doesn't understand,' Song said. He spoke in a low voice as a doctor passed by. 'I've heard that the frozen body bore the marks of trauma consistent with a blow from a blunt instrument, and that her neck was broken, and we know her father froze her body to preserve . . .' Song observed the teacher's pallor and halted mid-sentence.

'But can we even be sure the child was abducted?' The teacher was frowning, and he spoke in a low voice. 'I wouldn't dare say this at school, because the teachers all believe the child was kidnapped. But, for instance, everyone thought that two girls, Yanhua and Meimei, had gone missing, but they are back home now. I don't like to criticize Li Hetian when he's dead and his wife's in hospital, and besides, I would have called him my friend. But isn't it possible that it was her own father who killed her? Perhaps there are other explanations in each of the cases where the child has disappeared.' Teacher Ding looked embarrassed. 'I'm not from around here, perhaps there are things that I don't understand. These are just my own thoughts.'

Song nodded. 'It's a possibility,' he said. He thought that he had had three people now suggest to him that the frozen child had died at her parents' hands. He told himself he mustn't dismiss the theory just because he felt such guilt over Li Hetian's death.

He made his way back through the labyrinth of corridors and down the concrete steps into the entrance lobby. There were rows of seats where outpatients were waiting and queues at a series of windows marked Registration, Documentation and Accounts. He approached the last of these and stood in line.

'I want to enquire about the bill for Huang Xiuhong,' he said when it was his turn.

The accountant shuffled through files and thumbed through pages of fragile paper so thin that it reminded Song of Li Hetian's petition. She punched figures into a calculator and gave him a figure that sounded extortionate. He thought he might have misheard and asked her to write it down, which she did with no expression, as though she was asked to do the same thing a hundred times a day. For a moment he just looked at the figure. The amount was equivalent to several months' rent on a new office.

'Are you going to pay it or not?' the accountant asked. 'There's a queue behind you.'

He glanced behind him and saw a dozen people. He looked down again at the figure on the paper and thought of Huang Xiuhong, so heavily sedated. If only he had been able to ask her some questions. Then he thought that even if Li Hetian had killed his own daughter, the mother had to be treated.

He dug in his pocket for his bank card, which he handed her together with a crisp 100-*yuan* bill.

She put her head on one side, holding the 100-*yuan* bill towards him.

'What are you doing?' she complained. 'Why don't you pay it all with your card, what's the point in giving me this?'

He bent and brought his head close to the window so that the queue behind him couldn't hear.

'The card is for the patient's bill and the cash is a handling fee for the information I need, which is the address and telephone number of Huang Jianmin, the patient's brother. I believe he's her next of kin.'

Her eyes flickered to the queue behind him, but she slipped the note into her pocket, and while she processed the card and asked him to punch his bank code into the machine she scribbled an address on a piece of scrap paper. When she passed him his receipt she passed the address and telephone number with it.

Twenty-eight

Song made his way out onto the street and found his car. It was a black Audi with mirrored windows, bought as scrap by a dodgy dealer after it crashed on an expressway just outside Beijing. It should have been a write-off – its engine wouldn't last long, and on close inspection it looked as though it had been soldered together and spray-painted by a child – but from a distance it looked the part of a car belonging to the preparatory team leader of the investigation team.

He made a phone call to Huang Jianmin's house, and was directed to his place of work. He had to stop to ask the way, and found himself eventually on a street on the outskirts of Wanmei, where warehouses were set back from the road. He followed a truckload of pigs, so overcrowded that some of them were secured on the roof of the vehicle, lying on their backs with their legs stuck straight up in the air. The truck turned into a compound, and he realized that the address he was looking for was right next door. He parked on the road outside and walked in to the compound. There was a man there in a smeared apron and rubber boots.

'I'm looking for Huang Jianmin,' Song said.

'What for?' He was small, with a headful of black wiry hair.

'I want to talk to you ... you are Huang Jianmin, right? You look like your sister. I went to see her in the hospital. They gave me your home telephone number, and your wife said I'd find you here.'

'You know who I am, who are you?' the man challenged him.

This time Song did not give his false identity. If he was right about this place and how this man had helped his brother-in-law, then Huang Jianmin would clam up at the first whiff of official investigation. He had too much to lose.

'I'm a friend of the journalist Tang Ning,' Song said.

The man eyed him uncertainly.

'Tang Ning met your brother-in-law Li Hetian, and Li told him that his daughter had gone missing,' Song said. 'Tang Ning tried to get the government to investigate.'

Now the man was listening carefully, with his head cocked to one side.

'So,' Song asked, 'is that a slaughterhouse next door?'

The man grunted assent.

'And what do you run here, a meat-processing plant?'

'That's right.'

Song pushed at one of the double doors, and it swung open. He stepped inside. Pig carcasses hung from hooks at the back of the warehouse, and the whole place had the sweet smell of raw meat. There were half a dozen workers in there, all of them dressed in the same blood-stained aprons, hacking away at lumps of flesh in front of them. The floor was wet with blood and water.

'Is this a freezer?' Song hauled open a heavy metal door and bitter cold air poured out. He could see trolleys piled with packaged meat in a space as big as a room.

The man grabbed his arm and pushed the door shut. 'This is private property. If my boss sees you, I'll be finished. Just tell me what you want.'

Song stepped back outside and the man followed him.

'There's an investigation team coming to Wanmei tomorrow,' Song told him. 'They're going to see your sister in the hospital, but she'll probably be too heavily sedated to speak to them. With any luck, they won't come looking for you. Because keeping a human corpse in a freezer isn't proper use of these facilities . . .'

The man started to quake with fear. His eyes darted around the yard as though he was expecting an arresting officer to leap at him from the shadows. Song could tell he wanted to run away.

'I haven't . . .' the man started to protest. His whole body moved in denial, his head shaking his shoulders and his whole torso.

'I've just settled your sister's hospital bill,' Song told him.

'Why?' the man stammered, 'I don't understand.'

'I need you to answer some questions,' Song said, moving in close. 'If you help me out, I'm not going to tell the investigators where to look to find a freezer.'

The man started to nod his head frantically. 'All right,' he said, 'all right.' He pulled Song towards a bicycle shed at the side of the building.

'What do you want to know?' he asked. He wiped the sweat from his brow with his apron.

'I just have one question,' Song said. 'I know that Li Hetian's daughter was abducted in January. Then by the time Li Hetian wrote his petition, he was in possession of her body and had brought it here to be frozen. What happened in between? How did he find his daughter?'

'It wasn't like that. He didn't find her. The police brought her to him,' the man said.

Song frowned. 'I don't understand.'

'One day, after we'd been searching for her for a month, my brother-in-law was called to the police station in Wanmei County. They informed him that they had been contacted by the police in Yunnan province and that they had found the dead body of a child. They had her name and her home town, so they were sending her back. My brother-in-law was beside himself with grief. He waited twenty-four hours, and the body arrived in Wanmei. It was indeed his daughter, although it was clear that she'd been badly beaten. I went to meet him there, with my van, and we took her back to his house. It was winter, there was snow all around, so at first he kept her in the lean-to at the back of the house, where there was no heating. My brother-in-law went to the police in Yidong and told them that he had the body of his daughter back, and that she had been found in Yunnan province, which is thousands of miles away. He wanted them to investigate. He'd been told nothing about where she was found, or how. Instead of investigating they sent a young officer called Xu to take her body back.'

'But why did the Yidong police want to take the body away if the Wanmei police had given it to your brother-in-law?'

'I don't know.'

Just then a man walked around the side of the building.

'My supervisor,' the man muttered, and gave Song a beseeching look. Please, the look said, no more questions, not in front of him.

Song nodded, and walked away from Huang. As he went, he shouted over his shoulder, 'Call me if you lower the price,' as though they had been negotiating the sale of some item or other.

'It won't be any lower than that,' Huang shouted back, and Song could hear the gratitude in his voice. 'I'm giving you the best deal I can.'

When Song glanced behind him, the double doors were open, and he could see Huang at his post, setting to work on a carcass.

Twenty-nine

YIDONG VILLAGE

Song expected Yidong's police station to be a modest affair. It was a village, after all, and village police stations were usually small and simple, with a single counter manned by two or three bad-tempered women who thought their black uniforms had turned them into commandants. The men went out on patrol in their cars, and to restaurants where they demanded food and drink, while the women stayed in the branch and dealt with all the bureaucratic form-filling that was their lot in life. The people who came to seek their help were rarely rude, they couldn't afford to be, they needed the police to help them complete a multitude of permissions, and this only encouraged the rude female police officers to be ruder still.

But Yidong's station was a surprise. Set among the crumbling village homes, it was a substantial circular building of some black and highly polished stone, and without windows, so that it looked like an alien spacecraft that had landed in the dustbowl of north China. It was much smaller than the Party and government headquarters in the county town, of course, but instinctively Song felt the same disquiet here. The expensive building materials and the showy design suggested that the occupants of the building interpreted their mandate to 'serve the people' as an order also to bleed them dry.

Song drove into an official parking space. Yidong was only a village, but walking into any police station and pretending you were a government functionary when in fact you were not required both a strong nerve and a confident swagger.

He entered the building and paused to look around him. Inside, there was a marble-lined lobby. It was largely empty, its function apparently to impress. There was still, however, only the single counter, and two women behind it, and each of them looked as though she had walked off a propaganda poster.

He approached the counter. The women ignored him studiously.

He slapped his fake ID down on the counter. They continued to chat, and at the same time to stamp, one by one, a series of slips of paper. It was such a mechanical task that they didn't even need to look at what they were doing.

'I'm here on central government business,' he barked.

Startled, the women looked up at him. One of them opened her mouth as if to challenge him, but she thought better of it. Instead she reached out and picked up his ID, examined it, then passed it to the second woman. The first woman rose to her feet slowly.

'Haven't you received notification of the visit of the special investigation team of the ministry?' he demanded.

'I thought they were coming on Monday,' the woman who was still seated said.

'But there's preparatory work to do,' he said. 'I need to speak to Officer Xu, is he on duty?'

They looked at each other. One of them picked up a telephone and punched a number.

'There's an officer from Beijing here to see you,' she said.

After a few minutes, Xu came to the front desk, rubbing his eyes. He had clearly been asleep. He gazed up at Song as though he was a Martian, then glanced at the women, who shrugged.

'I want a room where I can question him in private,' Song ordered.

One of the women led them to a small office, and Song took the larger of the two chairs.

'I have some questions for you,' Song said, waving Xu to sit down. He wanted to get out of there quickly, before one of the women called their superiors.

Xu looked at him with big eyes.

'In the middle of January,' Song said, 'you went to the home of Li Hetian and his wife Huang Xiuhong, and you instructed them to hand over the corpse of their child. Is that correct?'

Xu looked at the glass door. Song could see the two women talking animatedly. They kept glancing towards the office where he and Xu were cloistered. He could see that one of them wanted to make a call because her hand kept straying towards the telephone.

'Is that correct?' Song demanded. He stood up, increasing his ability to intimidate.

'That's correct,' Xu said miserably. 'She cried and shouted at me. She wouldn't give me the body.'

'Who ordered you to ask for it?' Song asked.

Xu sighed. His knee was jiggling up and down nervously and he was wringing his hands.

'I can't remember,' he said.

'Sure you can,' Song leaned against the desk. Outside, at the counter, the two women had calmed down. Had they made a phone call while he wasn't looking? 'Tell me what happened before you went over there.'

Xu looked at the floor.

'Li Hetian came in one day,' he said. 'He was all worked up. Said he'd got his daughter's body back, and she was all beat up, and he wanted to make sure there was an investigation.'

'Who did he say this to?'

'He said it out there.' He nodded his head towards the counter. 'It was a busy day. He caused a real stir. Everybody heard what he had to say. Those two out there got rid of him, said he was causing too much of a disruption. Then, when he'd gone, there was an almighty row. The deputy here said there should be an investigation, but the chief said there would be no such thing. When everyone else had gone home, the chief called me in and told me to go and get the body back. That's all there was to it.'

'Did he say why you had to get the body back?'

Xu shook his head. 'I don't ask why anything,' he said.

'Do you know why the chief and his deputy argued?'

'No,' he said again. 'And I'm not interested.'

'What happened after she refused to give you the body?'

'Next day I went back but she told me it was too late, it was buried.'

'And was the chief satisfied by that?'

'I guess so. I didn't hear any more about it.'

Song wanted to know more about the relationship between the police chief and his deputy, but there was no time to ask, and anyway he doubted Xu could give him an adequate analysis of the situation. Right now he had to leave. A man had come into the marble hall and had approached the counter. He didn't look like a police chief, but from what Song could see, both police women were treating him with some courtesy. Song couldn't risk being caught yet.

'Thank you,' he dismissed Xu. 'You have been most cooperative. The investigation team will ask you further questions at a later date.'

Song waited for Xu to leave the room and then he tried a couple of doors until he found one which led directly into the car park. This meant that he didn't have to enter the hall again. He climbed into his car and manoeuvred out of the space. Only when he was on the open road again did his pulse rate start to slow.

When he had driven for some miles he pulled over. Jin Dao's mother had given him Commissioner Tang's telephone number, and now he rang it. A secretary answered. Song Ren introduced himself with his real name.

'I want to speak to the Commissioner,' he said.

Immediately she responded that the Commissioner was busy.

'Tell him I already know what he knows,' Song said. 'Tell him the little girl's body was returned to Li Hetian by the Wanmei County police. It had been transferred from Kunming. Are you getting this?'

The secretary began to bluster and to protest that she didn't understand, but Song started to shout at her.

'Tell him I want to know the rest of it now. Tell him that if he tries lying to me again, telling me the girl was killed by her parents, I'll find a way to embarrass him. I'll make sure it's known that he saw his nephew's report months ago and did nothing about it, showing his total disregard for the wellbeing of the rural population. I'm turning off this phone. I'll call him in ten minutes.'

He cut the connection, and buried his head in his hands. What was he doing, shouting at the Commissioner's secretary? Until now he had been cautious, he had been careful, he had so far avoided detection. Now this angry bluff. He had no way of knowing whether Tang Ning had shown the report to his uncle. How had he lost control so thoroughly? He looked at his watch. He gazed out of the window. On a map of China, Wanmei County and Yidong village would nestle so close to Beijing that they would be one dot. But it felt like a different world. The only tall building in the county was the Party and government headquarters, which cradled the procuratorate also under its marble wing. Apart from that, everything here was a scrabble-in-the-dirt struggle to become prosperous, a mess of workshops, warehouses, coal trucks, of grand plans and micro-finance that leeched out into the surrounding villages. Those who succeeded would leave this place behind.

After exactly ten minutes, he switched his phone back on and rang the Commissioner again. This time, the secretary transferred him immediately.

'Are you mad?' The Commissioner spat the words into the phone. 'You address my office as though I too am some small-time private detective who is beneath contempt? Do you know what I can do? I can squash you under my little finger like an ant.'

Song breathed in and out slowly.

'Commissioner, please accept my humble apologies. I don't know what came over me. It was thoughtless of me.'

'How dare you allege that I saw the report and did nothing . . .'

'As you say, a groundless allegation. I apologize. I won't repeat . . .'

'No evidence exists to suggest I saw the report.' It was both a statement and a question.

'No, Commissioner, no evidence exists. I got carried away.'

There was a long silence on the line, and then the Commissioner started to speak in a slow and weary voice.

'My nephew is dead, but you knew that when you came to see me, didn't you?'

Song hesitated.

'I feared that was the case, Commissioner.'

After a moment, Commissioner Tang began to speak.

'It's all in the petition the poor man dropped from the roof, and the police have confirmed the details with the police force concerned. In early February, in Yunnan province, just outside Kunming, the police were called to the scene of an accident – a lorry had gone into the side of a van on a country road. Witnesses reported that all the occupants of the van, several adults and children of various ages, fled the scene almost immediately, although the accident was not their fault. The police found one child trapped in the wreckage. She was pronounced dead at the scene, and according to the medical examiner all her injuries were sustained in the crash except for the marks which had been caused by restraints.'

Song ran his hand over his face.

'But how did they know that she was Li Hetian's daughter?'

'The occupants of the van had fled so rapidly that they left many things behind them which led the police to believe that they had driven an extremely long distance, and that they were involved in a child-trafficking operation. Most important was a notebook which had a list of children's surnames, their ages, genders, and the names of the counties where they had been seized.'

Song absorbed this information.

'They were able to match up the child with the list because . . .' and here the Commissioner's voice slowed further, as though he could scarcely push the words out, 'because she had scratched her name into the skin of her arm.'

Both men were silent.

'Why would a young girl scratch her name in her arm?' Song murmured. He didn't expect an answer, but the Commissioner attempted to respond.

'I've been asking myself that. It suggests she was afraid that she might soon forget her own identity,' he said, 'or that she feared her identity would be snatched from her, or . . .'

'. . . or that she knew or suspected she would die,' Song said, 'and she wanted to be identified.'

Again the two men fell silent.

'At any rate, the police in Kunming made arrangements for the child's body to be transported back to Wanmei. It was identified simply as "Li", but someone in the police headquarters must have remembered that Li Hetian had come to report his daughter missing. The body was returned to Li Hetian.'

'But then, for some reason, someone else decided he should not have it,' Song concluded, 'and Li hid the body.'

He thought for a moment.

'What about the other names in the notebook? Were there other children from Wanmei County?'

'My understanding is that there were not. They were from other cities that the van must have passed through on the way from Wanmei to Kunming. The Kunming police notified those towns, and it's possible that investigations are going on in those places, I have no information.'

Thirty

On the central thoroughfare in Yidong village, vegetables, fruit and cheap clothing were laid out on sheets on the dusty ground along the side of the road, and people were doing their shopping. He noticed parents holding tight to the wrists or the hands of their children. He parked and got out of the car to ask the way, keeping his voice low.

'I want to know where to find Chief Bo,' he said.

Surprised to find no guard, Song pushed open an iron gate, but he'd taken no more than a step inside the yard when a large black dog launched itself towards him, barking furiously. Song took a startled step backwards, and the dog skidded to a halt just in front of him, poised for attack, growling loudly, teeth bared, eyes burning. Another dog, its skeleton showing through pink, bare skin, hairless hackles raised, slunk from the shadows and joined its fellow, this one slavering, strings of saliva hanging from its jaw, its eyes a feverish yellow and sticky with pus. Song did not move. He had once read an account of a man who died of rabies baring his teeth like the mad dog which had bitten him.

A man, arms like sticks, emerged from the house.

'What the fuck do you want?' he shouted at Song.

'I've come to see Chief Bo.'

The man bent, his filthy vest hanging from his sickly frame, to pick up a stone from the ground. Song expected the missile to come in his direction, but instead the man launched it at the dogs. It glanced against the black dog's haunches. The second stone landed smack in the middle of the skeletal dog's back, and it gave a yelp of pain. The third stone had both of them in retreat, snarling.

The man beckoned him in with a jerk of his head and Song hurried across the yard and followed him inside. They passed into a foul-smelling shed that was like a zoo, lined with cages from floor to ceiling holding every kind of grunting and mewling wildlife, both birds and mammals, some of which Song recognized – a pheasant, a guinea fowl – and some, catlike, doglike, weasel-like, that he did not. Through into a scullery and then, deeper inside the house, Song heard voices raised in what sounded like drunken debate. A door was opened and he found himself shoved into a room where three men were seated at a round table that was piled high with food. Two of the men were in partial police uniform – their jackets were hanging over the backs of their chairs, and they sat there in their vests. Song could see that one of them, sitting far back from the table, had rolled up the legs of his uniform trousers and was busy picking a scab on his knee. Startled, they abandoned their chopsticks and scabs and stared at him.

'Chief Bo?' Song asked, addressing the only man who was not in police uniform.

'Who the fuck wants to know?' an officer with a red face challenged him.

The village chief shushed him, but the question stood.

'I've come from Beijing,' Song said, handing over the card he'd had printed. 'The centre is sending an investigation team to look into the rumours of child abductions in Wanmei County.'

'I received notification,' Chief Bo said slowly. 'They will visit Wanmei first, and we are looking forward to welcoming them to Yidong. But I was told they don't start until tomorrow, not today.'

'I'm an advance party,' Song said, thinking that he would probably go to hell for this. 'My job is to ensure that preparations are made for their arrival, and that you're clear beforehand about what they need to know, so there's no confusion . . . or obstruction.'

Song felt three pairs of eyes boring into him. He pulled out a chair and sat down.

'You should have been informed of my visit,' Song's tone was slightly aggrieved. 'Nevertheless, I expect you've done the preparatory work necessary. Do you have a report prepared?'

There was silence. Then Chief Bo cleared his throat.

'Isn't that the job of the investigation team?'

'The team will want to know at what points you've investigated the allegations of abductions from the village and what your findings have been.'

'Bring me a piece of paper and a pen!' Chief Bo declared.

One of the police officers went to the door, yelled at someone for a paper and pen, and returned quickly with both. He handed them to Chief Bo.

'A handful of children have been reported missing from Yidong,' Chief Bo said slowly, writing the words as he spoke them. 'Our investigation is in full swing. So far we have discovered that the child named Li died after sustaining injuries. A child has recently disappeared. It is possible that she has run away . . .'

'Or been sold by her parents,' one of the police officers chipped in, and Chief Bo wrote this down as well.

Song reached for the piece of paper, took it from Chief Bo's grasp, and tore it in two.

'A more serious approach is required in order to satisfy an investigation team from the Party centre,' he said softly.

Chief Bo looked up at him, his face dark. Deliberately, he turned to the officers who flanked him and dismissed them. He waited until the men had lumbered to their feet. They had a little trouble buttoning their jackets and looking for their hats and putting them on their heads. When they had left the room, Chief Bo addressed Song coldly.

'Two of the children who were feared missing have since turned up at home. I believe the Party centre would urge us to use the evidence of our own eyes and ears to assess the situation. We know what's going on in our village. Contradictions arise when the peasantry is misled by false expectations. They hear rumours of wealth and expect that it can fall into their laps. But for such as them – they work the land, their brains aren't up to anything more – it's inevitable that they're disappointed, and when they're disappointed there's the danger of cultish behaviour or of hysteria taking hold. I believe that explains the wild allegations about children. Here, you can speak to the mother of two of the children who went missing but weren't abducted in any way . . .'

He called for his maid and she came shyly into the room, a woman in her thirties, still pretty, poorly dressed. Song noticed that she kept her distance from Chief Bo, standing as far from the table as it was possible to stand.

'Tell this man what happened to your daughters,' Chief Bo ordered her.

She took a moment to look carefully at Song.

'They went missing, Chief Bo,' she spoke in a low, clear voice. 'We feared they had been abducted. They came back to us in a terrible state saying that they had got frightened out on the plain in the storm. Foolishly, they tried to shelter in the mine. There was an explosion, and the mine collapsed . . . when they got back to us their poor flesh was raw from digging.'

'So you see,' Chief Bo addressed Song, 'how incidents can be distorted. Two silly little girls, and another abduction rumour is born.'

'There was an explosion while they were in the mine?' Song asked.

'Yes,' the girls' mother replied.

'How did that happen?'

Chief Bo sent the girls' mother a warning glance.

'I don't know, I only know that it happened,' she said after a moment.

'You can go,' Chief Bo told her. 'But bring our friend from Beijing some of our speciality.'

She dipped her head to show that she had understood, and backed from the room.

'I'm interested in this explosion,' Song said to Chief Bo when she had left.

For a long time, Chief Bo did not reply. He seemed to be deep in thought, and this thought was fuelled by the food that he picked at, cold bean shoots sitting in oil, and the last remnants of fish that clung to the bones.

'There have been complaints about the miners,' he said eventually.

The maid reappeared with a dish of steaming meat that she placed among the detritus of the previous meal, and then she hurried to bring Song a glass and to pour *maotai* into it. Chief Bo raised his glass in a toast.

'To the wisdom of the Party centre,' he declared. He downed the alcohol in one gulp and belched loudly. Song replaced his glass, untouched, on the table.

'What kind of complaints?' Song asked.

'Eat!' Chief Bo urged him. With his chopsticks, he chose a piece of flesh and placed it on Song's plate. 'Our speciality,' he said. 'See if you can guess what kind of steak this is! Come on! The Party centre should accept the hospitality of the common man.'

Song took a piece of the meat and put it in his mouth and chewed. It had a firm texture and a light, slightly fishy, taste.

'It's crocodile!' Bo announced.

Song raised his eyebrows.

'You're clever to find a supplier of crocodile meat in northern China,' he said.

'Not so clever,' Bo protested, pleased at the flattery. 'Not clever at all. But you're right that I am a food enthusiast, as you can see. The juices of the natural world are the choicest nourishment for bodies that are drained and weary.'

'What have the miners done to cause these complaints?' Song persisted.

Chief Bo started to speak, but the girls' mother had been standing watching the two of them and listening to the conversation, and she interrupted him.

'My daughter Yanhua says that she was approached by one of the miners several times, and harassed,' she said.

'What do you mean by harassment?' Song asked.

'He asked her to go to the mine with him. He said they would have fun there. She says that on the night they were lost in the storm she saw him walking near the mine on his own.'

Song turned sharply to Chief Bo.

'Have you investigated this?'

Chief Bo jerked his head at the girls' mother to

indicate that she should leave the room, which she did reluctantly.

'The mines bring wealth to the village,' Chief Bo said when she was gone. 'People have to understand that there's a price to pay for prosperity. The newspapers flap about mine safety, but what do they expect? There have always been sacrifices to be made for the creation of wealth. If one or two miners flirt with the locals, the locals act like schoolgirls.'

'In this case it would appear they *were* schoolgirls,' Song pointed out.

Chief Bo spluttered.

'At any rate,' he hurried on, 'they forget they benefit from the coal the miners dig from the ground.'

Chief Bo stubbed out his cigarette and got to his feet. 'I didn't ask to see your ID,' he said thoughtfully, 'but I can see you're a good man, and we're all friends here. I will provide guides and a driver for you, and soon you will see that this is a fuss about nothing.'

'Good,' Song said. 'Then I'll begin by speaking to the girls who were buried in the mine.'

Thirty-one

The two police officers collected a third, then drove Song to the home of Yanhua and Meimei.

'There's no crime in this village,' the officer who'd been picking at his scab at the dining table said. 'When there's a problem we solve it very quickly. Like that.' He snapped his fingers.

Song nodded, glancing back at the officers, who were sharing the back seat of the car with a crate of cigarettes. They still had rosy cheeks from their lunch, and they reclined against the seat with their legs spread in such a way that their bellies had space to digest. Occasionally one or the other of them belched loudly.

'What about kidnapping?' Song asked. 'Don't you count that as a crime?'

There was a long silence from the back seat. Then one of them ventured, 'Of course. It's illegal, so from that point of view it's a crime. But . . .' His voice trailed off.

'But what?' Song prompted quietly.

'It's illegal, but from a financial point of view it makes a lot of sense,' said the scab picker. 'The only problem I can see is that the parents get upset . . .'

'It's all to do with market conditions,' the other said

sadly as they bumped along the dirt track. 'There are so many pitiable men in China, there aren't enough women to go around, so the traffickers have to redistribute the girls. It's a sort of social service . . .'

'The girls are a raw commodity . . .' the other explained, 'there's a clear profit to be made. Very few . . . you know . . . overheads.'

For some minutes Song stared straight ahead, frowning. Then he turned around again.

'Are you involved in these abductions?' Song asked. He thought, given what he had just heard – they sounded like brothers discussing a mildly shady family business – that they might just be drunk enough to confess there and then. But instead their faces turned from red to puce, and they quickly protested not only their innocence, but the innocence of everyone they knew.

The car drew up outside a one-storey brick house in the main street of the village. As they got out, one of the police officers yelled out, 'Cui Qinglei!'

'Their father,' he turned and explained to Song.

It seemed that Mr Cui had received word of Song's imminent arrival. He led Song into the house without asking for an explanation.

The two girls sat side by side on the edge of a bed, blinking up at the sudden crowd – as well as Song and the police officers, three or four men had followed them in from the street. Song saw that the girls were still badly bruised and scratched from their time in the mine, and that the younger one wore a sling. The older girl's hands were lacerated and swollen. Both of them looked terrified, and so did their father.

'I'm afraid,' Song turned to the police, 'that the investigative team, including myself, will insist on private meetings with witnesses. In the case of children, they will be interviewed in the presence of their parents.'

Grumbling, the villagers left the room. The officers left only after Song insisted.

'As you may know,' Song began, 'the central government is sending an investigation team to Wanmei County to look into allegations of child abduction. I have been sent ahead to do some preparatory work. Obviously, since this is a high-level government investigation, we need honest answers . . .' Song broke off. There was a desperate earnestness about the way that Yanhua was looking at him that he found hard to ignore. This was not the wild girl that he had imagined, a child who would decide to play around a dangerous mine.

'But we weren't abducted,' Yanhua said. 'I made a mistake.'

She was self-possessed, Song thought, and almost a teenager, not the small child he'd been led to believe.

'Tell me about your mistake,' Song said.

But it was the father who started to tell the story.

'The day after Fengfeng disappeared, my littlest one vanished,' he said, 'and because Yanhua is a responsible older sister, she went to look for her. On their way back they were caught in a storm. Perhaps it was foolish to shelter in the mine, but they were frightened and they didn't know that the shaft would collapse.'

'Because of me my little sister nearly died,' Yanhua burst out.

Her father shook his head and said, gently, 'Yanhua, you shouldn't be so hard on yourself.'

'But this investigator is sent by our leaders in Beijing. I can't lie to him. I was frightened, my imagination was too strong.'

'Yanhua . . .' her father interrupted again, but Song spoke over him.

'Let her speak,' he said, putting his hand on the man's arm. 'Yanhua, tell me what happened. Tell me why your imagination frightened you.'

Yanhua lowered her head. Song noticed that Meimei was shaking at the memory.

'After Fengfeng disappeared, I was frightened when I couldn't find Meimei. I went to look for her and I found the friends she'd been playing with, but they didn't know where she was either. The last time they'd seen her was in the amusement park.'

Song frowned, then remembered the roller coaster he'd passed on the way from Wanmei, and the boarded-up ticket office.

'By the time I found her in the amusement park I was very frightened for her. Silly thoughts were crowding my head as though I was having a nightmare, but I wasn't sleeping . . . We tried to run home, but then the storm came and we were soaked. Our shoes were so muddy we couldn't walk, and the sky was so dark that we could hardly see the path. Then I saw him . . .'

'Yanhua,' her father warned, 'think carefully about what you say. Can you be sure?'

'I've thought so much about it since that night,' Yanhua said eagerly. 'I'm sure it was him. There's a miner who keeps stopping us on the way to school.'

'He asks us to go to the mine with him and play,' Meimei said.

Their father shook his head.

'The sky was so dark you could hardly see the path,' he said to Yanhua, 'and the rain was pouring down. How can you be sure?'

She closed her eyes tight, trying to remember.

'When we were in the mine he came down looking for us before the explosion,' she said. 'I opened my eyes. I saw his face. I know it was him.'

'Was there enough light for that?' Song asked her gently.

'I saw his face,' she insisted.

Song stood and gestured to their father that he wanted to speak to him alone. Cui dismissed the girls, and they left the room without another word.

'Do you know anything about the explosion at the mine?' Song asked.

Yanhua's father glanced towards the window. Outside, the officers were waiting for Song, and a crowd had gathered. He swallowed nervously.

'It's not the first time,' he said, speaking in a murmur. 'The miners are in dispute with the foreman over wages. The foreman says there's nothing he can do, Chief Bo is in charge of the cash. When the miners get desperate they sabotage the mines.'

'It was the foreman who stopped you trying to dig the girls out,' Song said.

'He told us that the mine was dangerous and that he would be responsible if any of us came to harm. But we all knew it was an excuse. The foreman doesn't lift a finger unless it's on the instructions of Chief Bo.'

'Chief Bo seems to be something of an entrepreneur,' Song suggested. Yanhua's father nodded silently.

'The amusement park too?' Song asked.

'They lost their investor, they've run out of cash,' Yanhua's father said.

'There's always money to be made in selling people,' Song murmured.

'And many pockets to be filled,' Yanhua's father added so softly that Song could hardly hear him. 'The police are not our protectors here.'

Song sucked in his breath.

'You mustn't report any of this,' the man hissed, looking panicked.

'No one will know of it,' Song assured him.

When they went outside Song found that a large crowd of villagers had gathered around the house. He told his police escorts that he wanted to go to Fengfeng's house.

They climbed back inside the patrol car, as crammed in as ever, except that now the crate of cigarettes was topped by a large bag of oranges.

As they pulled out into the lane they found their way blocked by a handcart that had been left in the middle of the road and they had to stop again to negotiate its removal. Song glanced up and found Yanhua standing by the car watching him, her face unreadable. Behind him the police were debating loudly the relative virtues of two brands of mobile phones.

Song wound down the window. He saw a man he recognized standing behind Yanhua, then remembered where he had seen him before. This was Teacher Ding, who he'd met at the hospital delivering money he'd collected to help pay for the care of Huang Xiuhong. Song raised his hand in greeting and Teacher Ding nodded, smiling shyly.

'You didn't really tell me what your mistake was,' Song said to Yanhua.

She looked confused.

'If you're sure about what you saw that day then you were right to try to escape,' he said. 'You probably saved your sister's life.'

She bit her lip and looked as though she was about to say something, but then the engine roared and the patrol car lurched away from her, across a pothole and out into the street.

They had just pulled up outside Fengfeng's house when the police officer with the scabbed knee received a call on his mobile phone. His eyes darted towards Song, and Song braced himself. But when the call ended the officer turned towards him politely and informed him that Chief Bo had rung him to say there had been a development in the case and they were to proceed to the police station immediately.

Song didn't like the sound of this. He didn't want to be diverted from Fengfeng's parents – he could see the girl's mother standing watching for him in her doorway. Nor did he trust the village chief.

At the mirrored black police station which looked like an alien landing craft, they parked and got out of the car. Instead of entering through the front of the station and into the marble-lined hall, Song followed his guides to a back door. One of the officers made a great show of tapping in a code, and the door slid open to reveal a staircase. This they descended until they arrived at a row of windowless bare cells which were not marbled or mirrored. Song's heart pounded. Was this all a charade? Had they tricked him into jail?

Chief Bo was down there too, Song could hear his voice.

'Come over here,' he shouted to them, 'come and look at this.' They made their way to the furthest cell. Chief Bo was there, standing outside the bars, and next to him a uniformed officer who was marginally better turned out than those who were accompanying Song. Inside the cell, cowering in the corner, was a teenage boy. He was covered in coaldust, but his eyes shone white with fear.

'Here he is,' Chief Bo said proudly. 'We caught him trying to molest a girl.'

Song's eyes took in the blood that streaked the miner's face and hair, the arm that hung useless at his side. There was the smell of excrement.

'This boy's been beaten,' he said quietly.

'We had to restrain him,' the police chief said. 'He tried to get away. We used only the force that was necessary.'

'Hey, you,' Chief Bo called out, 'child molester!'

The miner's eyes darted like an animal's from Chief Bo, to the police chief, to Song.

Song pushed open the cell door and stepped inside. He asked the miner where he was from.

'Anhui, Zhouhua County,' the miner replied in a shaking voice.

'How old are you?'

'Fifteen.' The miner's eyes darted to the men outside the cell.

'Liar!' The police chief entered the cell. He took a handful of the miner's filthy hair and pulled his head back sharply, striking him around the face.

'Tell the truth!' he shouted at the boy. 'Tell the fucking truth.'

Song seized the police chief's arm and gripped it tightly until he let go of the boy. Fury was choking him, but he forced himself to speak calmly.

'The investigation team will be here either tomorrow or the next day,' he said. 'If he shows signs of beating, you'll bear the consequences.'

The police chief let out an exasperated grunt. Song released him. He thought he had probably just put off the beating. He knew he had imbued the investigation team with a moral righteousness that they might not, in fact, possess when they arrived. He had no idea whether they would beat confessions out of people.

He became aware that Chief Bo was speaking on his mobile phone once more, his back turned to Song.

'I see,' he was saying, 'I see. Thank you for clarifying the situation.'

He ended the call, turned and stared coldly at Song.

'We'll take you to your next appointment now,' he said.

Thirty-two

In the car no one spoke and Song knew that he had been found out. The only question was what happened next. It came as no surprise to him when they drove up to Chief Bo's compound. This time, as the car came to a halt, they pulled him out. He struggled, but these were big men and he was no match for them. He thought maybe they would just throw him to the dogs, which barked in ecstasy at his arrival, haunches raised, only staying back because of the kicks the police aimed in their direction. They dragged him past the shed with its cages of animals.

The woman who had cooked for them was there, Yanhua's mother, but Chief Bo shouted at her to make herself scarce and she ran away.

They dragged him across a yard and into an outhouse, where his first impression was of the stink of pigs. Inside the pigpen they pushed his head down and forced his arms up behind him, in the airplane position. He'd seen his mother forced to stand like this, and an image of her came to him now. When they'd dragged her away she'd managed to catch his eye and given him such a look of love.

'Who the hell are you, Mr Fake Fucking Government Official?' Chief Bo punched him in the side of the head.

Someone grabbed his head and jerked it sharply upwards. Then someone punched him hard in the kidneys. He collapsed, but they pulled him up again and forced his arms behind him.

A man walked up to him. Song could only see his lower half, but there was something about the shape of the broad feet in the leather trainers, the thick short legs, that was familiar. The man laughed and spoke.

'I know who this fucking joker is.'

Then Song knew for certain.

One of the feet shot out and caught him on the kneecap, hard. Song staggered. He recovered.

'It must be your breath that stinks in here, Psycho Wang,' he said. 'I should've known property deals in London wouldn't keep your snout from the pig trough for long.'

This time Psycho Wang's knee went into Song's face. He fell to the floor with his face in the pigshit. When he began to push himself upright they kicked his hands from under him and continued to kick him. Their shoes were thick with pig-shit too, and the stuff splashed and squelched around their feet as they slid and stamped. He curled into a foetal position, trying to protect his belly and his head. But the blows landed with great regularity, the pain spread across his back and down his legs, and into his head. He knew that wounds were opening and blood from his scalp would be mixing with the shit.

All at once they stopped. Psycho Wang squatted down beside him, his little head bobbing on his thick neck.

'I've always told you to keep your nose out of my business affairs. If you'd known this was mine you wouldn't have been so fucking brave, would you? Because you know what you've got coming.'

Song gathered his energy and his saliva. He lifted his head, twisting to spit in Psycho Wang's face.

Someone sat down hard on his back, a hand descended like a lead weight on his head, pushing his face into the manure. He twisted to the side, and gulped for air, then found himself breathing the stuff, drowning in it. He tried to gain purchase but could not. So he wriggled forward at speed, pulling himself on his elbows out from underneath the weight, pulling his legs up behind him, flipping the weight off his back and seeing his tormentor land on his butt.

Out of the corner of his eye he saw the woman again. She was standing in the doorway, watching intently. She should get out of there. If they saw her, there was no saying what would happen to her. The thought lasted a fraction of a second before they grabbed him. Both of them leaped onto his back, and brought him down. The one nearest his head grabbed it with both hands, then smashed it down onto the concrete underneath the excrement. He did this once, then twice, then three times . . .

When Song opened his eyes a snout was in his face, a quivering nostril breathing hot pig breath into his eye.

Song pulled sharply back as far as he could – which was not far – and gave a cry of alarm. The pig moved away. Song took stock of his situation. The sky beyond the roof of the pigpen was dark and filled with stars. Pigshit covered him, and the reek of it coated his mouth and his nasal passages. But he thought the filth might have saved him. It had slowed their kicks and dulled the smash of his head on the concrete floor.

Psycho Wang. The name went with the stench. Now he knew, it seemed so obvious. Where Chen Dalei was, where there were pockets to be filled, so was Psycho Wang. He was the missing link.

He tried to move his legs, but couldn't, then tried to move his arms and found them pinioned to his torso. They had tied him with rope. A pig's snout was shoved into his face again, the beast lumbering so close its bulk pushed against his shoulder. He flinched, but he was backed up against the barrier, and he couldn't get away. First one pig's snout, and then another, nudged his limbs, then with more aggression. The more he struggled against them, the more vicious they became. He had heard of instances where pigs had eaten human flesh. He tried to move across the floor away from them, pushing with his shoulders, then his feet.

He heard the clank of a metal bucket.

'Come and get it.' It was the woman's voice, hushed.

Song twisted his head around, but he couldn't see her.

At first, the pigs weren't interested in the bucket. Then, as though on second thoughts, they turned one by one towards the voice, away from him. He couldn't see where they went but he could hear them snorting, and hear the food move round their mouths and into their stomachs.

'Here.' Suddenly the woman was beside him, squatting, a knife in her hands. She sawed through the ropes around his ankles, then the ropes around his wrists. He wanted to thank her but his mouth was so swollen that he couldn't speak. He tried to push himself upright but his legs wouldn't cooperate. She half dragged, half carried him from the pen. Outside, he collapsed onto the ground. She stood over him, helpless. There was the sound of men's voices, raised in excitement, scenting blood. Song could hear the panic in the woman's breathing. He grabbed her ankle and she bent to listen.

'Get out of here,' he managed to say.

He didn't see where she went but when he next raised his head she was gone.

The voices came closer.

'How the fuck did he get out?'

'I left him in the pen.'

'So why's he here, idiot?'

They squabbled among themselves and then they turned on him, throwing curses thick and fast, and then from each a vicious kick, or a blow with objects he could no longer identify because his brain was busy registering hurt, joints dislocated, flesh bruised, lungs fighting for air, ribs cracking. Someone stamped on his hand,

and his fingers exploded in pain. He could hear himself screaming, and then nothing.

A column of light rose above him. Its warm embrace felt like liquid grace. He thought the phenomenon must be produced by a great fire, something like the sun, but without the sun's ferocity, because it created in him a great sense of calm. For a moment he thought he heard his mother's voice calling to him. His heart beat faster and he tried to respond, struggling to move his lips to form her name, but already doubt had set in and he was being wrenched from her. The column of light wavered above his head and his body lurched and jolted against something hard. The roar of an engine shattered the silence. He was travelling. He knew that much, he could feel the van's metal floor underneath him, the texture of the road as it moved underneath the wheels, every pothole and bump, every incline and turn.

A screeching halt. Hands seized his ankles and his wrists, and they lifted him and flung him like a carcass. He fell like a lead weight onto dirt and scrub, stones driving through the skin of his face, the impact sending blades of pain scything along nerves and neural pathways.

Perhaps it was the pain that saved him. Perhaps it was that hurling of his body, like a dead cow, that made him play dead. There was no decision involved. He was not capable of decision, only of primal instinct. If he breathed then his ribs screamed, so he scarcely breathed.

He could not have opened his eyes or mouth, they were so swollen. His limbs might have been severed from his spinal cord, so little did they seem to understand what he wanted of them. But he wanted nothing. He lay there with his body broken. At night the rain came, a deluge that rinsed the pigshit from him and soaked the ground under his back, and then pounded him for hours. When it stopped, he shivered until the sun rose and warmed him, and he slept.

Footsteps approached and came to a halt near his head. There was a sharp intake of breath, the sound of surprise.

'Is he dead?'

A foot made contact with his shoulder. His body no longer belonged to him. He did not react.

'Looks like it.'

'What happened to him?'

Swimming up through layers of unconscious, Song clutched at the voices.

'He lied to us all, he's an impostor . . .' Chief Bo's voice was unmistakable.

'I don't understand . . .' a hesitant voice, Yanhua's father.

'He lied to us and he's borne the consequences.'

'Who is he?'

'A filthy private detective, morally depraved, a parasite.'

'Why did he come here?' Yanhua's father gasped,

and Song knew that Chief Bo had seized him, perhaps by his neck or his ear, to threaten him.

'Your trouble-making daughter will identify our suspect for the investigation team,' Chief Bo hissed.

'I can't predict what my daughter will . . .' Yanhua's father moaned with pain.

'She'll say what you tell her to say. She knows it was the miner. Do-gooders from the centre are just as bad as hooligans like this one here, they'll stir up trouble out of nothing if we don't give them what they want. Go back to the village now and tell people what you've seen. Give them this warning: they should be cautious in what they say to the investigators, they should say that they are proud of their village and that it is a peaceful and law-abiding place. The miner's the one to blame. People who spread rumours will bear the consequences.'

'I don't understand . . .' Yanhua's father stammered. 'How . . . ?'

There was the sound of a blow. Vibrations ran through the earth as a body fell hard onto the ground next to Song. With his eyes swollen shut, Song listened. He could hear the man breathing next to him, a broken, sobbing sound. Then another impact as a foot made contact, and a yelp of pain.

'Understand now?' Another thud, another cry. 'Understand?'

'I understand,' the man who lay beside Song cried out. 'I understand.'

There was a snort of contempt and the sound of retreating steps. Beside him, Yanhua's father sobbed and swore. After a few moments he fell silent, as though he was listening. Song tried to quell his breathing further. Yanhua's father was leaning over him, examining his face. Warily, he reached out and touched Song's hand.

'Are you dead?' the man's voice asked. 'Did they kill you?'

Song tried to open his eyes, and the man stepped back so fast in surprise that he fell over. Song tried to move. He flexed his right hand. He heard Yanhua's father get to his feet and start to run away from him. Song passed out again . . . there was no more sense of time . . . Then more footsteps, hands at his ankles and his armpits, being lifted, a silent scream of pain that brought the darkness settling over him again . . . Deep in his unconscious the roar of an engine sounded.

When he awoke again he was lying on a pallet of what felt like wood. He could see nothing, his eyes seemed glued shut. When he tried to move, he seemed to struggle against invisible walls. He thought that he must be in the morgue, imprisoned now not only by his own paralysis but by a lid, buried alive. He was flooded with fear.

'We want to ask you about your daughters. We understand that they disappeared?'

The voice had come from nowhere, and now a voice grunted in assent. Song thought that the voices were coming to him either through a thin wall, or through some conduit like a pipe or a window. He could hear them quite clearly. He thought that he must be in a lean-to attached to the house. Again, that first voice, which had the tone of authority.

'Can you tell us what happened?'

'The little one ran away,' Yanhua's father muttered it nervously, 'and the older one went to look for her and they were caught in the storm. For a while we were frightened that something had happen to them. Later they returned home.'

'But someone tried to abduct them,' the investigator suggested impatiently. 'That's why we're here, to hear about the attempted abduction.'

'They thought they saw someone and they got scared,' Yanhua's father confirmed miserably. 'My daughter said it was a miner . . .'

'The villagers are right to distrust the miners,' Chief Bo cut in. 'Their educational level is low and they're far from home, there's no knowing what they get up to. The girls did well to escape from him.'

'Have they identified the man in custody?'

'I'll bring them in,' Chief Bo spoke again, 'they've just come back from the station.'

There was the sound of a door opening and closing. Song lay – he had no choice – and listened.

'Greet the officials from Beijing,' Yanhua's father prompted his daughters.

Only Meimei spoke clearly, greeting the uncles from Beijing.

Yanhua muttered something. Song thought it was not like Yanhua to mutter. Her father must have warned her about the danger they faced if they set a foot wrong.

'So, the man you saw at the police station, is he the miner you saw that night?' The investigator asked.

'I don't know.' It was Yanhua who replied. There was a long pause. 'I think it is.'

'Good girl. I believe you have a very good memory. So answer my question again, and see if you can please me. Do you think it is the same man or you know it is?'

'I'm sure it is,' she said, more confidently this time.

'You could see him clearly despite the storm? Well, I'm sure your young eyes are better than mine.'

Yanhua saw the sheets of rain, the figure walking towards them with the dog leaping at his feet. She remembered how she'd kept losing sight of him as he was hidden by the rain, and then how he'd appeared again, never where she expected. Had she seen his face?

'We took shelter in the mine,' she whispered. 'He came down to look for us. We hid from him. I opened my eyes. That was when I saw him. I saw him quite clearly.'

'It was so dark in the tunnel,' Meimei's high voice butted in, 'how could you see his face?'

But everyone ignored her.

'And you were scared when you saw him because he has harassed you on the way to school, is that right?'

'Mama tells us not to go near the miners,' Meimei put in, 'she says they're dirty, and some of them are not polite to girls.'

'He asked us to play with him,' Yanhua said.

'Did he sexually harass you?'

There was silence.

'Did he make any indecent suggestions?'

Still silence.

'Did he expose himself to you?'

Yanhua thought of the time that the boy had stopped them and his flies had been half undone, the front of his trousers hanging open, showing his underpants. At the time she'd thought it was just that he'd forgotten to do them up. His shirt was unbuttoned too, and his trousers were rolled up. He'd been more undressed than dressed, but so were half the men of the village in the summer.

'Maybe,' she said.

'I thought so,' the investigator said. 'It's often the case. Good girl. Sometimes silly girls don't tell us, but you see the importance of giving us all the facts. So, he exposed himself to you?'

'Yes,' she whispered, 'he exposed himself.'

Shortly afterwards, the investigator and Chief Bo left the house.

Fading in and out of consciousness, Song heard the murmur of hushed voices that he recognized as belonging to Yanhua, her father, her mother. They lulled him towards sleep. Then abruptly he was roused by Yanhua shouting, 'But I did see him, I did . . .' Her voice alarmed him, and for a moment he was startled and disoriented. He heard them quiet her and try to calm her. He felt his own pulse slow and time drifted again.

The door to the lean-to opened. There were footsteps. Song strained away from the noise. He struggled to open his eyes, but still he couldn't. The footsteps stopped next to him. He felt a warm cloth on his eyes, around his mouth and his nose. Again he tried to open his eyes, and this time saw a crack of light.

Someone held a cup to his lips. Song tried to sip through his swollen mouth, but half of the liquid ran down his chin and trickled onto his neck and then onto the floor. Now that his eyes were getting used to the darkness he could see that he was in a storage shed. There were coal briquettes piled around him.

He tried to speak, but Yanhua's father put his hand over his mouth. He withdrew as silently as he had entered. Song slept.

In the morning, Song awoke to shafts of sunlight that shone between the slats in the door. His first sensation was of intense pain, of ribs that screamed at him that they were broken, a head that ached as though he'd drunk for a week straight, of lacerations that stung like acid. His first waking thought was that because the pain no longer numbed him, he could feel it more. Tentatively, he stretched. He could feel his limbs at least. They felt as though, if they did not hurt so much, they would obey him. His left hand, which had been stamped on, lay curled and twitching and largely unresponsive.

Again the door opened. This time it was Yanhua's mother, the woman who had pulled him from the pigsty. She was carrying a bowl. She knelt down next to him and propped his head up, spooning *doujiang* into his mouth. He swallowed, and he could feel the sweet milky liquid work its way down through him. He tried to speak, as he had the night before, but she looked so alarmed and shook her head so fiercely that he stopped. He realized that the children did not know he was there. But if he spoke they would hear him as clearly as he had heard them.

After she had gone, he could hear them waking the girls up.

'Do we have to go to school?' Meimei asked. 'We're still all black and blue.'

'Teacher Ding says you'll be heroes,' their mother said. 'He says you don't have to do more than you can.'

'And no one will snatch anyone while the investigators are here,' said Yanhua's father.

'He's in a cell,' Yanhua pointed out. He can't snatch anyone.'

The door banged. Someone had gone outside. A moment later, from the other side of the wall, there came a commotion.

'How can he be dead? He's in a police cell, no one can get at him,' Yanhua's mother exclaimed.

'Old Wang just told me. No one got at him. He hanged himself.' Yanhua's father's voice, confused and anxious.

'Oh my lord,' Yanhua's mother moaned.

'Who hanged himself?' Meimei's voice rang out over her mother's.

'He can't be dead!' Yanhua shouted.

'It wasn't even him who scared us!' he heard Mei-mei's voice again. 'He didn't do anything wrong. It was Stupid Girl who scared us!'

'Don't say that!' Yanhua screamed. 'It was him. Of course it was him. He's killed himself because he's guilty, it's obvious it was him.'

Someone ran across the floor. The door slammed.

Song stared at the roof. He tried to move his limbs, and although they ached, they did respond. He rolled onto his side and manoeuvred his legs so that they hung over the edge of the pallet and his feet reached the floor. His head was telling him he had to move, and his bladder and bowels. Slowly he hauled himself upright, clutching his chest where his ribs stabbed at him. Tentatively, he tried to bear his own weight. All this took some time. After he had stood for a few seconds he had to sit back down again, wrapping his arms around his chest. He sat there, head lowered, trying not to think about the pain but only about what he had heard. It was Meimei's voice that rang in his head, 'It wasn't even him who scared us . . . It was Stupid Girl who scared us!'

He tried to call out, but at first his voice wouldn't work. He tried again.

'Mr Cui,' his voice rasped. 'Mr Cui!' This time it was louder. He heard an exclamation from the house and then the sound of someone hurrying out of the house and into the lean-to.

'Be quiet!' Yanhua's father hissed, as he entered the storeroom. 'Be quiet or you'll ruin us all.'

Song beckoned him over, gesturing that he must speak to him urgently, and Cui came close and squatted in front of him. Song leaned forward and spoke softly into his ear.

'Who is Stupid Girl?' he whispered.

Yanhua's father drew back, startled.

'I don't understand.'

'Meimei said it wasn't the miner who scared them,' Song murmured. 'It was Stupid Girl. Who is Stupid Girl?'

Cui stared at Song.

'Stupid Girl . . . ? I think I know. But . . .' he scrambled to his feet and hurried to the door. 'Meimei will know.'

Thirty-three

Yanhua's feet pounded along the path. She had never walked so fast. There was no way she could sit in a classroom all day, not with all the rage that was racing through her veins. How could they doubt her? How could Meimei say it was not the miner who had scared them? Hadn't her little sister heard the investigator praise her? He'd told her how clever she was. And why would the miner have killed himself if he wasn't guilty?

She hated herself. Here she was, trying to run away, to rebel, and yet she was on the way to school as though it was any other day. How could she sit in a classroom all day feeling like this?

'Yanhua!' A voice called her name. She halted, raised her head and looked around. She was by the amusement park, and Stupid Girl was standing under the gold-tiled entrance arch waving. For a moment Yanhua just gazed at her. The frisson of fear that she felt at the sight of the place was still there, but it had receded in the face of this great fury. By comparison, the fear was tiny. In fact, the fear was changing into something different. It was catching fire like a shiny, burning match that made her want to look at it and touch it.

Stupid Girl beckoned her.

'Come and play,' she called out.

Yanhua looked around her. She didn't want anyone to see her go in. She wanted them to worry about her and to search for her.

Yanhua walked down to where Stupid Girl was standing. Stupid Girl was wearing what she always wore, scuffed trainers, blue jeans that were tight around her sturdy thighs and a tight T-shirt with bright blue metallic strands in the cotton that glittered as she moved.

'You've come.' Stupid Girl turned towards her, smiling. 'I want to show you around. Your sister came once and she played on the swings but then she ran away.'

Yanhua nodded. This would show Meimei that she wasn't afraid. And she wasn't afraid because she'd told the investigator the truth. The boy in the cell was the boy who'd stopped them on the path. He'd been following them in the storm. He'd come down into the mine. She'd seen his face . . . She had seen his face, hadn't she? She couldn't have imagined it? She pushed that thought aside. Now that he was dead there was nothing to fear.

'What would you like to see? I've got keys to everything.'

'Do those work?' Yanhua nodded towards the bumper cars.

Stupid Girl shook her head.

'There's no electricity.'

'Not for any of it?' Yanhua asked. She gazed at the landscape of roundabouts and carousels decorated with animals. Metal pandas and enamelled horses, dogs and kittens, all with frozen smiles on their faces, gazed back at her.

'But you can sit in them, and I can push,' Stupid Girl said. 'Come on, over here.'

Yanhua followed her over to a roundabout which consisted of giant teacups that spun in smaller circles as the whole thing rotated around its axis. She climbed into a pink teacup, and Stupid Girl grabbed it and pushed. The whole thing creaked into action and began to move slowly around. Stupid Girl was panting with the effort of it. Yanhua tried to enjoy herself, but that too was hard work. The anger was still bubbling inside her. Still, Stupid Girl managed to speed up, and for a moment Yanhua found the amusement park revolving around her.

'OK, that's enough!' Stupid Girl stopped pushing, and bent over, panting.

Yanhua clambered out.

'Come on, I'll push you,' she said.

When Stupid Girl had her breath back they ran over to the carousel, and the two of them walked among the horses, stroking their noses and exclaiming over their flying manes.

'I'm going to ride this one,' the older girl said, climbing into the saddle and grasping the pole that rose from its neck. Yanhua tried to stand on the edge of the carousel and push it around but it was too heavy for her and soon she gave up. Stupid Girl continued to sit there on top of her horse with her head thrown back, as though she was galloping across the plains.

'I can't make it move,' Yanhua shouted to her. But all

the angry energy inside her was making her want to run and jump until she'd emptied herself out. She looked around, to see what was on offer, and spotted a trampoline. 'Let's jump, come on.'

They took off their shoes and ran up the metal steps. Yanhua was the first to step out onto the trampoline and start to jump. The last tendrils of anger flew away from her, and the air that raced over her skin cooled her cuts and bruises. Stupid Girl was still standing on the steps to the trampoline, her head bent over her mobile phone.

'Come on!' Yanhua shouted, and Stupid Girl put her phone back into her pocket and stepped onto the trampoline too. Cautiously at first, she started jumping.

'You're lucky,' Yanhua shouted, her hair flying around her head, 'you can do this every day.'

Stupid Girl didn't reply, she just jumped. Yanhua waved her arms around and kicked her legs, but Stupid Girl was more restrained. When they jumped close together, they found they could bounce even higher if they took it in turns, flinging the other into the air when they landed. Then they got out of synch, and first Yanhua and then Stupid Girl collapsed, laughing, onto the webbing.

'You're so lucky,' Yanhua gasped, lying on her back. The webbing rose and fell gently underneath her. Above her, the sky was blue, the sun burned down. When Stupid Girl still didn't reply, Yanhua turned on her tummy to face her. She had curled into a ball, hugging her knees to her chest, her head tucked in.

'Don't you think you're lucky?'

There was a long silence. The movement of the trampoline underneath Yanhua was soporific. She closed her eyes and lowered her head onto the webbing. She felt as though she was on a raft, bobbing out to sea.

'Would you like it?' Stupid Girl asked after a few moments, and her voice jolted Yanhua awake. 'You like school. You're always reading books. Everyone says you're clever. Teacher Ding says you're too clever.'

Yanhua took offence at the words 'too clever'. How could anyone be too clever? And what was Teacher Ding doing, saying things like that? She was his favourite pupil, especially now that Fengfeng was gone.

'I like school, but I like playing too.'

'It's no fun jumping if you're the only one,' the older girl said.

Yanhua thought about this. She felt sorry for Stupid Girl, not having a little sister.

'Why did you leave school?' she asked.

'I'm stupid, aren't I?' the girl said. 'That's what you all say.'

Yanhua was too embarrassed to reply. They'd all thought the girl was too stupid to know they called her stupid.

'That's what Teacher Ding said too. I kept failing my tests. He told my father he would give me private lessons . . .'

Her voice trailed off.

'I never heard of private lessons . . .'

'That's because you're so clever.'

'Did the lessons help you pass your tests?'

But Stupid Girl had scrambled to her feet and was standing over Yanhua, glaring down.

'Don't ask me about that any more,' she shouted. She ran awkwardly off the trampoline, and after a moment Yanhua followed her.

'What's the matter?' she asked, catching up. 'It was you who started to talk about it. It doesn't matter that you don't go to school. You've got a job, you're earning money, none of us has a job.'

Stupid Girl stared into Yanhua's face.

'You want my job? I don't think so.' She laughed acidly. 'You don't know what my job is.'

She walked in the direction of the gate, and Yanhua followed her. She turned into an empty cafe. There were tables with chairs stacked on top and a serving counter. Behind that there were shelves, and on these a handful of bottles and cans of fizzy drinks. Stupid Girl took down two glasses and a can. With her back to Yanhua, she pulled open the drink and poured it. After a moment she turned with a glass in each hand and came back to the table.

'Here,' she said, pushing one glass of the thick white juice towards Yanhua. 'You can drink it all, there's plenty more.'

Yanhua took a sip of the sweet liquid. She had never much liked almond juice, but it seemed rude to say so, so she took another sip, and another. The two girls avoided each other's eyes. Stupid Girl was staring at the table. She seemed uninterested in her drink.

'Perhaps I can help you with school work,' Yanhua said. 'Perhaps you can come back to Teacher Ding's class.'

The girl raised her eyes. Yanhua was shocked by the bitterness in them.

'There's no point,' she said softly. 'You don't understand.'

'Well, at least we can play together,' Yanhua said.

Stupid Girl shook her head slowly. Again she murmured, 'You don't understand. I'm not a child any more.'

Her eyes dulled. They shifted from Yanhua's face to a space behind her, and Yanhua twisted around to follow where she was looking.

Teacher Ding had entered the canteen and he was pulling the door closed softly behind him. Outside, she saw that a white van had pulled up.

She jumped to her feet.

'Hello, Yanhua,' he said, but he didn't smile and he didn't look in her eyes.

'Hello,' she whispered.

'Don't say hello,' the girl burst out. 'Don't waste your courtesy on him. Can't you see what's happening? I thought you were clever. Why did you have to come here?'

'What's going on?' Yanhua ran over to the girl and grabbed her arm, but Stupid Girl pushed her away and she found herself seized from behind by Teacher Ding.

He jerked his head at Stupid Girl. For a moment she stared at him rebelliously, and then she got to her feet and went to the back of the serving counter, where she bent down. When she emerged, she was carrying a red travel bag. She placed this on one of the tables and unzipped it. She brought out rope, and a bottle of something, and rags . . .

Yanhua struggled. She could tell how nervous Teacher Ding was. She could smell his sweat and feel his racing heart against her back.

'Don't fight,' he snapped at Yanhua. 'We're not going to hurt you.'

He gripped her more tightly, but she thought she might be able to escape. He was taller than her, but he wasn't big or athletic, he was bookish and spindly. She kicked her foot back against his leg and heard him exclaim with pain. She pulled hard over to the left, and he had to move with her, but he didn't loosen his grip.

'Did you give her the drug?' he asked Stupid Girl sharply. 'Why isn't she sleepy?'

She ignored him. She unscrewed the lid of the bottle. Yanhua's eyes went to the glass of almond juice. She hadn't watched the girl pour it. She was feeling dizzy. They had drugged her. Her heart raced.

Stupid Girl approached her. She was carrying a cloth soaked in liquid. Violently, Yanhua twisted her head away, first to one side, then to the other, so hard she thought her neck would break. Teacher Ding had loosened his grip on her arms, and had his hands on her skull, trying to hold her still. She raised her hands to claw at his fingers.

Then, just as she expected to feel the cloth descend

onto her face, Teacher Ding's hands left her head, and she thrust herself forwards, away from his grasp, making for the door.

'Help me!' Stupid Girl shouted behind her.

Yanhua stopped and turned. Stupid Girl had toppled him to the floor and was trying to pin him down, lunging to get the cloth over Teacher Ding's face, but he was fighting her like an animal, biting her hands and scratching at her arms and her face. There was blood running down her cheek, and on her hands. Yanhua hesitated, and Stupid Girl yelled at her again, this time with desperation in her voice. 'Help me!'

Yanhua turned back, but she didn't know what to do. When she got close, his foot kicked up at her.

'Sit on him,' Stupid Girl screamed. His hand snaked around her throat and pinched hard at her skin. She hit his face repeatedly with her bloody fist, and more blood spurted from his nose. She buried her knee deep into his groin. He screamed at that, but it subdued him enough for Yanhua to grab a chair from one of the tables and pin his torso in between its legs. With him momentarily subdued, Stupid Girl reached for the glass bottle that was on the table. She raised it and then, sobbing, smashed it against his head. The liquid spilled, and a strange smell filled the room. Teacher Ding stopped moving.

Whimpering, Yanhua stepped away from the still body on the floor. There was blood everywhere. More blood than she had ever seen in her life. Stupid Girl was covered in it. Her shiny T-shirt was covered in it.

Teacher Ding looked younger and skinnier like this, with his spectacles knocked off, like a boy, not a man. His face was swollen around the cuts, and blood was spilling from a gash in his head onto his hair so that it was matted and red.

'What have we done?' Yanhua clutched at her head. 'What have we done?'

'He's still alive, see?' Stupid Girl pointed at Teacher Ding's chest, which fluttered.

'Yes,' Yanhua was flooded with relief. 'Yes, he's alive!'

'You have to help me,' Stupid Girl said.

Yanhua stepped backwards, shaking her head.

'We have to tie him up. That's all, just tie him up. I'll do the rest.'

Yanhua looked at her sharply, but Stupid Girl had gone to pick up the rope. She found the end and handed the rest of the bundle to Yanhua. 'Just hold this, that's all you have to do.'

Yanhua held the rope.

'I can't do this,' she said. Her voice rose in panic. 'Let's call the police.'

'You still don't understand,' Stupid Girl screamed. 'He did to me what the men do at the truck stops when they need a woman.'

Yanhua squeezed her eyes shut.

'He did it again and again, and he told me I had to do it, and I had to keep it secret, because no one would believe me.'

'You can tell the police,' Yanhua whispered again.

'I can't tell the police,' Stupid Girl shouted, her face a mess of blood and tears. 'He threw me out of school. He put me here and told me to make friends with children when they came here, and he would come and collect them . . . I . . .'

But Yanhua couldn't listen to any more. She fled, letting the door bang shut behind her, never looking back. She ran and ran and ran.

Thirty-four

BEIJING

Lina watched in despair. There were police crawling all over her father's house. They had banned her and Doudou from the building and made them stand outside the yellow and red police tape. She stood at the bottom of the steps that led up to his front door and harassed the officers who passed her by. Doudou just watched.

'How can you be so disrespectful when the man's just been buried,' she protested, weeping, to one uniformed cadet who walked out of the house carrying a cloisonné vase a metre high that had stood at the base of the stairs. He ignored her, bearing his cargo carefully down the steps towards a removals truck which had been commandeered for the task. It was parked on the pavement, its rear end gaping, rapidly filling with the contents of her father's house.

Another uniformed officer emerged with an ornate gilt lamp. She waited for him to reach the bottom of the step, then pounced. 'These are his personal possessions,' she wailed. 'How would you feel if the police ransacked your father's house?' The young man shook her hand from his arm, but she followed him to the truck anyway.

That morning there had been an ugly scene with her father's staff – two maids and a driver – whom the police had thrown out of their rooms. They had gathered around her on the pavement with their few belongings around their feet and had refused to go away.

'There's no more work here,' she'd told them, raising her hands in despair, expecting their pity. 'You'll have to go home.' She had no idea where they came from.

But they had refused to go. Apparently insensitive to her distress, they demanded their wages and even train fare home, insisting that Detective Chen had agreed to pay for their journey to and from their home towns. On top of that they had presented her with grocery bills that had not been settled. She had cried and stamped her feet, trying to make them understand that these were her father's debts, and that he was dead. She, his daughter, was distraught, and had many things on her plate and should not be bothered with their material concerns. Still the staff had refused to budge. Eventually, Doudou had tugged on her arm.

'You should just pay them, Ma,' he said.

She stared at her son. His fat features seemed to resolve into Song's.

'You're just like your father,' she snapped. Still, there was no alternative. She would have to pay them off. For a moment she thought about stealing something from the removals truck to give them – a lamp, or a vase. It wouldn't really be stealing, after all, since everything was by rights hers. And any one of these objects was worth more by far than their paltry wages. She would be doing them a favour. But the officer guarding the truck caught her speculative eye, and she gave up. In the end she had gone to an ATM and stood there making withdrawal after withdrawal until the machine refused to give her any more cash. With cash in hand, she had returned to Manhattan Compound, and the staff had departed lugging their bags and their rolled-up bedding like refugees.

Her mobile rang, and she snatched it from her purse, glancing at the screen. It was Wang Rong. She heaved a sigh of relief. At last, someone who would understand.

'You're back,' she murmured into the phone. She thought she had grown fonder of him in his absence. Even his clumsy lovemaking had become wrapped in a more rosy hue since everything else had gone wrong.

'I came back two days ago,' Wang Rong said, 'I had business to take care of.' It wasn't a very romantic greeting, Lina thought. He sounded strained.

'Did you miss me?' she asked.

'I want to see you now,' he said brusquely. 'Are you at your father's house?'

'So eager! Did you bring me presents?'

'Do you ever think about anything else but presents?'

Lina squeezed her eyes shut. The criticism struck home. She did care about other things, like her father's reputation, but there was nothing to be done about that, so presents were as good a solace as any.

'Don't come to the house, it's crawling with police,'

she said, opening her eyes to the sight of her father's liquor collection being carried down the steps. She heard a sharp intake of breath from Wang Rong.

It was midday, so they met in a restaurant, Wang Rong arriving twenty minutes after Lina and Doudou had seated themselves in a booth near a window. Lina could see, as soon as Wang walked into the restaurant, that he was not in a good mood. His face darkened further when he saw Doudou.

'Did he have to come?' Wang Rong squeezed into the booth, pushing Lina along, his stomach wedged against the table.

Lina saw the expression on her son's face and she didn't know what to say.

'His school holiday's begun,' she said. 'He was bored at home. Besides, I thought if the police saw him with me they might be more sympathetic. Everything in the house belongs to me and to Doudou by rights. They're depriving him of his inheritance.'

'Why did you let them in?' Wang was impatient, tapping his cigarette carton against the table and summoning the waitress even as he spoke.

'I didn't have any choice.'

'I should have blown the place up,' Wang muttered as the waitress brought him a menu.

Lina and Doudou exchanged a glance. Lina thought that neither of them could have heard right.

Wang bent his head, stretching his chopsticks towards a small bowl of pickles.

'Do you still have the key?' he asked.

'I do,' Lina said, uncertainly.

'Give it to me, then,' he said, stretching his hand out, palm out.

Lina stared at his hand. She always tried not to frown, because it wasn't good for her complexion, but she knew she was frowning now.

'Why do you need it?' she asked.

He raised his head towards her and Lina was shocked by the expression in his eyes.

'It doesn't concern you,' he said, putting his hand on her thigh under the table. 'All that concerns you is that I have perfume for you, from London, and lingerie.'

'From London,' Lina echoed. Out of the corner of her eye, Lina noticed Doudou's excruciated expression. She pushed Wang's hand away.

'The house will be sealed up,' she pointed out. 'None of us will be able to get in even with a key.'

'We can break the seal and reseal it afterwards,' Wang said, letting his voice trail away as the waitress came to take their order.

They spoke no more of it while they ate, but Lina watched Wang's face. She was disappointed and a little frightened. She had been right to think him ugly and unpleasant. Why on earth had she considered accepting his presents? He was thinking about the house still, she was sure of it. She was not such a fool that she thought he would abandon his plan to get into the house just because she wouldn't give him the key. His threat to blow the house up scared her. Even empty, the house was still real estate. She hoped – although she couldn't be sure – that they would let her have it. But her father had let everything lapse, and as far as she knew he held no insurance policy for the house, if he ever had. A house that blew up would be no good to her at all. For a moment she caught herself wishing that Song was there. He had been right about so many things. She put him out of her mind. She was perfectly capable of handling this herself.

When they had finished eating it was Lina who brought up the subject again.

'We'll visit the house together tonight,' she said. She thought that in this way she could control the situation. She also wanted to see what it was that Wang believed was his. Wang nodded approvingly and grunted his assent. Lina thought that she had done the right thing.

At midnight, Lina and Doudou waited in the car. They were parked in a lay-by a hundred metres from the back gate to Detective Chen's compound. They waited in silence. Doudou had insisted on coming and Lina had given in.

'Your job is to keep an eye on Uncle Wang,' she told him. 'I don't know what he's up to.'

Soon another car pulled alongside and Wang Rong got out. He stalked over to their car, gesturing impatiently that she should open the door. When she did so he immediately laid into her.

'Why did you bring the fat kid? Two's already too many.'

'He's coming,' Lina said simply, 'and that's that.'

That afternoon Lina had tried to go into her father's compound and had found herself refused entry – the guards said they had been issued with instructions not to let her pass. Lina had fumed. It was Doudou who had surprised her by identifying a way in. There was a patch of wall along the perimeter, he said, which was not topped with glass and which seemed to be unguarded. Now they surveyed the landscape. There was heavy foliage on their side of the wall and, they hoped, heavy foliage to break their fall on the other side.

'I'll go first,' Doudou said. Neither Lina nor Wang demurred. But when it came to hoisting Doudou's considerable weight onto the wall, Wang swore and hurled insults at the boy. Still, after a moment of precarious balance at the top of the wall, the boy fell from view, and in another moment reported in hushed tones that it wasn't too hard. Wang insisted on going next, leaving Lina to scramble up the wall on her own and to drop down on the other side. She was glad she had thought to dress for the excursion in black leggings and tunic.

They kept to the shadows until they reached the house. There was a guard posted outside the front, but none at the back. They stepped over the crime-scene tape. There was a paper seal stuck across the maids' entrance, black characters giving that day's date. Lina unlocked the door and opened it, breaking the seal. She hesitated, thinking that the police might have installed an alarm, but there was silence. She and Wang had both brought torches, and these they took care not to shine near the windows.

Once inside, Lina went straight to her father's office, where the deeds to the house and to some other property had been filed. If they were still there she thought she would simply take them before another police removals team arrived. She did not see where Wang went, or Doudou, but she assumed that her son would carry out his mission to keep an eye on Wang. When she walked into the office she was relieved to see the filing cabinet there. They could easily have lifted it, lock, stock and barrel, into the removals truck. She selected the filing-cabinet key from her father's key chain and slid open the relevant drawer. It was empty. She slammed it shut and tried the drawer below, but it too was empty, and the one below that.

Suddenly, a voice came through a loudhailer from outside.

'Come out. Come out. You should not be in there.'

She looked quickly around the room. She saw that she had placed the torch on top of the filing cabinet and that it was shining out through the window.

She ran from the room, leaving the torch where it was.

'Doudou,' she shouted, 'Doudou.'

She heard a dull thud from somewhere upstairs and the sound of running feet. Then Doudou's bulky figure was there in front of her in the gloom.

'Quickly,' she grabbed him. 'Let's go.'

She expected to be seized at the back of the house,

but there was no one there. She could still hear the shouting through the loudhailer at the front. She thought that the lone guard must have seen the torch but been too nervous to enter the house without back-up.

They didn't bother with the wall on the way out, walking fast past the guards at the back gate to the compound with their heads lowered. Out of sight of the guard, they ran to the car and clambered in. Lina pulled out onto the road.

For several minutes the car was silent except for the rasp of Doudou's breathing.

Then Lina asked Doudou, 'Where's Wang Rong?'

Doudou turned his head away from her. From the corner of her eye Lina could see his chest heaving. He was making a strange rattly noise. After a moment Lina asked again, more urgently. When her son didn't reply she pulled the car onto the hard shoulder of the expressway.

'Where is he?' she demanded.

'He found the panic room,' Doudou wheezed. 'He had a card that opened the door.'

Lina stared at him. 'And?' she demanded.

Doudou turned to her with desperate eyes. He thrust something into his mother's hand, and when she looked at it she saw it was a card like the key to a hotel room.

'What's this?' She was frowning.

'He left it in the slot . . .' Doudou fought for breath. 'I locked him inside.'

Thirty-five

GANSU PROVINCE

Autumn was well advanced here. The red earth was bare and the cold wind whipped it into a dusty haze. At the gatehouse he stood in line keeping his head down, trying not to stand out. Everyone in the queue acted the same way, heads buried in scarves, eyes flitting uneasily. No one was engaged in conversation, no one quarrelled with the guards or raised awkward questions. None of them wanted to be turned away. They had all come too far. No one lived near to this place, except the guards and their families. Coming here on the bus from Lanzhou there had been wide expanses of land and no humanity. They had chosen the place well.

When his turn came, he signed in under another man's name. He placed his fake ID card on the counter.

'How long will I have?' he asked, in order to distract the guard from looking too closely at the card. He was careful to keep his tone polite.

But the guard ignored his question and scrutinized the card instead. He examined the photograph, tilting it against the light, then glanced up at Song's face, not once, but twice, and then again. Song forced himself to stand still. Any nervous movement would betray him. It was ridiculous, of course. Whoever tried to break into a prison?

The guard nodded him through, and turned to the next in the line. His knees felt weak, but he forced himself to keep pace with the man in front and the woman who was behind him. In turn they placed their packages upon a table, and these were examined. Song had brought soft blankets, thermal underwear, and a thick bright sweater knitted by her mother. There were vitamins too, and these were examined closely. He would have brought more, a suitcase more, but there were limits and he dared not challenge them.

'Move along!' The voice startled Song, but it was nothing, they were simply being herded like sheep.

A door opened in front of them, and they were in a corridor. It was concrete and bitter in this weather. They processed along it. He was directed to a door, which he opened. Inside, there was a small bare room, walls painted a greying white. There was a table, with a simple wooden chair on each side. He sat down. His heart was pounding.

And then, when he was telling himself to be patient, she was there in front of him, her expression perplexed, not understanding. She was thinner than he remembered, like a stick figure inside her padding, and her shoulders seemed to sag. Her hair was hacked into a regulation cut. He leaped to his feet. A guard followed her into the room, then stood with his back to the door.

For a moment Song thought that she would blurt out his real name.

'Don't look so surprised to see your brother,' Song said urgently.

She stared at him, blinking. Then, realizing, she glanced at the guard.

'Brother,' she murmured. 'I'm so pleased to see you.'

They sat down, facing each other across the table. The guard stared, unblinking, at the opposite wall. He was there to spy on them but you could never tell who would do their job and who would not. Still, Song could not think how to start speaking in a way that would not get them both thrown into solitary confinement. The claustrophobia of the situation engulfed him. He could not imagine being enclosed like this all day and all night. He saw that she was still shocked to see him there.

'I'm sorry, I didn't want to disappoint you,' Song said eventually. He had feared that this might happen, and had tried to prepare himself for it. 'I only . . . last time I saw you, you left in such a hurry . . . I brought you some blankets to keep you warm . . .'

He pushed the package towards her awkwardly.

'And thermal underwear,' he forced a laugh. 'It's not a romantic gift.'

She stretched her hand across the table towards him, and in an instant he had covered it with his and locked his fingers tight with hers. She smiled at him.

'This isn't brotherly behaviour,' she murmured, her

eyes flickering towards the guard, and reluctantly he surrendered her hand.

'I owe you an apology,' she said softly. 'I asked you to come with me and I put you in danger. I didn't know my husband's friend would telephone me that night. He . . .'

'They've arrested him,' Song told her quietly. He had to speak to her, he had to tell her what he knew. He couldn't have kept secrets from her even had he wanted to. But the danger of the situation – the guard could decide to pay attention any moment – made him lower his voice to the point that even he could hardly hear himself speak. Jin Dao dipped her head towards him to listen to what he was saying. 'He might have had a chance if he'd stayed where he was and stuck to his job, he'd have been just another bureaucrat. But he ran. When they heard he'd disappeared they knew they'd got their man and they went after him.'

'I guessed as much,' Jin Dao murmured, shaking her head.

It had been a difficult point at Jin Dao's trial. The proceedings had been held in secret, but he had heard a little about it from her mother. Jin Dao had confessed to posting the document online and had refused point-blank to show any remorse. Furthermore, she had refused to say who had given her the document. Even when the prosecution showed evidence that she had used a computer within the county government offices, she had refused to confirm that fact, knowing that it would implicate the man who had let her in. Her refusal to cooperate had contributed to her four-year sentence.

'How are they treating you?'

'There are endless lectures about socialist morality.'

'I don't imagine you stay silent.'

'If I argue they put me in solitary confinement.' She shook her head. 'I don't want to talk about it. I want to hear what happened.'

'There were so many people involved,' he said quietly, speaking quickly. This was a safer topic of conversation. In the end it had all been in the newspapers. 'It started when a new teacher, Teacher Ding, came to the school. He raped a girl who was his pupil. Chief Bo learned about the rape and blackmailed him. Chief Bo had fallen on hard times, his cash flow was drying up, and he'd been thinking about the money-making potential of trafficking. He enrolled the local police chief to run the thing. Chief Bo told Teacher Ding that if he used the girl he'd raped to gain the trust of children, and if he helped them seize the children, the police would overlook the rape. So the teacher put his victim to work in the amusement park, and together they lured children away.'

Song glanced at the guard, but he did not seem interested. Song turned back to Jin Dao. Her expression was bleak.

'Go on,' she said.

He sighed. It wasn't a story that would lift her spirits. 'When parents started to appeal to the police they were ignored, of course, since the police were running the trafficking operation under the direction of Chief Bo. When they wrote petitions to the central government they were passed to Chen Dalei, who had been made responsible for petitions concerning police work in Beijing and Hebei. But Chen Dalei was only interested in exploiting police abuses, not in justice. He sent Psycho Wang to Yidong to negotiate a cut in the trafficking business – it was a protection racket. Chen Dalei would ignore the petitions about the kidnapping in return for cash, which he split with Psycho Wang. In some cases, Teacher Ding himself helped them to write the petitions, and addressed them to Chen Dalei, knowing they would go no further.' The door opened. The guard was summoned into the corridor, and Song broke off. He couldn't bear the thought of leaving her here alone, with the weight of this story on her heart.

'Look . . .' he spoke rapidly, seizing her hand again. 'I got in here, maybe I can get you out.'

She lifted her face to him, then tore her eyes away from his and shook her head.

'This is my time of mourning,' she said. 'I think about Tang Ning, and what happened to him, and then I know I've been lucky. This is nothing in comparison. This will end if I can ride out their anger.'

Song nodded. He didn't know how to talk to her about the death of her husband, but he had to get it over with. Time was short.

'It was Wang Rong – the man I call Psycho Wang –

who killed your husband. I think the papers you sent to Tang Ning implicated Wang Rong, and that he killed Tang Ning for them. He's been arrested.'

Her head rose quickly, and interest burned in her eyes.

'He's been arrested?'

'He had the key to my father-in-law's safe room, and he broke in. Then – well it's a long story, but he got locked in there. The British police had already approached the Beijing police about him and informed them of their suspicions concerning your husband's murder. So when the Beijing police were told where to find him, they detained him on the spot. But I should warn you, it's not clear what will happen to him. Trying a Chinese for a murder committed against another Chinese on British soil is not straightforward . . .'

Song broke off, releasing Jin Dao's hand again as the door opened and the guard stepped back into the room.

'Time's up,' the guard said.

Song had no time to tell Jin Dao how Lina had called him at one in the morning to tell him what Doudou had done. Nor any time to tell her about Doudou's asthma attack that night, and how they'd spent the night at the hospital and left Psycho Wang to sweat. Nor any time to tell her how the safe room had yielded his father-in-law's papers detailing his part in the trafficking business.

'Get moving!' the guard ordered, irritated that Song showed no sign of moving. Suddenly panic-stricken, Jin Dao grabbed his hand.

'Come to see me again,' she begged. 'I don't want you to go.'

'Get out of here,' the guard ordered Song.

'I've got to tell her one last thing,' Song tried to plead, but the guard pulled him out of his seat. A female guard entered the room and took hold of Jin Dao, hauling her to her feet and moving her roughly away.

He didn't trust himself to look at her. He didn't trust himself to look at the guards. He didn't trust himself to do anything but retrace his steps, walking along the bleak corridor and through the guard house and out to the other side of the great prison gates.

On the bus, he stared out of the window until the labour camp was swallowed up in the fold of the hills. He thought that this land provided many crevices in which people could be hidden away. Now that he had seen Jin Dao he knew that she would not lose hope and that he must not lose hope either. But to leave her there, like that ... He wanted to jump off the bus and make his way back to the prison and hammer on the doors. He could hardly bear to sit, passive and unmoving on the bus, hemmed in on every side. He tried to distract himself and to think about what lay ahead of him. In Beijing, Wolf and Blue were moving the office into its new premises. Wolf's office hunt had not gone well because he was paralysed by indecision. Only when Blue returned from London and took charge did they find a place. It was in an old building, not too far from the city centre, and they had discussed whether or not they should take it because it too would likely be demolished. In the end they'd decided that they could not protect themselves against every eventuality and that if it was knocked down they'd simply have to start again.

A girl climbed onto the bus. She was about twelve or thirteen years old, carrying a school bag, and Song's mind went back to what he had not told Jin Dao. Even if there had been time, would he have told her? He was afraid she might think that he had done the wrong thing. He thought it very possible himself that he had done the wrong thing.

It was Meimei who told them where to find Stupid Girl, and Yanhua's father who commandeered a village truck. Cui drove them at high speed to the amusement park, and Song nearly passed out from the pain as they hurtled across potholes and ditches. They found Yanhua running, stumbling, from the amusement park. She wasn't able to speak for trembling at first, but she was splashed with blood and they understood from her wild pointing and gesturing that something terrible had happened. They drove on into the park and found Stupid Girl bent double, dragging the senseless Teacher Ding through the undergrowth into the lake.

Song and Cui launched themselves at her, trying to loosen her grip on the teacher.

'Why do you want to save him?' she shouted.

Yanhua grabbed Stupid Girl's hand, and tried to prise her fingers away from Teacher Ding's clothing. 'They don't want to save him. They want to save you. If you kill him, you'll be finished.'

Stupid Girl gave an ugly laugh.

'I'm already finished,' she said, releasing her hold on Teacher Ding.

Relieved of the need to struggle, Song and Cui stood and stared down at the teacher. The amateurish attempt to tie him up was already failing, the rope that bound him was already coming loose. The sagging rope and the untidy flop of his thin limbs made it impossible to believe that he had threatened anyone.

'Why did you do this?' Cui turned to his daughter.

'He grabbed me,' Yanhua told them again. 'He wanted to abduct me.'

'What are you thinking?' Cui shook his head sadly and spoke slowly. 'First a miner, now a teacher. Yanhua, you can't go around accusing people. Look at what you've done here. The consequences of this will be immense.'

Yanhua stared at him. Silently, she started to cry. Her father turned away from her. He bent down and started to pull the rope off the teacher's chest. Stupid Girl stood slouched next to the teacher's shoulders, no longer making any attempt to assault his unconscious form. She watched, without expression, as Yanhua's father started to free him. Then she spoke. Her voice was low and as unfeeling as her face.

'Your daughter's telling the truth,' Stupid Girl said. 'I helped him steal children.'

Yanhua's father lifted his head to look at Stupid Girl. Slowly he got to his feet.

'Why are you speaking in that strange way?' he muttered.

'Tell us what you mean,' Song said quietly.

Stupid Girl looked at him sideways, and Song thought that she was – or had become – sly.

'He called me his assistant.'

Yanhua's father stepped back in shock.

'Tell us what you mean,' Song said again softly.

The story fell from her mouth then like a foul river but still she showed no pain, only dull weariness. With her violent rage against Teacher Ding exhausted, she recited her story as though it had happened to someone else. Teacher Ding had raped her during a 'private lesson' in the same week that he'd told her parents she was a hopeless student and that they should waste no more money on her education. When he told them he'd found a job for her at the amusement park, her parents had washed their hands of her. From then on she slept and ate alone in the amusement park. Teacher Ding continued to visit her. He threatened her – others would find out what she was allowing him to do to her unless she cooperated. All she had to do was befriend children who wandered too close to the amusement park. Her job was to lure them inside. Then, when she called him, he would come and remove them . . .

When she stopped talking Song and Yanhua and her father stood in silence for some time staring down at the man who lay at their feet.

'We'll leave him here,' Yanhua's father said, and his voice was gruff. He knelt again to secure the man's bindings.

'He might die like this,' Yanhua said nervously. 'If he dies, we'll go to prison.'

Song and Yanhua's father avoided each other's eyes.

'Your father will call the Wanmei police later,' Song told Yanhua. 'You walk. I'm going to need the truck. Don't tell anyone that I was here. You must say the girl ran off.'

Yanhua looked at her father, and he nodded. A few moments later they had left, on foot, in the direction of their home.

When they were alone, Song noticed the way Stupid Girl looked at him, in weary anticipation of further assault.

'Get in the truck,' he said to her.

She clambered in and he stood watching her. She looked at him out of the window with that same blank face, as though numbing herself for whatever might come next. She had no social graces, he thought, no cleverness, and not much beauty. There would be precious little to save her. He had no idea what to do with her. He didn't trust the police, he didn't trust the courts. If there was a trial he could not be sure that the things she had endured would be properly weighed against the things she had done. Detention would only harden her further. Her parents would be ruined by her disgrace. Better, perhaps, that they should think her abducted with the rest.

He climbed into the truck and pulled out of the amusement park and onto the road.

They spoke only once. Song tried to ascertain what she knew about the other children she had helped to abduct. But she said she knew nothing and he believed her. The last she had seen of each one of them was as they were driven, unconscious, through the gates of the amusement park in the back of Teacher Ding's white van. She was not privy to the machinations of the men who had ruined her.

Song drove without knowing where he was going until they were many miles from Yidong. Then, at a train station in a remote town, he gave her money and he put her on a train. He thought this was all anyone could do: move on, start afresh, leave the ruins behind.

'Get a job,' he urged her, as she hung out of the window. 'There's enough cash there to buy a new name.'

She nodded, but even the defences she'd constructed could not hide the fear in her eyes. He avoided her gaze. He didn't know whether he was doing the right thing. What would she do far from home and in a strange city? He was afraid she would turn back to the things she knew. There would be a market for her terrible skills elsewhere. He waited until her train pulled out of the station and he lost sight of her. Then he got back in the truck, turned it around and headed back towards Beijing.